The Mutants Are Coming

By Isidore Haiblum

THE MUTANTS ARE COMING
THE IDENTITY PLUNDERERS
NIGHTMARE EXPRESS
OUTERWORLD
INTERWORLD
THE WILK ARE AMONG US
TRANSFER TO YESTERDAY
THE TSADDIK OF THE SEVEN WONDERS
THE RETURN

With Stuart Silver

FASTER THAN A SPEEDING BULLET—An Informal History of Radio's
   Golden Age

The Mutants Are Coming

Isidore Haiblum

DOUBLEDAY & COMPANY, INC.

GARDEN CITY, NEW YORK

1984

All of the characters in this book
are fictitious, and any resemblance
to actual persons, living or dead,
is purely coincidental.

Library of Congress Cataloging in Publication Data

Haiblum, Isidore.
The mutants are coming.

I. Title.
PS3558.A324M8   1984   813'.54
ISBN: 0-385-17513-2
Library of Congress Catalog Card Number 83–45108

First Edition

The Mutants Are Coming

CHAPTER 1

I hauled myself out of the beige easy chair and crossed the room for another chat with the receptionist. My third one in an hour. But who was counting?

"Excuse me, miss."

She looked up at me. Blue eyes, blond hair. A creamy complexion. She was nifty all right, but I hadn't come here to inspect the sights.

"Yes, may I help you?" she asked.

"I hope so. I'm beginning to feel old age and decrepitude setting in."

"I beg your pardon?"

"If your boss doesn't get to me soon, I just might be too feeble to hold up my end of the conversation."

"Mr. Morgan—"

I winked at her. "A word to the wise, as they say."

"Mr. Morgan, the senator knows you're waiting. He's occupied at the moment."

"Uh-huh. But he doesn't know the goodies I'm bringing from Moon Base. If he knew *that* he'd be all over himself trying to get unoccupied. This isn't just any old courtesy call. Take it from me, your boss *wants* to see me."

The receptionist looked doubtful.

"Go on," I said, "ask him again, you'll see."

The girl got to her feet; she didn't look any too eager.

"Thanks," I said.

She went away.

I glanced around the waiting room. Two middle-aged men and a woman shared the place with me and a tel-viser. One of the men was dozing. I looked up at the senator's portrait behind the blonde's desk. It looked back at me imperturbably; the senator wasn't giving away a thing. I tried to remember if I'd ever voted for the old goat. I gave it up. Five years on Moon Base had addled my brain.

The receptionist came back. "I'm sorry, Mr. Morgan, I gave the senator your message."

"And he didn't buy it?"

"I'm afraid he expects to be tied up all day."

"No kidding."

"Perhaps if you left your card, Mr. Morgan, we could get back to you."
I got my card out, scribbled the name of my hotel on the back and handed it to her. Maybe they *would* get back to me. I wasn't going to bet my last Credit on it.

I nodded at the blonde, turned on my heel and headed for the door. None of the waiting trio even bothered to look up. I'd come and gone without making a ripple.

I went back into the hallway. The door snapped closed behind me. I was alone. I stopped short, wondering what the hell I was supposed to do next.

This whole business with Fulton was cockeyed; he should've come jumping out of his office with open arms to greet me. It wasn't every day an official Moon Base ambassador showed up for a powwow. For all Fulton knew he was missing the chance of a lifetime by giving me the cold shoulder.

As a matter of fact he *was*—along with me, Moon Base, and if the chief was right, everyone else on the North-Am Continent.

Everyone else could look after themselves, but I was getting kind of worried about me and Moon Base; especially me. Old me stood to lose a bundle if I couldn't swing a deal with Fulton. And old me was the only me there was.

I took the chutes down to the lobby, went hunting for the doorman and found him in the local whoopy bar. Whoopy came in all shapes and sizes, liquids, solids and dainty little pills. I was glad to see the doorman was still on his feet. Someday, maybe, I'd find out just what a doorman did.

"You folks got a maintenance office in this building?" I asked him.

"Sure, whaddya think?"

I flashed my Moon Base buzzer at him, the one that got me into Moon Base canteens at half price. Since there were no Moon Base canteens on Earth the damn thing was absolutely worthless. Except for every now and then. "Computer inspection," I said. Most office buildings were computer run; it stood to reason *someone* would inspect them sometimes. I hoped reason wasn't about to let me down.

The doorman said, "Take the chutes to the sub-basement. Go left, you can't miss it," and went back to reading his racing form.

My faith in reason upheld, I went back to the chutes, rode to the sub-basement and headed left.

The sign over the door said: "Maintenance. Authorized personnel only." I went in without knocking.

The chubby guy holding down the battered desk looked up from his crossword puzzle. "Yeah?"

"I was just wondering," I said, "if you got any openings?"

"Any *what?*"

"I mean, do you need some help?"

"Do I *look* like I need help, mister?"

"No jobs, huh?"

"Jobs? Where you been, mister, the Moon? We ain't had no jobs here for three, four years. Me and another guy handle all the chores there are—and that ain't saying much. What's this talk about jobs?"

"I've been down on my luck," I explained earnestly.

"So, what's the matter, too proud for the dole?"

No one was too proud for the dole; two thirds of the nation was on it. Even *I* knew that. "Just asking." I shrugged. "No law against that."

The guy waved a hand. "Aw, go on, beat it."

I beat it.

By then I'd taken in all I could handle of the building floor plan; it was conveniently tacked up on the wall, which saved me the trouble of coming back during lunch break and frisking the joint. I was thankful.

I headed down the corridor.

Even with the damn floor plan fresh in my mind it was no cinch finding the service lift. Running the maze in an outsized, sprawling government building wasn't fit work for a grown man. And I was going to put in a complaint if I ever found my way out.

I turned left, right, a number of other tricky directions. It took a bit of doing. First I reached the fire stairs. Since it was a seventy-four story climb to Fulton's floor and I was still in my right mind, I ignored them. After a while I hit the service lift. I put off congratulating myself until I made sure the darn thing was working. Stepping in, I pressed the lift button and was rewarded by a rumble deep in the shaft.

We lifted.

What the ride lacked in speed it made up for in security; a building that was 98 percent computer-run wasn't apt to have nosy handymen dropping around to ask embarrassing questions. At least, I hoped not. Hope was all I had going for me at the moment. Maybe soon I'd have more.

I stepped out on Fulton's floor. I was somewhere at the rear end of the building. A storage area. Crates lined the walls. No sounds came through the heavy walls. I started working my way toward Fulton's suite.

The first door I went through led into a large chamber; computers rose from floor to ceiling. Small red and yellow lights blinked at me. Something was going bleep-bleep. Wrong door. I went back to the hallway. The next door was locked; I decided against breaking it down. The third door took me through a narrow passageway. I found myself in a room full of filing cabinets. Very old-fashioned. Just like the senator. And exactly what I needed.

I dug into the files, came up with a thick leather-bound sheaf of papers. I didn't bother looking through them. I left the room through a second door with the folder neatly tucked under my arm—a sure sign that I belonged—

went down a short corridor. Sounds of activity came from up ahead. I followed the sounds; they led me into a large hall. Round windows showed clouds, sky and the Central City skyline. Bright lights on the ceiling looked down on rows of desks, view-phones, tabletop computers and lots of personnel.

Nobody lifted an eyelid in my direction. I liked that.

Stepping over to the nearest desk, I asked a thin middle-aged man, "Which way to the senator's office?"

The guy didn't even look up; he pointed toward a door over his shoulder. "Through there and down the hall."

Good old human personnel, they'll do it every time—I knew from personal experience; I'd been one myself.

I followed the guy's instructions; he seemed honest enough.

The large, ornate double doors I came to certainly looked as though they might lead to a U.S. Senator. Just so there could be no doubt about it, his name was on the door too. Probably he was up to his ears in work; maybe he even had some committee holed up in there with him. For all I knew, I'd stepped square in the middle of some terrible crisis. That would sure account for my getting the run-around.

But I couldn't let any crises stand in the way of progress—especially mine and the senator's. He'd never forgive me if I let mere formality louse up our historic get-together; not once he got wind of my offer.

I didn't bother knocking. I just pushed open the doors and went on in. What did I have to lose? After all, the chief was behind me all the way. Even if he was back on the Moon.

CHAPTER 2

Forty-eight hours ago the chief had me ushered into his office, waved me into a padded armchair. He was a short, plump man with a full head of snow-white hair and a large white mustache. Some of the Moon Base crew kidded around that the chief looked like Joe Stalin. But compared to the chief, Uncle Joe had been a cream puff.

The chief glared at me from across his desk, which wasn't much smaller than a two-ton tank and said one word: "Trouble." It was enough; right away I started sweating.

"What is it, Chief?" I asked. "The dome spring a crack? The air-pumps stuffing up? Is the food supply contaminated again? I don't think I could stand that!"

"No," the chief said simply, "none of those."

"Thank goodness," I said, exhaling and sinking back into the chair. As Moon Base's top troubleshooter I got to tackle all the tough ones. And the last couple of troubles had almost shot *me*.

"This is much worse," the chief explained.

"Worse?" I had to suppress a giggle. I was becoming hysterical. "What could be worse?"

"Earth."

A brief picture flashed through my mind of Earth blowing up, leaving a large empty space in its place. I considered the possibility. I could live with it. But could Moon Base? Probably not. Moon Base still had a good dozen years to go before it became self-sufficient.

"Okay, Chief," I said, "let's have it; lay it on the line. Whatever this is it can't be any worse than the time all the generators conked out, eh? Or the time the dome filled with exhaust fumes; right, Chief; right?!"

The chief just looked at me with his little gray, steely bloodshot eyes. Mentally I substituted "wrong" for "right"; I was used to it by now. I'd been doing a lot of substitutions lately. Pretty soon it would become second nature. I could hardly wait.

"How long since you've had a vacation, Morgan?" the chief asked.

The question surprised me. "Five years; five long years, Chief. Not that I'm complaining. I was all set to go last year when Kempton had his nervous breakdown and I had to take over. And the year before that Richards hung himself, so naturally I couldn't go. And the year before that poor Millard went berserk and it took weeks to get everything back into order. Oh, there was always a good reason. And it could have been worse. I always managed to get a couple of weekends to myself. Why just seven months ago I got a whole Sunday off."

The chief nodded sympathetically. "You're all a bunch of swine, aren't you?"

I thought it over. "Some more than others, I suppose."

"Malingerers, backsliders, idlers," the chief said. "It's the younger generation. It's gone soft, turned rotten. No backbone."

"None at all," I admitted. "But don't worry about *me;* I'm aging fast. A couple more years like this and my youth will be a dim, distant memory."

"Where were you going to spend those vacations you never took. Earth?"

"No. In bed. This job takes a lot out of a fella."

The chief narrowed his eyes. "Don't think you have me bamboozled, Morgan; not for a second. I know what you're up to."

I shook my head. "As the only civilian of senior rank who hasn't gone crackers yet, I think I deserve a bit more respect. If you don't mind my saying so."

"I do," the chief said. "Listen, Morgan, Moon Base is just a hollow shell of its former self. I know that. But I'm not blaming you."

"Thanks, Chief."

"A decade of operating on a shoestring has all but brought us to our knees," the chief said bitterly. "We've had to make do with what we could get—namely *you*, Morgan, you and your rotten ilk."

"Let's leave my ilk out of this," I said.

"Shut up, Morgan."

"Yes, sir."

"The one thing that is still reminiscent of Moon Base's former glory is its public relations department. We can thank our lucky stars for that. On Earth they still think of us as a going concern. It's your ace in the hole, Morgan."

I raised an eyebrow. "Ace in the hole? Mine? What game am I supposed to be playing, Chief?"

"A game for the highest stakes."

"Those are usually the worst kind, the riskiest and meanest."

"Precisely. You are to return to earth, Morgan, at once."

I glanced at him. "At once, no less."

The chief nodded glumly. "That's an order, Morgan."

"An order, eh? Well, that settles it. Count me out! Earth of all places! Look, Chief, you can send me through the tubes of the heating system up here, or out on the other side of the dome for inspection. But you can't send me back to Earth. You haven't got the authority. I don't *want* to go back. It's messy, noisy and terribly congested down there. Without a pile of money the place is a nightmare. And I've still got three years to go for *my* pile; yep, three years and I retire at pay and a half. *Then* I go back. But rich! It'll make all the difference in the world, Chief. Believe me!

"Anyway, whatever dumb problems Earth has is none of *our* business, is it? With all these budget cuts, we've got our hands full just staying alive up here. Let *them* handle their *own* problems . . ."

"But it *is* our problem, Morgan."

"Sure it is. Tell me another one, Chief."

"Listen, Morgan, your little sidelines are common knowledge. The numbers game; the joy-seed concession; the floating crap games; the gambling parlor. *Those* are the reasons you don't wish to return."

I shrugged. "So what? I do my job, that's what counts. My off hours are something else."

The chief nodded. "Perhaps. But you're making a big mistake. You may have a tidy nest egg laid away, but you'll need every red cent of your pension to live in the extravagant and disgusting style you no doubt desire. And that is far from certain. In fact, there may be *no* pension *at all.*"

"Come on, Chief, cut it out." I grinned. "You'll have me rolling in the aisles. I'm too old and tired to buffalo. I know my rights."

"*What* rights? If you mean the law of the land, it's been changed four times in the last nine months. And the next change could very well wipe out your pension. Along with the whole of Moon Base! You'll go back to Earth then, all right, with the rest of us, but it won't be for a life of ease. Far from it."

"What in blazes are you talking about?" I demanded.

"Four coups in less than a year. And the last one brought Raymond Hess to power!"

"So?"

"Raymond Hess, Morgan! The new Chairman of the People's Council is called Balanced Budget Hess. Know how he's going to achieve that goal?"

"Start another lottery?"

"Bah! There are too many lotteries as it is. No, he plans to do away with Moon Base pure and simple!"

"The public will never stand for it!"

The chief shook his head. "You don't understand, Morgan."

"What's to understand?"

"Elections have been suspended for over a year. Anything is possible now. It's a time of chaos! We have a man on the spot, Morgan, a paid informant whom Moon Base has relied upon for years. He's close to both the Hess faction and General Manning West. Hess, he tells us, has no intention of holding elections; he plans to annul the constitution and name himself dictator. One of his first acts will be to totally abolish Moon Base."

"Dictator, eh? I could go for that myself," I chuckled. "So, what's he waiting for?"

"General West has been trying to line up the army behind him."

"That'll be the day."

"Our agent says he's making progress, that it is only a matter of time."

"Who *is* this wiz kid?"

"Malcolm Lane."

"Never heard of him."

"He is highly placed."

"Uh-huh."

"Listen, Morgan, it's still not too late. All the factions are jockeying for power. Hess can be stopped. Senator Scott Fulton and his party support Moon Base development. We can throw Moon Base prestige and resources behind the senator in a power play. We need a good man down there, one dedicated to our cause, someone completely unscrupulous. For once, Morgan, your full talents can be utilized on behalf of Moon Base."

"Thanks a lot, Chief! I stand to lose a small fortune if I take off now. And what if this Malcolm Lane joker got his facts wrong and the whole trip is just a wild goose chase? I go right to the cleaners, that's what."

"If you determine that Lane is in error, scrap the mission and return home at once. You'll be paid handsomely for your time. If Lane is right, get to work, do anything you wish. Just see to it that Moon Base comes out on top. As for your many enterprises here, they can surely be looked after by some of your trusted colleagues."

"Let's not horse around, Chief. You know damn well the reason I haven't taken a vacation in five years is that I don't *have* any trusted colleagues. They're all a bunch of crooks; they'll rob me blind!"

"You really are a wretch, aren't you, Morgan?"

"It takes all kinds, Chief."

"I have mentioned Moon Base resources. Let me assure you they exist in ample quantity. We have a numbered bank account, at least for the time being. I am offering you five hundred thousand."

"Five hundred thousand *what?*"

"Credits, you fool!"

"No kidding?"

"If your mission is a success."

"That's a big if."

"Take it or leave it," the chief said.

"H-m-mmmmm," I said smartly.

CHAPTER 3

I got off the space shuttle a little past 10 P.M. No brass bands were there to greet me; not even a third-class cultural attaché. I was merely one of the crowd. That suited me fine. My ambassadorial papers were tucked away in my briefcase. No one even knew I was coming. Just a bit of cover, till I got the lay of the land. It couldn't hurt.

I trailed after my fellow passengers as we headed for the check-out terminal. It felt damn funny strolling around without a glass dome over my head. I figured I'd get used to it. If I could get used to Moon Base I could get used to anything. And five hundred thousand Credits was just about the right incentive.

At a distance, in every direction, Central City glowed and twinkled in the darkness: narrow, luminous skyscrapers; pale, translucent domes; elevated mobile walks spiraling around and over buildings; rows of domed autos heading to and from the city on raised highways. Not bad. Especially for the real estate outfits that owned the works.

The terminal was packed. I claimed my suitcase from the baggage rack, made my way outdoors, climbed into an auto-cab, told the machine where I was going and was carried off to city center.

I checked into the ninety-floor Hilton, used the view-phone up in my room to order a snack, washed up, removed my chow from the meal chute and dined on a steak sandwich washed down by a mug of beer.

So far everything had gone like clockwork. But so far was only an hour. I decided to postpone slapping myself on the back for a while yet. Maybe tomorrow. If things still looked as rosy. *If.*

CHAPTER 4

I stood in Fulton's office.

Six windows looked out over the city. Giant skyscrapers, patches of blue sky and lots of clouds looked back. Hover crafts bounced around like yo-yos. No sounds from outside penetrated walls or windows. A thick brown rug stretched across the office floor, almost rose ankle-high. A bookcase on the east wall displayed three rows of gold-embossed leather-bound volumes which, I was willing to bet, had never been touched by human hands. A liquor cabinet, a very wide desk, eight padded chairs and the senator's portrait rounded out the picture. The only thing missing was the senator himself. Maybe he'd stepped out to the john?

I made my way across the carpet and over to the desk. It was clean as a whistle, no papers in sight. The senator was probably a stickler for neatness. All on its own, my hand crept to the top desk drawer, quietly slid it open. Pens, pencils, blank paper, a box of paper clips. Hardly worth the effort. But then I was only rifling the senator's desk to keep in practice; I had no great expectations.

I tried the second drawer. Copies of the *Congressional Record,* a set of speeches by the senator. Again, nothing to write home about. There was only one drawer left. I pulled it open, took a long hard look. The good grades I was giving the senator for neatness suddenly went down the chutes. Papers had been tossed pell-mell into the bottom drawer as though some irate chambermaid had lost all patience with her job. Minicomputers, recorders, were part of the mess too. I pulled out some of this paper work, smoothed it out on the desk top: handwritten notes for a speech on a new hover-port in Mid City; itinerary for a tour of the border states; an appointment schedule. Everything was dated two or three weeks ago. How about that?

I rummaged in the pile of papers till my fingers touched the hard plastic base of a desk calendar. I yanked it out for a quick look-see. The pages were blank after April the eighth, two weeks ago. I stood there staring at them as though expecting writing to magically appear and tell me where the hell Fulton had gone. The chick at the reception desk certainly wasn't going to do that; she'd been mum as a clam when it came to giving me the straight goods. In fact she'd even gone to the trouble of pulling off a senseless charade just to keep me in the dark. But why bother in the first place? A guy like the senator could write his own ticket when it came to taking a breather, didn't need anyone's permission for a vacation. The whole thing was goofy.

I thumbed the calendar back to the eighth. Frank Broderick was the only name listed that day. Maybe *he'd* know where the senator had gone. I could always start pulling some strings on my own; Moon Base had lots of strings. Only I wasn't looking forward to that much activity. I sighed, ripped off Broderick's page and stuck it in my pocket.

The sooner I got out of here, the quicker I could get my senator hunt going. Just what I needed to fill up my spare time, a real live senator hunt. I hoped there was some reasonable and logical explanation for all this, something that would surface after an hour of digging and let me call it a day. Somehow I had my doubts.

I moved toward the door.

The door swung open, as if in greeting. Two large men stepped into the office, closed the door behind them. They stood there eyeing me expectantly as if I were a star performer on a stage about to deliver my most famous lines. I wondered what the hell I was going to say.

The first one, the taller of the two, spoke. "Waiting for a bus, palsy?"

The other one grinned. "Maybe he's the new charlady, eh, Greg?"

"Where's his mop, his pail? Na, he gotta be waitin' for a bus, right, pal?"

"Poor guy, a bus ain't stopped here for years—if ever."

"Ha-ha, guys," I said, "I appreciate the routine, no kidding. But I'm really here on a legitimate errand. Like they say, I can explain everything. Ha-ha," I added for good measure. When they catch you with your hand in the till, a little friendliness never hurt. On the other hand, looking at these two guys, I didn't think it was going to do much good, either.

The big one shook his head sadly. "Look, pal, the last guy who tried to explain everything took months."

The little one said, "We ain't even got hours."

I fumbled for my wallet. Maybe they could get me for trespassing. But they'd have trouble making it stick against a bona fide Moon Base rep. And for the moment that was me.

I got my credentials out and waved them at the pair. "No need for any lip, gents; I know this looks bad, but just give me a chance. What are you, security?"

"Uh-huh," the shorter guy said.

"Got this place wired, huh?"

"What else?" the shorter guy asked.

For a shorter guy he was pretty tall. And the other guy was even taller. Charm wasn't going to work, that was plain to see. It was time to use irrefutable logic. Too bad I didn't have any handy. Maybe authority would carry the day; *something* had to. "My name's James Morgan, fellas, and I'm an authorized Moon Base rep. I got business with the senator. It's strictly confidential, of course, but I can tell you this much: the senator's going to be real glad to hear what I have to say. Take it from me, you guys will probably pull down a bonus if you can put me in touch with Fulton. I'm bringing him a deal from Moon Base that'll have him sitting pretty in no time. That's why I took the liberty of barging in like this. Time means a lot and I was afraid the senator and I had maybe got our wires crossed. I wanted to explain things to him firsthand. I didn't know he was off somewhere. But as you can see, especially if you'll take a gander at my papers, it's all on the up-and-up. And no damage has been done."

"Not yet," the shorter guy said.

"Because we been patient," the taller guy said.

"Only now we run outta patience."

They both started for me.

"Wait a minute, guys," I yelled. "Hold it. Didn't you hear what I was saying? Moon Base rep. Heap big deal. Authorized, licensed, and approved by *Good Housekeeping*. Come on, guys, be reasonable. Who needs trouble?"

The tall guy was pulling a sap out of his pocket. "We do."

The shorter guy produced a small wooden billy club from somewhere. "We gets paid for trouble."

I started backing up; it seemed like the smart thing to do. "What this'll get you is fired," I explained cleverly, looking around for somewhere to run. "You think the senator's going to *like* your lousing up his deal? You think he's going to hand you a medal for roughing up a Moon Base rep? I told you I'm the guy who can have him sitting pretty."

"He's already sitting pretty," the tall guy said.

"Don't you know *anything?*" the shorter guy said.

By then I'd backed around to the other side of the desk. "Apparently not."

"You'll learn," the shorter guy said.

"Uh-huh. We'll teach you, palsy."

"Thanks a lot."

"Don't mention it," the tall guy said.

I stooped down, pulled open the bottom desk drawer. "If you want to act irrationally, guys, that's okay with me. This is where your boss dumped all his important papers, see? Very messy. But not to worry, the clean-up squad's on its way. Watch." I fished my lighter out of a pants pocket, snapped it on. "You aren't the only guys who can act irrationally," I pointed out, dropping the lighter, flame and all, into the drawer. "Your boss is sure going to get a kick out of everything being in cinders," I said brightly.

"Shit," the bigger guy said, making a dash for the drawer around the left side of the desk.

I headed right, remembering to scoop up the senator's wastebasket in the process. I bounced it off the shorter guy's head. He blinked and that was his big mistake. I kicked his ankle out from under him. The guy hit the floor as I ran for the door.

A glance over my shoulder showed me smoke and flame rising from the desk drawer. The tall guy was trying to beat it out with his jacket.

He needed help.

I pulled down the lever that said fire alarm in the hallway.

I raced into the large work-hall.

"Fire! Fire!" I screamed. I didn't need any help putting panic in my voice; the mere thought of the two goons in the senator's office was enough to bring on a whopping case of it.

Office workers sprang to their feet, took off in all directions as if competing in the treasure hunt of the year. I went with them. We hit the chutes, one solid mass, and poured down to the ground floor. No one paid me the least attention. As I sprinted through the lobby, I had the comforting feeling that can only come when forty other sprinters are all around you.

Out on the street I kept going. I had nothing to brag about. Maybe I'd managed to save my skin back there at the senator's office. But as far as advancing my mission, I'd just laid a big, round egg.

CHAPTER 5

I used a handy view-phone on the main drag, slipped my rate-card into the pay slot—after wiping my brow and getting my hands to stop shaking— punched the Moon Base Public Relations Office co-ords, and was instantly connected with a blue-eyed, blond-haired girl who broke into a dazzling smile at the mere sight of me. Whenever they do that I know something's wrong. I gave the view-screen a closer look-see. The darn girl looked perfect; too perfect. I was ogling a mech-image. "This is Ambassador Morgan," I said in some disgust. "Get me the director."

The director was a white-haired, sleepy-eyed, mild-voiced sixtyish gent named Timins; he flashed on a second later. "Morgan?"

"Yeah, it's me. Since when does Moon Base stoop to mech-image?"

"Since the budget crunch; where've you been?"

"The Moon."

"Why, so you have, Morgan. Well, there've been lots of changes since you last dropped by."

"I'm sure."

Timins sighed. "And not all of them have been for the better."

"Have *any?*"

"Probably not, but who can be sure?"

"Uh-huh."

"Well, Morgan, what can I do for you? Need some vacation pointers? A couple of free tickets to the girly shows?"

"Not this time, Timins. I'm here on business. Moon Base business."

"Didn't know we had any left."

"No kidding? I thought you guys were getting the big bucks."

"By Moon Base standards, yes; by anyone else's, no."

"Great. But don't worry, Timins, they've made me the new ambassador; I'm here to straighten things out. Get things rolling again. Put Moon Base back on its feet. And if none of that works out, I can always buy you a drink, eh, Timins? But I'll need your help."

"No sweat, Morgan, I'll go fifty-fifty with you on that drink."

"Not that part, Timins, the other parts."

"Well, you know, Morgan, the P.R. office is at your disposal—what there is of it."

"What's that supposed to mean?"

"We've got more mech-images around this place than people."

"Dig up a people, Timins, and get him working on the Scott Fulton skip-out. The senator's blown the coop and Moon Base needs him found."

"Really?" ‑

"Honest injun. But keep it under your hat."

"I don't wear a hat, Morgan."

"Uh-huh. Better get me a rundown on a Frank Broderick, too. He was the last guy to see Fulton two weeks ago."

"Where do I reach you if and when we turn something up?"

"Not sure yet. I'll have to call you."

"The plot gets thicker."

"Darn right. I ran into some flack at Fulton's office, and there's just a chance I'm in dutch with the law. Or the senator's strong-arm boys."

"Strong arm? Is that like in muscle, Morgan?"

"Just like, Timins. Truth is, I can't spare the time for that kind of squabble. So I'm going to duck for a while. But don't worry, I'll be in touch."

"I wasn't worried."

I rang off and went back to my hotel. I skirted the front door and lobby. That was for ordinary citizens. Ambassador types like me deserved something special. I used the back entrance, took the service chutes up to my floor. I didn't think the pair from Fulton's office was going to make trouble here at the hotel. But then, I hadn't thought they'd make trouble for me in the first place. Obviously, my thinking had been a wee bit off. And until I found out what was what with this Fulton business, I was going to pretend that trouble was nipping at my heels. I hoped pretend was all I'd have to do.

No one was lurking in the hallway. I got into my room, packed my one suitcase on the double and was out of there in five minutes. The service chutes took me down. I stepped into the alleyway, closed the back door behind me. My hotel bill would have to wait; I could always pay by remote with my rate-card. The thing to do now was make tracks out of here. If Fulton's boys wanted my hotel, they could have it for the asking. I'd used my own name to register and waved my credentials at the pair of goons just so they'd know who I was. As an official Moon Base rep it had seemed the smart thing to do. Too bad smart wasn't holding up its end. A remote check with Central Registry would turn me up in an eye-blink. Fulton was supposed to be on *our* side; if I was having so much trouble with friends, I wondered what would happen if I ran into an enemy?

I got out on the street, flagged down an auto-cab and headed for the other side of town. Tall buildings began to diminish in size. Multilevel highways fell away in the distance. Bobbing copters sank to metallic pinpoints behind me. When an occasional tree began popping up I knew I'd reached home base. No one would think of looking for an ambassador out here in the wilds—it would be uncivilized.

I checked into a small nondescript hotel, using a phony name and ended up in a cozy fourth-floor room with a view of a park across the street. It was a nice place to unwind, but I had other things on my mind.

I went outside, found a view-phone conveniently located a few blocks away. It seemed a darn sight safer than using the hotel's facilities, not to mention the fresh air I'd be getting. I stuck my rate-card in the slot and punched the co-ords I'd been given for Malcolm Lane. The phone buzzed up a small storm in my ear, but the screen stayed blank. Lane was probably off somewhere with his eye to a keyhole bent on getting the latest dirt for Moon Base. Or maybe he'd taken the day off and gone to the racetrack. Either way, I didn't figure Lane was going to be much help. On the other hand, you never know.

In quick succession I dialed Fulton's home, the Senate Chamber and a lobbyist I had known years ago. The first two wouldn't give me the time of day. My old pal, the lobbyist, told me it was two-fifteen but when it came to Fulton's whereabouts, he didn't know from beans.

The old view-phone was chewing up my rate-card, adding tidbits of revenue to the phone company's coffers. Aside from that, nothing very much was happening. To change things for the better, I hoped, I used the phone three more times, set up a trio of appointments. I left the view-phone waiting for another mark, hunted up an auto-cab a few blocks away and rode back downtown. Time for the personal touch again. I hoped I hadn't lost it.

CHAPTER 6

Tom Bossly was a short, fortyish balding man with black hair, shrewd gray eyes, a trim mustache, a perpetual leer or grin on his face, a cigar in his mouth or a drink in his hand. He was a big wheel on the signal-nine news-alert network. We'd been buddies in the good old days, whenever that was. Now, up on the sixty-first floor of the Eastern Network Building, I was holding down an easy chair in Bossly's office. He finished pouring me a drink, reclaimed his own chair, nodded jovially and grinned.

"But I trust you didn't come here just to chew the fat, did you, Jim boy?"

I shrugged. "Sure. What else? What are friends for?"

Bossly laughed. "Cut it out, before you shake my faith in human nature."

"Well," I admitted, "there is one *very* small question I might ask."

"I'm all ears."

"Yeah. I noticed. But I was too much of a gentleman to say so. What do you know about Senator Scott Fulton, Tom?"

Bossly shrugged. "What's to know?" He picked a half-smoked cigar out of his ashtray, began chewing it.

"I'll settle for anything."

"Wellll, his political life's a matter of public record. He's been pretty good to you folks up on Moon Base; supported you all the way, correct, Jim boy?"

"Can't be faulted on that."

"Fine. He pulls a lot of weight in the People's Council, and is maybe even working his way up to the top slot of chairman."

"You think so?"

"It's just conjecture. It would take a lot of doing. Raymond Hess has brains to spare, he's holding up his end real good. If he calls elections in the next couple of months, his party just might bring home the bacon."

"So I've heard. What about Fulton's personal life? Any skeletons in his closet?"

"You mean women?"

I shrugged. "Anything'll do. Woman, graft, kickbacks. You name it, I'm not particular."

Bossly waved a hand at me. "Forget the money angle. The senator doesn't need it; he was to the manner born."

"So, make it women."

"Wellll, his wife passed on a couple years ago. What's Fulton now, sixty-six, sixty-seven? Anything's possible, I suppose. But if the senator's been playing house with some female, it's news to me."

"Uh-huh. Could you get me a rundown of the guy's hangouts, his cronies, stuff like that?"

"Sure. What gives anyway? Why this sudden interest in the good senator?"

"You wouldn't believe me if I told you."

"Still, what have you got to lose?"

"You drive a hard bargain, Tom," I said earnestly, "but your flawless reasoning has brought me around."

Bossly grinned.

"Fulton's taken a powder. He's dusted out. In short, vanished."

Bossly nodded good-naturedly. "I see. So maybe you can explain this: If Fulton's disappeared, how come no one knows it?"

"That's an easy one, Tom. There's a cover-up."

"Indeed. A cover-up."

"You probably wonder why, huh?"

"You might say that."

"Me too."

"Jesus H. Christopher!"

"Yeah. That goes without saying. Maybe I should just give you the facts."

"Maybe."

"Well, Moon Base put me down here on a small errand. Suffice it to say part of this errand was getting hold of the senator."

"Easy enough, I'd imagine."

"That's what I figured. Guess again."

"He wouldn't see you?"

"He wasn't *there* to see me. And in the process I almost got my head handed to me by a couple of his goons. I didn't even know he had any goons on his payroll."

"Anyone who is anyone has goons these days, Jim boy. Why, I'm even thinking of buying a few myself. Keep my social standing up to snuff."

"Great."

"Wellll, there has been a lot of violence abroad lately. But you said something about facts." Bossly removed the cigar from his mouth, looked at it quizzically, and placed it in the ashtray. He still hadn't lit it. He took a swig out of his half-full glass of hooch and sat back to listen to me.

"So I did." I went on to give him my sorry yarn in most of its grizzly detail. When I was done, Bossly wagged his head at me.

"You're sober, I trust?"

"Your trust is well-founded."

"Wellll, if there's anything in this wild and woolly tale of yours, it would make a real dandy item on the news-lines."

"A nice feather in your cap too, eh, Tom?"

"I notice you haven't sworn me to secrecy yet."

"An oversight, all right. I bet you'll go blab to the whole world now." Bossly's gray eyes were glittering. "That's what I have in mind. *If* this pans out."

"It'll pan out okay. You can count on it. My mess is your scoop."

"You don't look too broken up about it, Jim boy."

"Yeah. The first thing they teach us on Moon Base is to keep a stiff upper lip. Hurts like hell when you're trying to smile."

"What's the second thing they teach you?" Bossly asked with some interest.

"To save your paycheck so you can get the hell off Moon Base. I'm working on that angle right now. Only this Fulton business has me up a stump. Maybe a little publicity will help smooth the way, huh?"

"Can't hurt."

"Uh-huh. Might even keep the senator's goons off my back. Once the news gets out that the senator's beat it, there won't be much incentive to shut my mouth, will there?"

"Probably none at all. Unless, of course, there's some other small grievance these boys have got that you aren't talking about. Or maybe even something you don't *know* about?"

"What would that be?"

"What indeed, Jim boy?"

The Darrell Building was located on Central and North streets. I took the chutes up to the ninth floor, went hunting for room 9B. The decal on the door said Brian Litkey Confidential Investigations. The decal had no reason to lie. Pushing open the door, I stepped in. The anteroom was empty. A thin coating of dust lay over easy chairs and magazine stand. Litkey was too tight to hire a cleaning lady and too lazy to do the job himself. Good old Litkey. It was reassuring to see that some things hadn't changed. I went through the anteroom into Litkey's private office.

Litkey was a very tall, heavyset man somewhere in his early fifties. He had thinning brown hair, huge shoulders, a large nose, a squarish jaw, and a permanent scowl etched into his massive head. The scowl had been known to turn to a sneer at a moment's notice. He was seated behind his desk in a wrinkled suit. He looked tired. But then, he always did. "You're late Morgan," he said as I came in.

"Five years you don't see me," I complained, "and that's the best you can do?"

"You owe me thirty Credits."

"Since when?"

"Since five years ago. The poker game, chump."

"Oh, yeah. Put it on my bill. Add a twenty for interest."

I pulled up the client's chair, sank into it.

"You're a real sport, Morgan. How's Moon Base treatin' you?"

"A poor place for a growing lad to make his fortune."

"Trying your hand back on Earth-side?" Litkey sneered. "A little over-aged for the job market, ain't you, sonny?"

"I'm on Moon Base business, Litkey."

"No shit. Whaddya know about that? And you're offering poor old Litkey a slice of the pie, huh, buster?"

"A few crumbs, maybe."

"Still the big spender, ain't you, Morgan?"

"Don't forget the thirty Credits, Litkey. Bet you never figured on seeing them, eh?"

"Can the crap, Morgan. Just give me what you're peddling, okay?"

I told him. "It'll make the holo soon enough. Senator Scott Fulton's turned up missing."

Litkey stared out of his office window for an instant. Other office windows in buildings across the street stared back, hardly an uplifting exchange. But to be expected.

Litkey said, "Everyone and his cousin'll be out chasin' after the old bozo; you don't need me to hunt him up."

"Right. But if you should run across him in your travels, you might let me know."

"You got business with him?"

"Moon Base does. I'm just the messenger in this. What I want from you, Litkey, is to find out what kind of goons Fulton has working for him. And why."

"Goons?"

"Uh-huh. At least a pair." I described my two playmates from Fulton's office. "Find out who they are."

"How'd you run across these guys?" Litkey wanted to know.

"They jumped me."

"What were you up to, buster, crossin' against the light?"

"Frisking the senator's office."

"That figures."

"Maybe. But I was very neat about it. And for all those guys knew I was the senator's long-lost brother."

Litkey nibbled his thumb. "Well, Morgan, going up against the senator's hired help ain't gonna be no picnic. Poor old Litkey ain't as young as he useta be. It'll cost you some."

"Cost Moon Base, not me. Don't let it worry you, Litkey. Moon Base is good for it. At least, I hope so."

"Let's both hope so, buster."

One last stop and I could call it a day, at least as far as my appointments went. I flagged down an auto-cab, settled in for a long ride. Good thing it was automated; where I was headed, a real live cabbie would've probably wanted a double fare—one for hazardous duty.

I sat back, let the scenery shoot by and thought over my last hour's doings. Poor old Litkey, eh? The guy had more Credits salted away than I had worries—and I had plenty. He could've retired yesterday without batting an eye. Only the notion of a bit more icing on the Credit pie kept him hopping. And always would. Greed had him in a headlock—just like a lot of other parties I knew. Litkey was a bastard, all right. But he knew his stuff and didn't often switch sides in mid-game. That counted for something. I wondered just how much.

The cab buzzed along, its computerized motor humming placidly to itself. The dumb cab was in a better mood than me and why not? So far, I'd hardly set the world on fire. Even with Fulton in tow, knocking Hess off his pedestal would've been no cinch. But at least we'd've had a fighting chance. Now it was anyone's guess what might happen. If Fulton wouldn't play ball, or stayed missing, I'd have to try and rig some kind of coalition myself. After five years on Moon Base what I knew of Earth-side politics was next to zero. And half my contacts had no doubt moved on to greener pastures. Or even worse, turned honest. Some mess.

Far in the distance the first signs of urban blight began to appear. Bright, colored lights twinkled and winked at me as if they were old friends welcoming me home after a long absence. Multicolored free-form structures groped skyward. I was still a long way off but the sounds of merrymaking seemed to drift over the small houses and crooked streets and find their way right into the cab. No use crawling under the padded seat. The damn racket would reach me anyway. I was headed straight for Whoopy Complex, the Fun Capital of the Eastern Seaboard. Some laugh.

Slipping my rate-card into its slot, I paid off the cab, stepped out onto the concrete. Fun houses lined both sides of the street. Loudspeakers blared, colored lights blazed away, the crowd rose like a wave around me. Out of a corner of my eye I saw the cab beating a hasty retreat. Smart cab.

Shoving and pushing I made my way through the hubbub. When I reached the first side street, I turned left. In the middle of the block I found a gate, opened it, walked into a small narrow cobblestone alley. I was alone here and glad of it. Old-fashioned four-story houses were on both sides of the alley. The third house on the right was my target. I rang a bell, an answering buzz let me through the door. I went up two flights of stairs, turned left and there it was. The door said Consultations. And underneath that: J. Procter Ambrose.

I went in.

A little man sat behind a desk in a one-room office. J. Procter Ambrose looked up and smiled. He was maybe five-foot-three, bold, had a long hooknose, bushy white eyebrows, wore rimless glasses and was somewhere in his late sixties or early seventies.

"Well, as I live and breathe," he said, "if it isn't James Morgan. And right on time, too. Come in, my boy. Do."

"I'm already in, Joey."

"Ah, yes. Not Joey, please, Procter. Pull up a chair, Jimmy. It's good to see you again."

I pulled up a chair.

"You haven't changed much, Procter."

"Well now, at my age that's good to hear. It certainly is. Yes indeedy. Prospering on Moon Base, are you, Jimmy?"

"Holding my own."

"Now, Jimmy, no need for excessive modesty. Not between old friends. I'm certain you're doing quite well in all things. Now aren't you? Isn't that so, Jimmy?"

"Stop running off at the mouth, Procter. This is business."

"You have a problem, then? One that requires my expertise?" Ambrose made a steeple of his fingers, regarded me inquisitively. Smiled. Unsteepled the fingers. "But then you always do, Jimmy. Have a problem. Of one sort or another."

"Yeah, I suppose so. The sort I have now can earn you a couple of Credits."

"Well, I certainly can't complain if you've come for a consultation, can I?"

"Nope."

"My bread and butter, after all."

"Uh-huh."

"Personal matter, Jimmy?"

"I'm here for Moon Base."

"Ah, then, you must have an expense account. A huge one, I'd imagine. Yes, indeedy."

"Try not to drool on your desk, Procter."

"Well, some of my consultations *do* run to a pretty penny, you know."

"Yeah. I know."

"But well worth every last Credit, you'll agree." The little man smiled at me. The thought of Credits was making his day.

"Uh-huh. Look, I've been trying to get hold of Senator Scott Fulton—" Ambrose held up his hand. "Wasted effort, my boy. The senator is *nowhere* to be found. Been absent about two weeks, perhaps."

"Well," I admitted, "I've got to hand it to you, Procter. You're the first guy I've bumped into who's had the straight goods on that one. It's a cockeyed wonder. Now if you could only tell me where he's at."

"There *are* rumors."

"Yeah?"

"I must say, Jimmy, that I do not put much stock in them."

"Okay, you've said it. What are they?"

"Mutant Village." The little man let out his breath.

I gave J. Procter Ambrose a long, hard look. "Have a heart," I told him.

"Moon Base is shelling out good old coin of the realm for your inside track. If you start dispensing a lot of eyewash, think what it'll do to your reputation."

Ambrose smiled sweetly. "That bit of information did come with a disclaimer, Jimmy. Oh, yes indeedy."

"Some information. Look, a savvy politico like Fulton wouldn't touch Mutant Village with a ten-foot pole. That place is poison. Who loves a mutie, huh? Besides, the village is legally out of bounds."

Ambrose held up a hand. "Mutant Village *does* have its supporters."

"Sure, a lot of fringe crackpots. What have they got to lose? But Fulton's up there on top. Fulton's opponents would make mincemeat of him if they ever found out he was playing footsie with the mutants. They'd probably have the law on him, too. Come on, Ambrose, you can do better than that."

Ambrose tilted his head sideways, as if he were listening to some small, private voice. "Perhaps his association with the village isn't entirely voluntary?"

"That's just as hard to swallow, Procter. Public opinion is dead set against the muties. Even I know that, and I've been camping on the Moon for half a decade. If the muties pulled a stunt like making off with Fulton, they'd find themselves behind barbed wire quicker than you could say 'crime does not pay.' "

"My dear boy, I do not believe that I have ever seriously suggested to anyone that 'crime does not pay.' And for all practical purposes the mutants *are* behind barbed wire."

"Sure. With all the comforts of home, and then some. It's not the same thing. And why would they want to put the snatch on Fulton anyway?"

"Have you ever heard of People's Counsel Barnabus, Jimmy?"

"Uh-huh."

"A most able politician."

"So how does he figure in all this?"

"For some reason, Counsel Barnabus has taken up the hated mutant cause. And he is, of course, only a chamber away from the People's Senate."

"Maybe I'm missing something. I still don't get it."

"There is a move afoot to remove the legal restraints which have been placed upon the mutants. As yet it is a fledgling effort. Barnabus is a part of it. In some way Senator Fulton has become embroiled in this controversy. Rumor has it that his disappearance is linked to the maneuvers around the mutant issue."

"Pretty vague."

"Of course. But then until *you* arrived on the scene, Jimmy, no one had employed me to be more precise. What I have given you so far is merely hearsay. What you will get in the weeks ahead will be facts. Solid facts."

"Better make that days, not weeks. This job won't keep."

"As you say. In this office Credits talk. And bring results. But you know that, Jimmy, or you wouldn't be here, would you?"

"I suppose not, Procter."

CHAPTER 7

By the time I got out of Ambrose's office, dusk was starting to settle over the streets. Man-made implements fought the darkness. Brilliant lights flared: red, green, orange, yellow, blue. They winked and blinked: "Fun! Fun! Fun!" loudspeakers blared. "Play me! Play me!" game shops screamed. "Eat me! Eat me!" eat shops howled.

It was murder back on the main drag; all of Central City seemed to be out on the town. The Whoopy Complex was booming. Half the attractions were licensed by the Leisure Guild; its director, my old pal and drinking buddy Harley Stokes, must've been raking in the Credit hand over fist.

I didn't envy him—not too much anyway. A guy with all that responsibility had to be having a pretty tough time. At least I hoped so. It would only be fair.

"Mr. Morgan," a voice said.

I looked around, sure that I was hearing things. No one could find me in this mob scene.

"Over here, Mr. Morgan."

I glanced over a broad-shouldered guy, past a young couple holding hands and saw him. He was a skinny kid in a checkered suit and straw hat. He couldn't have been more than twenty-two. I didn't know him from Adam.

Reluctantly I pushed my way through the crowd. Whoever this guy was I didn't think I'd enjoy meeting him.

"Put it there, Mr. Morgan," he said, extending a limp hand.

I gave the hand a shake, said, "You've got a name, friend?"

"Name? Oh, sure. Billy Williams, that's me."

"Okay, Billy Williams. Who are you? How do you know me? What do you want? Have I left anything out, Billy?"

"Na, I think you covered it all."

"So?"

"So, let's say we step into this here drinking joint, knock off a couple-a joy-juices and I'll give you what I got."

"As long as it's on you, kid."

I followed Williams into the dive. The place was jumping. We made our way to the bar. Williams had a high-up special. I settled for an old-fashioned beer.

"Okay," I said. "Let's hear it."

"Sure. I work for the Speedy Service Agency, Mr. Morgan."

"Yeah? What does it do?"

"Service."

"Figures. And what service do you perform?"

"I'm a messenger, kind of."

"Uh-huh. And you've got a message for me?"

"That's right, Mr. Morgan."

"Don't be bashful, kid, spill it."

"The message is: Lay off."

"Lay off?"

"That's it."

"Nothing more?"

"Just lay off."

"Some message."

"For more you gotta see my boss, Mr. Henderson."

"He's got more, huh?"

"He's always got more, Mr. Morgan."

"This act you and Henderson put on, you do it for others, not just me?"

"It's one of the services."

"You got more?"

"Sure."

"Like what?"

"Deliveries."

"Anything special?"

"Whatever Mr. Henderson wants."

"Yeah, that makes sense. Sounds like a real neat service."

"You bet. Lotsa folks need messages and deliveries."

"So tell me, Billy, how did you find me?"

"No trouble at all."

"No, huh?"

"Just waited where Mr. Henderson said I should."

"And where was that?"

"By the alley back there."

"Uh-huh. And you recognized me how?"

"This picture."

The kid reached into his jacket pocket, pulled out a snapshot. It showed me getting off the Moon Base Shuttle. I was wearing the same suit I had on two days ago.

"Henderson give you this?"

"Sure."

"Know where he got it?"

The kid shrugged a shoulder. "He had lots of copies made and gave them to more than fifty messengers just like me, had them cover all the places you might show up at."

"He knew the places, eh? Your Henderson must be quite an operator."

"He's aces."

"When do I see him?"

"Tomorrow."

"Time?"

"Mr. Henderson said you should see him after lunch around two."

"Sounds swell," I said. The whole thing was as depressing as hell. This Henderson—whoever he was—seemed to have all the answers, while I was still stumbling around trying to figure out what the questions were. What kind of a game was *that*?

I said, "Where do I meet him?"

"His office." The kid gave me a card. Henderson had a midtown address in an ordinary business section. There was no knowledge to be gained from the location.

"Okay," I said, "tell him it's a date."

"Sure thing. This is my lucky day, all right."

"Yeah?"

"I get a bonus."

"You do, eh?"

"For finding you."

"Hell, I didn't even know I was lost."

An auto-cab carried me back toward city center. I wasn't chipper at all. I was starting to wonder if I'd go the distance on this caper. When the opposition begins calling the shots, it's high time for some second thoughts.

This Billy Williams shouldn't've been able to pick me up so easily. In the old days when I was turning an honest Credit on Earth-side as trouble-shooter, I'd used J. Procter Ambrose more than once. That was hardly a secret. But for someone to come up with that item now—and stake out fifty other joints, no less—showed too much effort. I didn't like it. Fulton shouldn't've done a fade, either. And the muties shouldn't've figured in this at all. I sighed. Far too many shouldn'ts bouncing around to suit me. I wondered if I'd left any out. Yeah. Hoods and goons shouldn't've been cluttering up Fulton's office. Brother. I glanced back out the rearview window just to make sure I wasn't being tailed by goons and hoods this very moment. The Whoopy Complex was far behind us and city center off somewhere ahead. We were sailing along on a wide highway, trees, fields and small clusters of houses on either side of us. Out of the darkness behind us only one pair of headlights glistened. I looked at the headlights. The headlights looked at me. Not much to be gained by that. We rode along for another twenty minutes. Other cars came and went. The headlights stayed right where they were.

Jeez.

This was the time to ask the cabbie if he'd noticed anything. But the cabbie was a stupid machine. I wasn't about to let that stand in the way of enlightenment. I was beginning to get real nervous.

"Oh, cabbie," I said.

"Yes-s-s-s?"

"I think we're being followed."

"You do?" The mechanized voice was coming out of the gridwork on the dashboard. Rotten voice.

"Yeah."

"Well, you're absolutely right!"

"*I am?*"

"In *my* cab the customer is *always* right. But you're *more* right than most."

"More right."

"Exactly. As soon as you climbed in my cab I noticed. That car was waiting at the curb. It took off right after us. It's been behind us ever since. I'd call that being followed, wouldn't you?"

"Yeah, that's what I'd call it."

"With my sensors on, I notice lots of things."

"I'm sure you do. Can you shake that car?"

"Only if I had hands."

"I mean lose it."

"I'm only a machine, why should I risk life and limb chasing around in the night? After all, it's not as though I needed a tip. What would I do with it? They grease me enough as it is in the garage."

Grease him enough. Just great. I'd hit a loquacious machine.

"Does that mean no," I asked, "or just maybe."

"It means no."

"Okay. To the Central City Airport, cabbie."

"It's none of my business," the cabbie said, "but by the time you get a ticket to blast off, they'll catch you for sure."

"We'll see about that!"

I hopped out of my auto-cab in front of the large double doors of the airport's main entrance. The crowd at this hour was just so-so. Maybe I'd do better inside. I went through the double doors. Loudspeakers blared away. Electric billboards listed arrivals and departures. Passengers streamed along in all directions. Not bad. I could've taken to my heels and lost myself in this hubbub without much trouble. But then I'd never know if I was really being shadowed. And by whom.

That wouldn't do.

I hid behind a large beam and watched the main entrance. I didn't have long to wait.

There were four of them, big hefty guys in trench coats, their hands stuck in their pockets. The fact that they immediately spread out and began peering at faces in the crowd might have given them away. The mean look on their kissers would've helped too. If I'd needed that kind of help. I didn't. Two of the guys were far from strangers. Although they weren't pals of mine, either.

The pair of strong-arm hoods I'd tangled with in Fulton's office were back on the scene. And this time they'd brought along some help.

I had at least a couple of choices open to me:

I could slip my laser loose and fry 'em where they stood. Except that I didn't have a laser. And the prospect of spending the rest of my life in the pokey didn't exactly appeal to me.

I could raise a holler, ring in the cops and have it out with this pair here and now. Except that for all I knew, their two buddies *were* the cops. And instead of going about my business, I'd be fighting trumped-up charges down at the courthouse for the rest of the month—if not longer.

That left a third ignoble course: I could run for it. It didn't take much thought. The third had it hands down.

I slipped away from my beam, turned my back on the main entrance and fell into step with a group of folks heading for the information desk.

Both sides of the wide walkway were lined with shops. I caught my reflection in a succession of plate glass windows and an occasional mirror as I hurried along. I looked no different from any of my fellow travelers. And the same could be said for the four mugs dashing along after me.

Double Jeez.

I ducked into a side aisle, took off as best I could. The narrow corridor was jammed. I wasn't going to set any record in this crush, that was for sure. But the foursome behind me might not be as considerate of people, might even knock a couple down to gain a yard or two. And that's about all they would need.

I got out at the first exit I came to, found myself back in the great hall.

I didn't waste time scouting the territory. I took it on the heel and toe.

No track star ever tried harder. The thought of the four goons behind me gave me all the incentive I needed.

I passed eat shops, clothing shops, newsstands, game shops and a number of exits leading into the dark, lonely night. I ignored them all. Especially the dark lonely night. There were better ways to get beaten to a pulp. But none surer.

I was looking for a whoopy joint and found one down on the far right. Lou's Neo—Pub, the sign said. Dodging bodies right and left I picked up speed. I caught one glimpse of my pursuers far behind me, before I hit the pub's swinging doors. By then I was ready for the hurdles.

Inside was dim, crowded, the bars and tables full. Soft music whispered to the customers. Some of them were tanking up on liquor. Most were having a go at the stronger stuff. I didn't hang around to cheer them on. I made straight for the rest rooms in back. Ignoring the gents, I pushed open the door marked ladies and stepped in. Bright pink walls greeted me. But not half as pink as my face was getting. A sink, mirror, and three closed toilets were the room's only furnishings. One of the cubicles was occupied. I made for an empty one, closed and locked its door.

I sat there on the toilet seat sweating from every pore of my body. The cubicle's designers had left a foot-long space between floor and door. My men's shoes and trousers would be a dead give-away. I leaned back against the wall, lifted my feet and jammed them up against the door. Better an empty, locked toilet than the wrong kind of feet on view. Immediately my legs began to tingle with the unaccustomed strain. I gritted my teeth and sat tight. I heard women coming and going outside. I waited. Probably I was safe. My shadows might go through the joint with a fine-tooth comb, but odds had it they'd skip the ladies' room.

Odds didn't quite carry the day.

I heard the outside door open, and I heard a lady scream. A gruff male voice said, "Sorry, ma'am." And the door closed again. Thank God for that lady!

I sat around for another twenty minutes wondering why I was worth all this attention. And what I was going to do about it. Darned if I knew. Every now and then I'd lean over to rub my legs and change position. By now I could hardly feel them.

Putting an eye to the crack between door and frame, I peeked out. No customers present. Enough was enough. Even hand to hand combat seemed preferable to another ten minutes of this.

I stood up and almost fell down. I hobbled out of the ladies' room on legs that felt as if they belonged to a dime-store mannequin.

The four hoods were nowhere to be seen. Just as well. I'd've been a sitting duck. Even a wheelchair case could've made better time than me.

I turned, went back to the bar and had a whiskey sour. It didn't help much. Probably nothing would.

CHAPTER 8

I changed cabs twice, got off half a mile from my hotel and hoofed it the rest of the way. As far as I could tell, no one was dogging my heels. On the other hand, I was hardly a wiz these days in outwitting the opposition. In fact, I still didn't know who the opposition was. I hoped no one found out I had grown old and incompetent before I did something to improve the situation.

Back in my hotel room I used the view-phone to order a late dinner, put in a call to Ed-Out Backlog, rented a batch of tapes—mostly current events and personalities—and charged the whole shebang to Moon Base. I showered, changed into pajamas and lounging robe, found my dinner waiting for me in the meal chutes, hauled it out and proceeded to dine. As meals went on old terra firma, it wasn't half bad.

Flicking on the News Alert Network on the tel-viser, I sipped cognac and waited for developments. Developments came some ten minutes into the newscast. Tom Bossly's boys hadn't come up with hard evidence, but they did demonstrate beyond much doubt that Senator Scott Fulton had failed to frequent any of his known haunts for at least a couple of weeks. And that included the Senate. The newsy, looking professionally concerned, asked: "Where is he now? His family, colleagues and friends all want to know." They weren't the only ones, I thought.

I turned off the set, took another swig of cognac and realized I was feeling better. Now that Bossly had started the ball rolling, it was only a matter of time before the authorities got into the act, began beating the bushes for old Fulton. I was off the hook. The senator's stooges could go crack someone else's skull. And with all of Central City on the alert, Fulton should be a cinch to track down.

I leaned back in my easy chair, glanced out the window at the dark park below and wondered what the hell I was feeling so cheerful about. I was no nearer to completing my mission than the day I landed back on Earth.

And for all I knew, Fulton was pushing up the daisies in some vacant lot. Or had gone bananas and decided to join the muties. And the guys after me would never let up because they just hated my guts. And a grudge was a grudge. Oh, brother. Talk about rotten scenarios. Before my mood hit rock bottom I decided to do something positive. But something that wouldn't take much effort—I'd used up all the effort I had going for me this day.

First, I reached for the view-phone, dialed Brian Litkey's home number. For an instant I thought of playing it safe, dashing outdoors to use the corner phone. Only my arms and legs wouldn't go along with the notion. Let's hear it for the old arms and legs.

Litkey was out. But his answering mech was a lot friendlier than the private eye would ever be. I left a message concerning the following day and rang off.

Next, I got to my feet, went over to the Ed-Out chutes; the spools I'd ordered were there. I took them out, slipped them into their slots in the tel-viser, peeled off my lounging robe and crawled into bed. I adjusted my headset, flicked off the lights and in no time was off in slumberland.

Ed-Out transmissions, broadcast while the subject slept, provided unconscious education. Some were live or taped broadcasts received directly through the tel-viser. Others—like the ones I was using—were taped backlog transmissions stored in the Ed-Out archives and shot to the customer through inter-city chute. A third kind existed, too: subliminal broadcasts under the regular entertainie and news features.

An elaborate system of checks and balances—including Senate committees, electronic monitors, and production overseers—in which all factions took part—kept Ed-Out honest and neutral. And a good thing too. Because if one side ever got control of Ed-Out, they'd have the whole hemisphere dancing to their tune. And some dance that would be.

I got up bright and early. But I hadn't slept all that well. What with Ed-Out buzzing through my brain and a couple of nightmares I'd concocted on my own, featuring large burly men chasing me down dark, crooked streets, I was giving my unconscious more of a workout than it needed.

While shaving and brushing my teeth I tried to take inventory of the new data carousing through my cranium. I kept a special lookout for brand names that might be going off in my mind like neon signs. Not that I mistrusted the keepers of Ed-Out; too many watchdogs were breathing down their necks for them to slip in some unauthorized data. But with all those advertising Credits floating around, old temptation was wearing a special grin these days. I remembered years ago sleeping through a build-your-own-houseboat tape and waking up with an overpowering urge to get drunk on Drummond's Beer or Ale. I'd have landed in the drunk tank for sure if I hadn't got the damn thought erased by a specialist.

Nothing like that this morning. The tapes I had rented were supposed to clue me in on the political doings hereabouts. But the more I mulled over my new-found knowledge, the less I seemed to know. The whole thing was one huge muddle. Politicos ditching their own parties, splinter groups taking off right and left, bigwigs grappling for advantage. In this game, it looked like you couldn't tell the players even with a score card: they wouldn't hold still long enough. I gave it up.

What I had to do was forget all this trivia and start at the top.

At least I knew where that was:

Raymond Hess.

CHAPTER 9

"Do come in," Hess said, extending his hand, "what a great pleasure."

He took the hand I gave him, pumped it as though I were a local ward healer he was bent on winning over. And in a way, he wasn't far wrong.

"Good to see you, Mr. Chairman," I told him. My first lie of the day; I wondered how many would follow.

There was no desk in his office, just a low designer table with the latest model mini comput-processor on it, a number of ritzy easy chairs and, of course, a large utility computer in the west wall hooked up to Computer Central. A thick blue carpet hugged the floor. The five large priceless modern paintings on the wall, along with the two busts over in the corner, clearly showed that the Treasury hadn't gone broke yet. I took one of the chairs and planted myself opposite Hess.

This Hess was a large burly man in his mid-fifties with close-cropped steel-gray hair and a jutting jaw; his voice was deep, his eyes blue and forthright. He looked swell on the tel-viser. Very sincere. He was dressed in a simple gray suit that couldn't have set him back more than a couple of months' Credits.

Hess cast another glance at my Moon Base credentials and returned them to me.

"Well, Mr. Ambassador," Hess said, showing me a row of white, even teeth, which I took to be a grin, "let's get right down to issues, shall we? I know what brings you here."

For an instant I wondered who he was talking to. Then I remembered *I* was Mr. Ambassador. Now all I had to figure out was how Hess knew what I wanted.

"You do?" I asked smartly.

"Moon Base thinks I'm against them. Right?"

"You might say that," I admitted.

"They think I'm out to scrap the whole project, right?"

"There *have* been a couple of rumors to that effect, Mr. Chairman."

"Let me ask you something, Mr. Morgan."

"Sure. Fire away."

"How well do you know my record?"

Mentally I tried to conjure up a picture of the chairman's record. No dice. My Ed-Out research hadn't included it.

"Actually," I said, "I wouldn't call myself an expert."

"There you are," Hess said, showing me his teeth again.

"There I am *where?*"

"Barking up the wrong tree."

"You don't say?"

"I'm no foe of Moon Base."

"You're not, huh?"

"I have never voted against a Moon Base appropriation."

I thought that one over. "Have you ever voted *for* one?"

"Of course not."

"So?"

"But think of how many have voted against the appropriations."

"Lots, huh?"

"Obviously, or Moon Base would be a thriving concern."

"Are you saying, Mr. Chairman, that you're a *friend* of Moon Base?"

"Not an enemy."

"That's nice."

"I plan to schedule elections soon."

"No kidding?"

"I would be grateful for Moon Base support."

"Who wouldn't? But what about all this talk of closing us down so you can balance the budget?"

"Idle chatter."

"You willing to go public on a pro-Moon platform?"

The chairman shook his head. "I'm running a spend-less campaign. I'd never be able to square that with the voters."

"So what are you offering *us?*"

"My private assurances."

"Uh-huh," I said, trying not to sound too skeptical, just skeptical enough.

"Those who know me, Mr. Ambassador, also know that my word is my bond."

"They do?" That was a new one on me. And probably the nation, too. But I was beginning to get the hang of this guy. With his deep bass voice and blue earnest eyes that never left my face, the chairman could say just about anything and still come out sounding sweet and sensible. Not bad. The act must've gone over great on the election stump. But just now, it didn't have me cheering. I told him, "Actually, Moon Base was hoping for something more *concrete.*"

"Do try and be realistic, Mr. Ambassador."

"I'm trying. The thing is, Moon Base has no political party of its own."

"Of course it doesn't."

"Yeah, so if you made a behind-the-scenes deal with us and for some unexpected reason—like you're *really* trying to balance the budget— couldn't keep it, all we could do was go jump. And from the Moon that's quite a distance. But, Mr. Chairman, if you made a deal with a couple of our supporters, brought their factions into your coalition, that would be a different story, wouldn't it? That might even prove good faith."

"Good faith?"

"The words are in the dictionary."

"Any specific supporter in mind?" The chairman was eyeing me as if I might pull a supporter out of my sleeve.

"Senator Scott Fulton."

"Aha."

"Fulton and Moon Base go way back."

"So they do."

"We *trust* Senator Fulton."

"Who doesn't? An admirable statesman."

"If you could work out a deal with Fulton, Mr. Chairman, you'd have a Moon Base endorsement in your back pocket."

"I don't doubt it. And nothing would please me more than to have you and the senator in my corner. But there is one small difficulty. The senator seems to have vanished."

"Gone on vacation, maybe."

"Perhaps."

"Enjoying a long-sought rest."

"That is, of course, a possibility."

"He's bound to turn up sooner or later."

"I decidedly hope so."

"And you could always help things along by looking for him."

"Everyone seems to be looking for him now."

"That many?"

"More probably," Hess boomed at me heartily.

"That's sure a lot. But if you looked too, that would be one more."

"So it would."

"And I'm sure, Mr. Chairman, that you have resources available to you that even the police don't dream of."

"They dream of them, all right; they just don't have them."

"Uh-huh," I said.

"You are quite right, Mr. Ambassador. It has, in fact, always been my aim to work closely with Senator Fulton. And I would surely treasure the backing of Moon Base. Why, Moon Base is a national shrine, you know."

"Yeah, I know."

"And Senator Fulton is one of our ablest leaders."

"He'll be glad to hear that. Three months ago you called him a crooked, scheming four-flusher," I said, recalling a tidbit from last night's Ed-Out session.

"That was three months ago, and he *was* a crooked, scheming four-flusher then. But three months is a long time, politically speaking. I don't have to tell you that, Mr. Ambassador. Things change. Today the senator is an honored and revered colleague. One I can *use* in my coalition."

"To use him, you've got to find him."

"So I do."

"That's the spirit, Mr. Chairman. I knew we'd see eye to eye sooner or later."

The tel-viser was churning away in the Senate cafeteria. I got a pot of coffee through the meal-chutes, chose an empty table and gave my attention to the life-size images the tel-viser was projecting. It was one of Senator Scott Fulton. He was being treated as a genuine Missing Person. Even the capital police were out on the hunt. I sat there admiring what was—essentially—my handiwork and wondering who else I could sic on the senator. The more people out there doing my job, the better I liked it. I didn't think Chairman Hess was going to dash around beating the bushes for Fulton. But you could never tell. And, if nothing else, I'd let him know Moon Base wasn't going to sit this one out. We'd be in there come election time, pitching away. Especially if there was an election. That was the catch, all right. Along with a whole lot of other catches I probably didn't even know about.

CHAPTER 10

The Leisure Guild took up ten square city blocks. Its showpiece was the domed Hall of Electronic Distortion. Inside both computers and humans labored to set up illusions for the masses through the tel-viser system. With a lot of time on their hands and a negative income tax to keep their pockets loaded at the subsistence level, the masses needed any illusions they could get. And they got plenty.

Harley Stokes stepped out of his inner sanctum to personally greet me. He was the director of the Hall, which made him one of the most important guys in the nation. But Moon Base packs a lot of punch. And besides, I'd known Stokes when he was a mere technician, fooling around with wires and circuits. We'd been pretty thick.

"Son-of-a-gun, you've come up in the world, old man," Stokes said.

"Yeah, but not half as much as you, Harley. Talk about the big time. You're so high up it gives me a nosebleed just to think about it."

Stokes patted me on the back. "Nothing to it, old chum. All it takes is backbreaking labor, endless effort and knowing the right people. Especially the latter. And, of course, getting the right breaks doesn't hurt either." We went into his office, a circular room with changing amoebalike shapes jittering along the walls. Colors bled into one another, twinkled, blinked and vanished to be replaced by other colors. Some show. One I could do nicely without.

"Can you douse the fireworks?" I asked.

"Sure thing, old bean."

Stokes went over to a control panel, pressed a button. The wall was just a wall again.

"Thanks," I said. "My nerves are shot as it is."

"Really?" Stokes said. "Drink?"

"Why not?"

Stokes had one ready, handed me a tall glass with a white liquid in it: a mild form of joy-juice. Nonalcoholic, nonaddictive, nondetrimental. And left your mind clear as a bell. If you lived on the dole and needed a lift because there were no incentives worth feeling good about, joy-juice would do the trick. I took a swig and felt better already. Damn thing always worked. Vaguely, I wondered what I was feeling better about.

Stokes chose a padded green and yellow armchair; I plunked down on the solid black couch, sank into a mound of foam rubber. Damn thing was so comfortable, I was all but ready to suck my thumb and grab a quick snooze.

Stokes grinned at me. "Is this a social call, Jim, or does Moon Base have business with me?"

"A little of both," I said, trying to wake up.

Harley Stokes was a trim five-foot nine. He had lots of long blond wavy hair, heavy sleepy lids over wide-awake hazel eyes, a longish nose. And a chin with a cleft in it. He was forty-one, and looked maybe ten years younger. There wasn't much about the good life that Stokes didn't know. Or wasn't willing to find out. He hardly seemed the type to head up the nation's illusions. But what sort of a type would that be anyway? He had on a solid brown suede suit, with an open-necked yellow shirt and brown leather boots. I thought of asking him where he kept his six-shooter but thought better of it.

I said, "What do you think of Hess's chances in the election?"

Stokes shrugged a lean shoulder. "Not quite a shoo-in, but fairly close."

"Can he be trusted?"

"About as much as any politician."

"Sorry to hear that."

"What did you expect, Jim? You become an elections buff?"

I shook my head. "That's part of the business that brings me here. Moon Base has been getting short-changed for years. Maybe I can line up some support."

"You're wasting your time with Hess; he couldn't care less about Moon Base."

"That's not what he told me, Harley."

"If you start listening to what he *tells* you, old chum, you'll really land in the soup."

"Yeah, that's what I figured."

"What you need is someone like Fulton."

"I figured that, too."

"Clever lad."

"So where is he?"

Stokes raised a finger. "That's the rub, all right."

"Word has it, Harley, that you're kind of buddied up with the senator."

"Well, word's wrong on that score. We've shared a drink or two, sure. But that goes with the territory." Stokes waved his arm at the room.

"Got any bright notions about his whereabouts?"

"Nary a one. I know as much as I get on the news-lines. Less probably. Because I don't pay attention. This job keeps me tied to my desk."

"What desk?"

"It's in the other room."

"Just asking. Ever hear of a Frank Broderick?"

"Can't say I have. Anyone special?"

"Last guy to have seen the senator."

"Well, the Security boys will get to him."

"Maybe." I remembered tearing Broderick's name off the calendar. And wishing I hadn't.

"Spoken with Senator Tarken yet?"

"Uh-uh," I said.

"He's a good bet, Jim."

"For what?"

"Tarken was Fulton's second-in-command."

"Think he had the senator spirited away?"

"Not too likely; they're a team."

"How's he on Moon Base?"

"Solid. You haven't done your homework, old man."

"On-the-job training. I didn't plan it that way, of course, but who can plan anything these days?"

"I can."

"I suppose so."

"I plan the nation's illusions, you know."

"Yeah, I know."

"You'd be surprised how many illusions this nation's got."

"I doubt that."

"And they all need planning."

"So how *is* the job, Harley?"

Stokes shrugged. "It's a living," he said.

I used an outside view-phone to dial Malcolm Lane. Pedestrians, traffic and aircraft all added to the tumult around me. I wouldn't have been able to hear Lane even if he'd come to the phone. He didn't. Some Moon Base agent! What good was he if I couldn't reach him in a pinch? And if this wasn't a pinch, what was?

CHAPTER 11

An auto-cab drove me the thirty blocks to the Science Fed complex. I could see the white buildings rising up toward the sky way before I got there. This was the third and last establishment center on my list. When I'd covered this baby, I could go back to hobnobbing with the hoi polloi, provided I found some willing to talk. At least I couldn't be accused of not touching all the bases. But was I making progress? If nothing else the Science folks would be receptive to helping Moon Base. What would Moon Base be without science? Just a hunk of undeveloped real estate. But today Moon Base was a glowing endorsement to scientific achievement. Scientists the world over could bask in its reflected glory. And would continue to do so as long as our P.R. department kept grinding out the propaganda. Which, come to think of it, wouldn't be too long, if Moon Base didn't get some more funding. I had a feeling that the Fed would understand my viewpoint perfectly. And if there's one thing a lonely ambassador could use on a strange planet, it was a little perfect understanding. Of course, Earth wasn't a strange planet. But the longer I fooled around with this mission, the stranger it seemed.

Melissa Sussman was Fed president. She was a late-fiftyish lady in a no-nonsense blue tweed business suit as befits a president. In fact, if she wore anything else, they'd probably have taken her presidential seal away. That would still leave all the medals and awards she'd won as a top-grade scientist. I figured she could handle the situation either way.

Her brown hair was tied back in a bun. She had brown eyes and over them large round glasses.

Her sidekick, Valerie Loring, was in her late twenties. She had shoulder-length black hair, large gray-green eyes, full lips, a neat complexion and delicate bone structure. She wore green slacks, an orange blouse. She was maybe three inches shorter than Sussman, which made her five-foot four.

The three of us sat at a table nibbling very small triangle-shaped sandwiches, drinking hot herbal tea and occasionally noting the sun's progress —through a large overhead glass dome—as it made its way over Central City. It didn't take me long to explain the situation—the situation was simple enough; it's what I was going to do about it that had me over a barrel.

Sussman waited until I was done, nodded and said, "Hess was lying." Her voice was deep, musical.

"I can believe that," I said. "But just what part was the lie?"

"He hates Fulton."

"Yeah?"

"They have been at odds a long time."

"Is it mutual?"

"Fully."

"Political?"

"Personal."

Valerie said, "Hess insulted Fulton's late wife once." Her voice was more in the upper register.

"How's that?"

"Hess called her Mrs. Creep."

"Sounds like an insult all right," I agreed.

"Fulton called Hess a would-be tyrant," Valerie said.

"Hess took offense," Sussman said.

"Thin-skinned, huh?"

"No," Valerie said, "Mrs. Fulton *was* a creep."

"I see," I said.

Sussman said, "Hess was under the impression that he was merely stating a known fact. Naturally he took it amiss when the senator struck back."

"Naturally," I said.

"Besides would-be tyrant," Valerie said, "he also called Hess a bloodsucker, snake in the grass and skunk." She took a dainty bit of her cucumber sandwich.

I helped myself to a second.

"The senator had a zoological turn of phrase," Sussman said.

"Well," I said, "Hess sure sounded like he meant it. But then, he's had lots of practice sounding that way."

"It's what he does for a living," Valerie said.

"Not that he would categorically rule out a Moon Base alliance," Sussman said.

"No, eh?"

"Not if he needed it, or thought it might do him some good."

"Does he need it?" I asked.

"Probably not," Sussman said. "Tea adequate?"

"Can't complain. Next to booze, I dig the old herbal brew. Can Fulton put a crimp in him?"

"Perhaps," Sussman said, "but not alone."

"We think," Valerie said, "that Senator Fulton had three options open to him."

Sussman said, "A coup. A coalition candidacy. Or an outright win in a future election."

"An outright win would be quite a long shot," Valerie said.

"So that leaves a coup or a coalition?"

The pair nodded in unison.

"How would Hess feel about that?" I asked.

"He wouldn't like it," Valerie said, "but why should he?"

That made sense. "What are Fulton's chances of pulling it off?"

"The coalition," Sussman said, "is certainly a possibility. The coup?" She shrugged.

"And Hess?" I asked.

"He wouldn't be found sitting with folded arms," Sussman said, "while all this was going on."

"He'd try to stop Fulton of course," Valerie said.

"How?"

"Use your imagination, Mr. Morgan," Sussman said.

"My imagination," I said, "is old and tired and out of touch."

"Raymond Hess is an ally of General Manning West, the State Security chief," Sussman said. "The general backed Hess in the last coup."

"So he did," I said.

"West would move to protect his interest," Sussman said.

"Who wouldn't?" I asked.

"West would move decisively," Sussman said.

"You mean he'd knock off the old guy?" I asked.

"He'd do whatever he thought he had to," Valerie said.

"That's swell."

"These are high stakes," Sussman said.

"All this is pretty iffy," I said. "We don't even know if Fulton was planning anything."

"But *you'll* find out, won't you?" Valerie said. "And tell us."

"Sure," I said.

"The Science Federation is on your side, Mr. Morgan," Sussman said. "Don't hesitate to call on us in any way."

"I won't."

"It's been very nice," Valerie said. "Come again."

I promised I would and took my leave.

The chutes carted me down to the main floor. Outdoors, I began making my way through the hive of buildings. All in all, it hadn't been a bad session. The refreshments had been okay. And the ladies, friendly and informative. But had they been completely honest with me? Was there any reason *why* they *should've* been completely honest with me? I didn't know.

What I did know was that according to Ed-Out, Sussman had been a West ally too. And not so long ago, either. Was she on the outs with him now? Or was I being played for a sucker?

CHAPTER 12

I still had time to kill before my date with Henderson. Only auto-cabs around. The thought of having some deadhead machine for company didn't really leave me panting with joy. I decided to stretch a leg instead.

Above me, as I walked, medium and high walks spiraled around the Federation Complex, ducked above and under the sky-drives. Midgi-copters and hover crafts were out in full force as though making a concerted effort to blot out the sky. Around me eat parlors blinked their neon lights invitingly behind their plate glass windows; meal chutes clanged open and shut as if they were part of a ravenous assembly line. Central City was going to lunch. The walks, side streets and shops were full of people. It took a while for me to leave them behind.

The blocks began to change, the buildings grew smaller, the streets less populated. A little of this and gray factory buildings started to rise up in front of me. The closer I got, the taller they became and the emptier the streets. Soon I had no company at all. Only an occasional auto-cab scooted by. Here auto-mat factories held sway—an area given over to wires, gears, metal and lubricants. Wires crisscrossed under the metal sidewalks and flooring, and computers clicked and murmured, plotting the next week's work load. The only humans who ever came calling were the inspection crews. The factories hummed night and day. Machines needed no unions, never asked for more pay or better working conditions. Good old machines.

I picked up my pace, almost regretting that I'd chosen to hoof it through the district. The tall windowless buildings seemed to whisper as I passed them. Any second now I expected one of them to call me by name. I turned a few corners, headed down a long metal drive and I was out of the industrial complex.

Humans began to appear again. They weren't the spic and span sort who had filled the Fed walks and drives, but that didn't bother me at all. I was in the southwest business complex, an unplanned region where dissimilar buildings rubbed shoulders and no two enterprises were alike. I went looking for the Speedy Service Agency.

Some ten minutes later found me standing before a nondescript six-story building. I pushed open the door, noted the out-of-order sign on the chutes and used the stairs to take me up.

"Mr. Morgan, is it not?"

He was a small man with a short nose, narrow face, large glasses and a thin, graying mustache. His hair, what there was of it, was the color of ashes. He had on a gray business suit. His smile was pleasant enough.

"Mr. Henderson?" I asked.

He nodded. "Pull up a chair, sir. I can't tell you how glad I am you were able to keep our little appointment."

"You don't have to tell me," I pointed out. "The question is, how glad will *I* be?"

"Oh, very, very much, indeed."

"That's nice. I can use an extra touch of gladness, Mr. Henderson; I've been running kind of short lately."

"How opportune, then, that we, as it were, came on the scene."

"Yeah, no doubt. Just how did you manage that little thing?"

"Why, our client, of course."

"Of course. This client got a name?"

"I should hope so."

"You telling?"

"His *name?*

"Uh-huh. That's what I had in mind."

"But my dear sir, how can I? That part is strictly confidential."

"Yeah. I'm sure it is. But why?"

Mr. Henderson smiled. "I can only guess. But I do believe I know. Your benefactor wishes to remain anonymous, Mr. Morgan. It is certainly a legitimate and cherished tradition. One that I imagine you will be more than delighted to honor, once you become aware of your anonymous benefactor's enormous generosity."

"Enormous, huh?"

"Oh, yes."

"Generosity."

"Indeed."

"H-m-mmm."

Mr. Henderson grinned at me.

"The guy likes to dish it out, huh?" I asked.

"He delights in it."

"And I'm the lucky Joe on the receiving end?"

"Precisely."

"I can hardly wait to hear what I'm supposed to get."

"Credits, Mr. Morgan. Credits."

"No kidding?" I grinned. The grin was halfway honest, too. It must've showed.

"I was certain you'd see it our way." Henderson beamed.

I shrugged. "Who can knock Credits? Only an ingrate, right?"

"You are a man of keen perception, sir."

"Thanks; so how much have I got coming?"

"Twenty-five thousand Credits!"

I whistled.

"A man can go far on twenty-five thousand Credits, eh, sir?"

"Darn right," I said.

"Money from heaven, so to speak," Henderson said.

"You don't have to convince me. The advantages of twenty-five thousand Credits are obvious even to a dimwit. Just wrap up the certificates, Henderson. I'll take them with me."

"You have that rare gift, sir, humor."

"Thanks."

"There *is* one other *small* point, of course."

"Isn't there always?"

"It is *quite* insignificant."

"Thank goodness. I was starting to worry."

"A vacation, Mr. Morgan. A South Sea island perhaps."

"That's what I gotta do for the Credits?"

"It can hardly be called *doing.* The exact opposite is indicated, stipulated, in fact. You benefactor desires that your vacation be complete. You may choose whatever destination your heart desires. But it must be at least a thousand miles from Central City. Your benefactor knows of your love of hard work—"

"That's more than even *I* know."

"So he is making certain that you *rest!*"

"The guy is a veritable saint."

"Indeed, a most generous spirit. When you arrive at your chosen destination, sir, a deposit of ten thousand Credits will be made in your name at the Mid-Continental Bank."

"You guys take no chances, huh?"

"Not I. Indeed no. Were it left to my discretion, Mr. Morgan, I would pay you right on the spot. A mere glance at you, sir, is sufficient to reveal that you are the soul of honesty. However, my latitude in this area is circumscribed by the express desires of your benefactor."

"Uh-huh. I don't get the Credits till I take a powder."

"You *do* have a way with words, sir. Ten thousand down, the rest after you have completed your vacation, say, in three months."

"That long?"

"Perhaps two and a half. Rest, ease, relaxation. I envy you, sir, indeed I do. You will be notified."

"You got some service here, Mr. Henderson."

"Service is my life, sir."

I nodded. "Mr. Henderson, I'll be frank with you."

"Why, my dear sir, I expected nothing less from you."

"Yeah. The thing is, I can't touch this Credit, no matter how much I might want to, unless I know whose it is."

"But that is impossible. Not to mention unreasonable!"

"Not quite. From my side, it's the very essence of reasonableness. I've got a little Credit of my own tucked away; bet you didn't know that, Henderson."

Henderson shrugged.

"I'd be willing to share some of those Credits, Henderson, share it with *you.*"

"Oh, *no,*" Henderson said.

"Oh, yes."

"But really I couldn't."

"Live a little, Henderson; who's to know?"

"But *I'd* know, Mr. Morgan."

"A thousand Credits, Henderson, think of it. For only five seconds of work."

Henderson actually blushed. I stared at him, starting to feel embarrassed myself.

"How about just a hint," I suggested. "Five thousand Credits, as long as your hint makes some kind of sense. It's a bargain, Henderson, you can't beat that anywhere."

Henderson lowered his eyes. "My life is the Service," he said simply.

"The Speedy Service Agency?" I asked with some wonder.

"Integrity is my motto. The agency is founded on trust. What sort of service would I be offering if I betrayed my clientele?"

"Smart service, Henderson. In this case at least. You don't know what's involved, what the stakes are. This is big-league stuff."

"Five thousand Credits is big league?"

"Make it six, Henderson, what the hell. Just call me Morgan the Big Spender. With that kind of Credit you could redecorate your office and even have enough left over for lunches at the Ritz."

Henderson shook his head. "My dear sir, if you paid me enough to move my office from here to, say, Park Plaza, that might be something to think about. But as long as I retain these humble quarters, I need hardly worry my head about redecoration."

"I get your drift, Henderson. The thing is, I'm just a bit player in this big-league game. That's the plain truth. Six is my top offer."

"I'm truly sorry, Mr. Morgan; that's not top enough."

I sighed. "Well, you can't say I didn't try."

I stood up to go.

"But Mr. Morgan, what of *my* proposition? Surely you haven't forgotten *that?*"

I shrugged. "How could I? Twenty-five thousand Credits buys a lot of laughs. But like you said, Henderson, it ain't exactly Park Plaza, now is it? When I'd blown the bundle, I'd be back on the street with a tin cup in my hand. My name would be mud. Why, I bet I couldn't even land a job at the Speedy Service Agency if I tried."

"I would surely give you top consideration, Mr. Morgan."

"Yeah. But no thanks. I'm sorry, Henderson, your anonymous benefactor will have to get himself another boy."

"You are making a grave error."

"It won't be the first time, Mr. Henderson."

The chutes were still on the blink. I started down the stairs.

Sounds from below reached me. Footsteps moving up, more than one pair. I listened for voices, heard none. There was something about meeting at least two strangers in a narrow, confining space that just didn't appeal to me. Especially here. It hadn't slipped my mind that the last time I'd been chased was right after my chat with Henderson's messenger. I hated being chased.

I began backing up.

That's when I heard the second set of feet. These were somewhere *above* me, heading down.

Nothing strange about that. With the chutes out, the stairwell would be seeing a lot of activity. So why was I worried? Probably my mistrustful nature. One chase too many had made me leery of my fellow humans. For that matter, I wasn't too keen on mechanicals either.

I decided to table further introspection and get the hell out of there.

I was a couple of steps away from the fifth floor landing. I reached it, opened the door and found myself in the hallway.

I didn't waste any time. I moved. The first two offices I came to were locked, their frosted glass windows dark; the third was open.

The decal on the pane read: Astrological Sightings, Inc.

I stepped in.

A small bearded male secretary looked up from his word processor and said, "Yes, can I help you?"

A simple enough question. I sifted through my mind for an answer.

"I'd like to see some charts," I said, glancing around the place. The

setup was pretty much like Henderson's—another door led into the office
—except that these rooms faced the front of the building.

"Sorry," the guy said, "we only do mail order business here."

"Actually," I said, "I don't *really* want charts. That was just something
I said."

"Yes?" The guy seemed vaguely interested.

"What I really want is someplace to hide."

"I beg your pardon?"

"Like in there." I pointed to the exec office.

"Oh no," the guy said, "Mrs. Shafer is in there."

"It wouldn't be for long."

"I don't think she'd like it."

I started for her door. "We could ask her."

Mrs. Shafer's door opened. A brunette of startling proportions stood
before me. She was somewhere in her late twenties, curved and filled out in
all the right spots. But her height is what got and held my attention. If this
lady was an inch under six-foot six, I was a midget. She peered at me
through large aviator glasses. "Ask me what?"

"This gentleman—" the secretary began.

"Wants to hide in your office," I said.

"Why in the world—?" Mrs. Shafer asked.

The outer door opened.

The fearsome foursome stood there: my two pals from Fulton's office
and their two helpers.

"Because of them," I said, jerking a thumb at the new arrivals.

"Hi, palsy," the shorter of the pair of goons said, "we been lookin' for
you."

The taller hood said, "You oughtn't to run out on us like that. You don't
wanna hurt our feelin's—do you?"

"He already hurt our feelin's, Greg," the shorter guy said.

"Yeah, that's right," Greg said. Good old Greg, he sure had a way with
words.

The four started for me.

"Sorry about this," I told Mrs. Shafer and her secretary.

"Gentlemen," the secretary said, "please. You don't want to irk Mrs.
Shafer."

"Good point," I said, backing past the lady toward her office. There was
nowhere else to go.

Mrs. Shafer removed her glasses, placed them carefully next to the word
processor.

Greg was in the lead.

"That will do," Mrs. Shafer told him.

Greg stopped. "Listen, sister—"

Mrs. Shafer interrupted sternly. "I don't know what quarrel you have with this gentleman, but whatever it is, I do not want it continued in this office. Understood?"

"Don't get her miffed," the secretary yelled.

"Smart advice," I said brightly.

"Shit," Greg said and started forward.

That was his mistake, all right.

Mrs. Shafer put one large hand on Greg's coat lapels, the other on his belt, lifted him off the floor, held him aloft. Complete silence filled the office, awe-inspired silence. Mrs. Shafer hoisted Greg overhead as if she was raising an empty paper carton and threw him out the door. Just like that. Greg let out a yelp you could hear out in the street. He landed in the hallway with a loud, bone-crunching smash.

In the stunned silence which followed the secretary said, "I told you not to vex her."

"You." Mrs. Shafer pointed at the shorter hood.

"Me?" he said.

"Out!"

"The hell with that," he told her, reaching toward his trench coat pocket.

Mrs. Shafer grabbed his arm, twisted it behind his back.

"Hey!" he yelled.

Mrs. Shafer lifted him off the floor, heaved. The guy seemed to sprout wings. He flew out the office door after his pal. Another loud, unseemly scream and crash!

Mrs. Shafer hadn't even worked up a sweat yet.

The two remaining goons began backing up. Smart goons.

"See," the secretary said, "you got her nettled." The guy hadn't even gotten up from behind his desk. But then, why should he?

I turned to Mrs. Shafer gratefully. "That's some act you've got there—"

"And what are *you* waiting for?" she demanded.

"Eh?" I said.

"Out!" she bellowed.

"Lady," I said, "have a heart. I'm the good guy and those are the bad guys—"

The next thing I knew I was in the air sailing after the strong-arm bunch, right out the door. This time the voice I heard screaming was mine; it sure put a damper on my rising spirits. I landed on the shorter one who was just getting up. We went down together. Shorty had saved me a couple of lumps; he made an okay pillow, but I didn't think he'd appreciate the compliment. I lay there trying to catch my breath.

From inside the office I heard the secretary howl, "Anyone who riles

Battling Shafer, the Female Grappler, gets what's coming to them!" The guy seemed to be enjoying himself; he was the only one.

The office door slammed shut.

I was alone in the hall. Alone with my four companions.

"Roll off me, punk," the shorter hood growled.

I rolled off him. It seemed the decent thing to do. I took a deep breath. "Look," I said, "now that we've all had our fun, maybe we can let bygones be bygones, eh? Square the beefs, whatever they are. Talk this over man to man. What do you say, guys?"

"Uh-uh, palsy," the taller goon said with a tight grin. "Now you got us really pissed." By this time he was up on his feet.

"Sorry to hear that," I told him.

He aimed a kick at my head.

I caught his shoe in both hands and twisted. "Yowwww," the guy said and joined me on the floor again.

This lying around in hallways was for the birds. I began climbing to my feet.

The two other goons started for me.

"Don't do that," Brian Litkey said in a low voice, stepping out of a shadowed doorway across the hall.

"Louder," I yelled. "Make sure they understand. Understanding's what counts!"

"Yeah, yeah," Litkey said, "understanding."

The two stooges turned from me to the new arrival.

Litkey grinned, stepped in close, clobbered one with a hard right to the head. The guy half turned as though he'd suddenly noticed something very interesting on the wall, leaned against it, slid down to the floor.

Litkey ducked a punch from the other guy, popped him in the guts; he doubled over, fell to his knees as if in prayer. Litkey kicked him in the face. The guy closed his eyes, as though ascending to heaven, and went to sleep.

"Rotten crumbs," Litkey said.

Litkey took a laser out of his coat pocket, pointed it at the two hoods lying next to me.

"On your feet," he said.

Greg and his pal slowly got to their feet. They looked stunned.

"You sure took your sweet time," I complained, standing up myself.

Litkey shrugged. "So what?"

"I think they're armed," I said.

"Yeah?" Litkey grinned; he put two fingers in his mouth, whistled. Four men detached themselves from the shadows, each held a gun. "You don't say?"

"Jeez," I said. "Five guys following me all over town. That's not tailing, that's a parade."

"You don't like the way poor old Litkey works, chump," he said, "buy yourself another boy." To the goons he said, "Move." They moved. To me he said, "Got held up in traffic. If you guys hadn't been so noisy, we'd never've found you." The whole procession started down the hall.

"I know someone who can take you, Litkey," I called after him.

He looked back. "Yeah?"

"She's in there," I said, pointing to the Astrological Sightings door.

Litkey shrugged; he and his crowd went away.

They weren't the only ones.

CHAPTER 13

"Mr. Morgan?"

"Yeah."

"Golly, gee." She was a short plumpish girl with curly blond hair, a pink sweater and gray skirt. "I bet you're here to see Mr. Timins," she said.

"You'd win that bet, too. But only by default. Is there anyone here *besides* you and Timins?"

"Forty-nine mechs."

"Not counting them."

"Eight humans. But three are part time."

"Timins only looks human. Twenty years on the job has sucked him dry. You're . . . ?"

"Ellie Fenwick."

"You don't say?"

"Sure."

"And you were expecting me?"

"Uh-uh."

"So how did you know I was me?"

"Gee, Mr. Morgan, you're a hero."

"Me? A hero?"

"Everyone here knows of your dedication to Moon Base."

"All eight of you, huh?"

"We even have your picture up on the wall."

"No kidding?"

"In the basement."

"Uh-huh." I jerked my thumb toward the outer office. "You've got a mech greeting visitors out there."

"It's okay," Ellie Fenwick said, "we don't get a whole lot of visitors. Follow me, Mr. Morgan."

I followed her. The place looked none the worse for wear. But then it had been built at a time when Credit was no problem. I could almost remember that time on days when I was clearheaded. "How long've you been here?"

"Two whole years."

"Well, you appear to be holding up okay."

"Golly, yes."

"Sometimes looks are deceiving, Miss Fenwick. Moon Base can take its toll even by remote control. Only the P.R. copy is optimistic these days."

"It's done by mechs."

"What isn't?"

We took the chutes up to the top floor. Long ago Moon Base used to occupy the entire building, but now more than half the floors were rented out. It didn't take much to figure out why Timins' hair had turned white.

Miss Fenwick left me at her boss's door. I went in. Timins was busy catching forty winks on his office couch.

"Don't get up," I told him. I sank into one of his three black upholstered office chairs.

George Timins had on a rumpled blue suit and red tie. Probably he was sleeping it off. If his upper desk drawer didn't hold a quart of gin, vodka and rum, it was only because the whiskey had squeezed it out. Timins opened his eyes, smiled sweetly, clasped his hands behind his head and said, "Moon Base hasn't changed you much, Morgan; too bad, I'd harbored some hopes."

"Just older, Timins; not even wiser."

"Come up with anything on this mission of yours?"

"Sore feet. How about you, George?"

"Well," Timins said, "I didn't find the senator if that's what you mean."

"I didn't expect you to; but it would've been nice anyway."

"Nothing's been nice lately."

"I was trying not to notice."

"Remember Captain Charles Ryder, Morgan?"

"Sure. The hotshot astronaut. Retired now."

"And your friend."

"Yeah, we used to be chummy. That was a while back though."

"He's our good senator's friend, too."

"No kidding?"

"And he's put in more than a couple of good words on our behalf."

"To Fulton? Didn't know he needed any encouragement when it came to our noble cause."

"That's the old Fulton. The new one isn't all that sold on Luna real estate."

"This job of mine gets worse and worse," I complained.

"But Ryder's been holding him in line."

"How?"

"Friendship. You name it."

"How'd you get all this?"

"Our files. And Ryder kept us informed, too."

"Good old Ryder; didn't know he had it in him. Any idea why Fulton was starting to slip?"

"Perhaps he saw the handwriting on the wall? Ryder thought the senator had a short attention span. And his attention was being directed elsewhere."

"Any idea where?"

"Ryder didn't know."

"Anything else?"

"Isn't that enough?"

"Yeah, I guess it is."

"Any time, Morgan, provided there still is a Moon Base P.R. operation."

"Yeah, provided. Get a line on this Frank Broderick, maybe?"

"Almost forgot. Broderick works for an outfit called Environment Inc."

"What's it do?"

"Worry about the environment—what else?"

"Broderick fits in how?"

"He's a lobbyist, Morgan."

"Sounds legitimate."

"The firm's quite respectable."

"I don't think I could stand another dead end, George."

"You've had lots?"

"More than my share."

"Why should you be different from the rest of us?"

"Thanks loads. Mind if I make some calls from here?"

"Morgan, I want you to consider this office—what's left of it—your home. Within reason, of course."

"Of course."

Timins closed his eyes, went back to sleep.

I used an unoccupied office to dial a couple of numbers.

Malcolm Lane's view screen was still blank. I didn't know if it mattered or not. Maybe Lane had some hard evidence that Hess was going to do

away with Moon Base. If nothing else, it'd be worth a look-see. But politicos like Hess changed their minds like other guys changed their socks.
Before I started pushing my weight around I needed to exchange a few
words with Fulton, find out where he stood in all this. Lane, as far as I
knew, had nothing to do with Fulton. Probably I could put our so-called
agent on the back burner for a while without damaging our cause. But
what if I was wrong?

Using the scrambler I filed a report for the chief up on Moon Base. So
far my progress was nothing to brag about. I didn't think the chief would
be too pleased. On the other hand, I wasn't exactly jumping for joy myself.
You win a few, you lose a few. Mostly I'd been losing. But how long could
that go on? I didn't want to think about it.

Next I dialed J. Procter Ambrose. The little man was at his post.

"How's tricks, Joey?"

"Procter, my boy; never say Joey, always Procter."

"Sure, Procter."

"Thank you, Jimmy."

"Come up with anything?"

"You might say so."

"I'm impressed."

"It is only a morsel."

"Right around now I'd settle for anything. Can this find be disclosed
over the viewer?"

"That is always a bad habit, Jimmy."

"Want me to drop by?"

"That would be agreeable."

"Being agreeable is one of my many virtues."

It didn't take me long to get to Ambrose's office. All I had to do was flag
down an auto-cab, make my way through the four o'clock rush hour, four-
eighteen traffic jam, and four thirty-seven stalled vehicles syndrome. Nothing to it. Especially if you're used to it as your daily diet. Too bad I wasn't.
When I finally hit the Whoopy Complex I was fit to be tied. I'd probably
developed a couple of brand new complexes to boot. The fun crowd, I saw,
was out in full force again. I wrestled my way through the crush, just
about holding my own, and managed to reach the side street. I turned left,
nimbly keeping myself from being trampled, and made it through the gate.
I stood there panting and wiping my brow. I was getting too old for this
kind of workout.

Two flights of stairs and I was back in the consultations chamber. What
I needed was a rest cure, not a consultation.

"You're looking somewhat peaked, Jimmy."

"It's that gang out there. Why don't you get yourself a decent location?"

Ambrose shrugged. "Peaceful enough in here, quite cozy, in fact. And the rent's dirt cheap."

I sank into his client's chair. "Yeah, it would be. What a day. All I got was the runaround. I hope you didn't drag me over here just to hear some wild and woolly yarn. I'm bushed with a capital B."

"Well, Jimmy, you know I can't guarantee complete accuracy. Oh, no indeedy. But I *do* have something of a reputation in the field. If I do say so myself."

"Some field."

"My, you have had a hard day, Jimmy."

"It's just envy, Procter. You get to sit around all day taking viewer calls while I've got to hoof it all over town. So what's your news?"

"You recall my mentioning Counsel Barnabus?"

"Uh-huh. The guy whose heart bleeds for muties. So?"

"I have an informant, Jimmy."

"I should hope so; at least one. Stop bragging and get on with the story."

"He too believes in the mutant cause."

"It takes all kinds, Procter."

"Don't sneer, Jimmy. My contact is hardly a hothead or bum."

"How about patsy?"

"I would doubt that. He is a man of vast erudition."

"Look, Procter, with Ed-Out nestled under everyone's pillow, that's not much of a trick, is it?"

Ambrose shook his bold head. "As you wish, Jimmy. My job isn't defending the mutants."

"The mutants," I said reasonably, "don't have any defense. And don't need one. It's not their fault they're muties. It's just one of those things. But Mutant Village is no concentration camp. They're doing okay. What's their beef? If we had them running around all over the place, first thing you know, they'd be interbreeding with everyone else. Wouldn't be able to tell who belongs in the zoo and who out. Some mess that'd be, eh, Procter?"

"Jimmy, why would a normal want to breed with a mutant?"

"Hell, some of the muties look as normal as you or me!"

"They have my sympathies."

"Save it for their offspring, Procter, that's where the dirty work starts to show up. It's nothing you'd want to run into on a dark night."

"You're hopeless, Jimmy. My informant has attended some meetings of the mutant underground."

"Jeez, you've got to be kidding."

"Why, for goodness' sakes?"

"I didn't even know they *had* an underground."

"There are probably many things you don't know."

"Yeah. But none as disgusting as this. Just who makes up this underground, Procter?"

"Well, it does not consist solely of mutants."

"Supporters, huh?"

"Supporters."

"With muties calling the shots?"

Ambrose raised a narrow shoulder. "It is, after all, their cause."

"I suppose so. Well, get on with it. Whatever you're going to spring on me, I know it'll be just dandy."

"My informant believes that he has, more than once, recognized a noted celebrity at these gatherings."

"Believes? He's not sure?"

"Our celebrity was disguised."

"Don't tell me it was Fulton?"

"It was People's Counsel Barnabus."

"That's more like it. Barnabus is no concern of mine; he can do what he damn pleases."

"Well, on one occasion, Jimmy, Barnabus had company."

"Oh-oh. I see it coming."

"That was Fulton."

"Your spy is sure?"

"Informant, Jimmy. Not sure, but reasonably certain. This guest of Barnabus was also in disguise."

"That figures."

"You will have to take it from there, Jimmy."

"Great. What do I do, brace Barnabus? He'll have me chucked out of his office. Where's the proof?"

"I have something better."

"What could be better?"

"Your chance to find the proof yourself."

"I can hardly wait."

Ambrose shook a finger at me. "You won't have to wait long."

I sighed. "This underground group of yours, Procter, I bet it's having a get-together real soon. Maybe even tonight, huh?"

"Why, how in the world did you know, Jimmy?"

"Easy. I just asked myself what was the worst thing you could come up with. And here it is."

"Now, now, Jimmy, it's not that bad."

"You got some way to get me into this powwow?"

"Of course."

"That's what I was afraid of."

An auto-cab carried me back to my hotel.

I dialed Timins from my room. "Working late, George?"

"Just about to pack it in, Morgan. What is it?"

"I hesitate to even mention it."

"Go on. I'm all fortified with alcoholic beverage."

"Nice going. What's so tough about your job? Just because they've fired most of your staff and given you machines to work with is no reason to complain. They haven't cut your paycheck yet, have they? Try a couple of years up on Moon Base. You'll see how soft you've got it."

"What a malcontent!" Timins complained. "So what *is* it you want?"

"Hear anything naughty about People's Counsel Barnabus lately?"

"Barnabus? That stuffed shirt? Nothing that wouldn't make the family news-lines. Why? The gossip mongers have been at work again?"

"Working overtime. Word has it Barnabus is hot for muties."

Timins shrugged. "That's the first I've heard of it."

"Does that mean it's a lot of baloney?"

"Can't tell. Barnabus has never been our concern. We don't keep an eye on him. That your big news?"

"Uh-uh. Word also has it Barnabus may have led our Senator Fulton astray."

"How?"

"Sold him on muties."

Timins laughed.

"Yeah, I know," I said. "Sounds silly."

"Sounds *ridiculous.*"

"Nothing came your way about it?"

"Not a whisper."

"Think Ryder might've picked it up?"

"He wouldn't have kept a thing like that to himself."

"Nuts."

"Disappointed, Morgan?"

"Yeah."

"Good gracious, why, man?"

"The 'word' I've been quoting knows a thing or two. And the 'word' thinks it might be the straight goods."

"So?"

"So now I've got to check it out."

"But that's what you're getting *paid* for, Morgan."

"Uh-huh. Here I go sticking my neck in the noose and all my team can do is cheer me on."

"What more do you want?"

"Some cooperation wouldn't hurt."

"I can start the wheels rolling, if you wish."

"Yeah, do that. Maybe you'll turn up something worth knowing. But for me, it's gonna be too late. What I got to do, I gotta do now."

"And just what is that?"

"You wouldn't want to know, George; not over the public lines."

"Well, whatever it is, Morgan, good luck."

"I don't need luck. I need a reprieve."

" 'By, Morgan."

" 'By, George."

CHAPTER 14

Night covered the city like a black patchwork quilt. I walked through twisted, narrow streets, hunting for the right house. The neighborhood was old, decaying, a throwback to yesteryear. Small, gutted houses lined both sides of the street. Some were boarded up, chunks of wood or tin sheets nailed over doors and windows. Others were mere skeletons. But some houses still had one or two lit windows. And an occasional face peered through a cracked pane, surveying the refuse below. I could have done without those faces.

Gaunt, leafless trees stretched their branches skyward, a mute testimony to the poisoned environment around them. Crooked streetlamps offered scant light. Vacant lots grew wild, a no-man's-land for trash, weeds and rodents. None of the benefits of civilization reached into this section. No meal chutes clanged open and shut. No hookups to Computer Central provided for Ed-Out, banking-Credits, home-work or the entertainies. Even view-phones were a rarity. On second thought, the place did have a sort of charm at that.

I turned a couple of corners, found the street I was looking for. No streetlamps here at all. For once I'd come prepared. Fishing a flash out of a rear pocket, I continued on my jaunt. The house numbers came and went until I hit mid-block. The building I wanted was right there before me. Four sagging stories of wood and shingles. The windows were covered by thick boards. The roof was half caved in. I didn't try the front door, I knew it wouldn't open. A narrow alley led to the back of the house. I made my way through it cautiously. The back yard was fenced in and empty. I listened for sounds and heard none. *What the hell was I doing here?* For all

I knew old Ambrose had sold out and I was walking straight into some trap. What I should have done was send a stand-in, some poor Joe who, if worse came to worst, wouldn't be missed. The trouble was, *I* wouldn't be missed either.

I went to the back door, pushed it open. Hinges creaked as if in pain. A sound like that could be heard on the next block. Good thing the next block was probably empty, too. I stepped into the house; stairs led to the basement. I made my way down, smelled dust, mold, decay. Tough to imagine Senator Fulton letting himself in for this kind of an expedition. Fulton might not've come this way: According to Ambrose a hundred routes led to the meeting place, some more private than others. Mine took the cake when it came to privacy. Somehow I didn't figure the others would be much of an improvement.

The cellar was a nest of cobwebs, broken cases and rusted water pipes. I found the sewer lid where it was supposed to be. I didn't have much trouble lifting it. Soon I was trotting down a long, dark tunnel somewhere underneath the city.

I stepped through the doorway.

There were no windows in the joint. The ceiling was domed and held up by square columns. I smelled rotting wood, stale air. A small stage was in front, and three elderly men were seated on it in wooden folding chairs. No one was at the dais yet. There were maybe a hundred men and women on benches below the stage. They were all sizes, shapes and ages. If any of them were muties they weren't flaunting the fact. These people appeared as tame a crowd as could be found on any street corner. I heaved a sigh. Mutie supporters, not muties. I didn't mind one bit. I didn't think a bunch of muties was going to help me find Fulton anyway. I'd have been too distracted to ask the right questions. I looked closely at the faces. In the pale blue light none of them looked even vaguely familiar. I wondered if a celebrity like Fulton would've escaped notice even in disguise. I'd soon find out.

A burly guy ambled over to me. I'd been standing by the entrance as though someone had planted me there. The big guy nodded, "Greetings, brother," he intoned.

I searched through my mind for the right comeback. I'd been so busy giving the joint the once-over that I'd clear forgotten the drill. Ambrose's phrase came to me:

"All men are brothers."

"Even those who are different?"

"Especially those who are different."

I managed to get this last bit of wisdom out while keeping a straight face —no mean trick.

The big guy seemed satisfied. "New here?" he asked.

I admitted it.

"Got a name to go with the pass-phrase, brother?"

"What do you think? Walter Karmack."

"Right on the button, brother."

This Karmack was one of the first muties. He'd grown an extra hand. Very useful for doing manual labor, no doubt, only his fellow citizens hadn't quite seen it that way. Karmack was strung up from a tall tree by a very irate lynch mob. All this happened some thirty years ago. Karmack was a bookkeeper, a meek little guy who, by all accounts, never bothered anyone. He hadn't even been a fetus some fifty years before when the Big-Blast or World War III went off. No one knew the joker the Big-Blast had in store for unborn guys like Walter. If Karmack's hand had come along a couple of years later, he might have been able to save himself. By then a string of underground surgeons had sprung up to turn an illegal Credit and take care of little problems like his. But Karmack was born at the wrong time. He went up on the tree limb and into the history books. The little bookkeeper, the last guy you'd tag as a martyr. It was just the breaks.

"Quite a place you got here," I told the big guy.

"Yeah," he said. "It's like the catacombs. We got a hundred ways in and out. Mostly the old sewer system with a few extras we provided."

"Pretty elaborate."

"Why take chances? If we had people lining up to get into our gatherings, we'd give the show away. What brings you to the mutant cause, brother?"

I had my answer ready for that one. "Want to see everyone get a fair shake."

"Not worried about the chance you're taking?"

"Got to take some chances. Besides, you guys seem to run a tight ship."

"We do, brother. We figure you got the pass-phrase, you got the name, you're one of us. At least for tonight." The big guy grinned.

"You got more than one meeting place, huh?"

"Only common sense."

"That figures."

"We got steps, brother, steps that take you to the inner circle. You'll find out all about that once the show gets underway. But it's a long route, brother. It's only for the patient."

"And where am I now in this route of yours?" I asked.

"Where else, brother, but step one?"

"Where else, indeed. When do things get underway here?"

"Maybe fifteen, twenty minutes. We like to give everyone an opportunity to show up. Just make yourself at home, brother."

I waved so-long to the big guy and went to make myself at home.

Procter Ambrose had earned his pay by getting me this far, but this far wasn't far enough. A big shot like Fulton would hardly start at the bottom. The crowd here would have no inside track on the muties. They'd know just about as much as I did—which was next to nothing. If Fulton had been around at all, it would have been on an inspection tour. Maybe Barnabus was some kind of official like the guy who'd met me at the door. But even in disguise, I couldn't see him taking this kind of risk. I was beginning to figure maybe I'd come to the wrong place.

I didn't want to be tied down to a seat yet. Some of the crowd here was circulating. I went over to a fat party, exchanged words for a while. I didn't bother asking him if he'd seen two funny-looking guys in disguise who might've been Senator Scott Fulton and Councilman Barnabus. The fat guy was a first-timer too. So were the other four folks I managed to corner before the chairman banged his gavel and the meeting got underway.

As meetings went what followed was no great shakes. The chairman, a small, pudgy man with lots of white hair, greeted the crowd assuring them that they were all high-class citizens because of their interest in the less fortunate. The audience liked that and gave the old guy a hand. He applauded back. I kept looking around for someone I knew. No soap. The first speaker—a thin, wispy guy—droned on about man's inhumanities to man. I already knew all about that, and then some. A lot of it was firsthand experience. My mind started to wander. For a moment I was back on the Moon. Not many kicks in that. I pulled my attention back to the business at hand. The second speaker—a bold, pot-bellied fellow—was no better than the first. His pitch was that we were all muties under the skin. I could do without that notion too. The third guy—an elderly gent who seemed to be having trouble with his dentures—said he had a surprise for us. The lights dimmed, a screen had already been set up on stage. We were being treated to an old-fashioned movie.

The shapes that suddenly flickered on screen were nothing you'd want to take home with you—not if you were in your right mind, you wouldn't. The guy with the three eyes wasn't so bad, and neither was the Joe with the four arms, once you got used to him. (They had him working a shovel and pickax all at once; a pretty neat stunt and worth at least time-and-a-half in the good old days. Too bad the good old days were kaput.) But it was the two-headed wonder who took the cake. Both heads were grinning and nodding at the camera, and that made it all the worse. Then the gang on screen rolled out a large tub. The thing splashing around inside was big as a horse, but was mostly a head: it had eyes, nose and a tiny mouth; the mouth even talked. This thing was nothing less than one of the mutie leaders. The gruesome sight made me want to crawl under my chair and hide. But since everyone else seemed to be taking it in stride, I sat still.

I figured by now I'd seen their best shot. But I was dead wrong. The muties had just begun to uncork their set of marvels. Next they trotted out the ladies. I'd been hoping that common decency, fair play and advanced logic might make them think twice about that. But I'd just been letting my optimism run away with me. The ladies came in all shapes and sizes. Their ages varied too. But after a minute or so the last thing you thought about was age. What had been merely awful on the men was absolutely hideous in the women. Some looked normal enough; the surgeons had seen to that. But you just couldn't toss a coin when it came to chopping off an extra head. And neither head was likely to volunteer for oblivion. Some extra limbs were too close to vital organs to fool with, and anyone who had four eyes or two mouths was beyond help. A little while of this and I was the one who needed help. I glanced around at my neighbors. Some of them seemed a bit squeamish too. At least I wasn't the only one. I was willing to lay odds that a lot of the true believers in this crowd were starting to have some second thoughts.

The ladies frolicked on screen and then the men joined them. Any resemblance to normal folks, either living or dead, ended right there. I wanted to look away, but I couldn't keep my eyes off them.

At least one thing seemed perfectly clear. Whatever happened next on screen couldn't be worse than what I was watching now. That was my big mistake.

A bunch of mutie kids suddenly popped up right out of nowhere. They were like kids everywhere—except for the usual mutant additions to their anatomy. Those additions were more than enough. The kids cavorted about like no one's business, seemed to pay no attention to the camera. Then the grown-ups joined their offspring, making the picture complete. Here it was, the mutant family up close: Everyone on screen was grinning at the camera, a collective grin I would probably never forget—although I was sure as hell going to try.

The house lights finally snapped on.

The old geezer with the dentures came tottering back. "You have seen it yourselves," he said, "and who but we are responsible? Society must bear the blame for the great atomic war which wrought such havoc. And these, our brothers and sisters, are the ultimate victims of that terrible conflict.

"The war was long ago, a thing of the past, which none of us can alter. But we *can* ease the vast suffering, pain and isolation of these mutant victims, and we are honor-bound to do so.

"Despite what you see on the news-lines, my friends, we are not alone. Men of good will on all levels of society must ultimately take heed of our stand. And I can assure you, that process goes on at this very moment. Many on the highest rungs of authority—while publicly castigating us—in their heart-of-hearts wish us well. For they secretly acknowledge the rightness of our cause. And wait only for the correct moment to stand up and be counted.

"Yes, my friends, what a day that will be when our hidden backers make their voices heard. And how our ranks will swell then, sweeping aside all barriers, transforming society. Yes, my friends, we shall build a just and noble nation in which the principles of brotherhood reign supreme.

"Believe me, my friends, it is not long off. But each and every one of us here must do our parts to hasten that glorious time, must join in the struggle against injustice *now*.

"I will tell you what must be done. . . ."

I figured the old geezer was going to hand us some line about manning the barricades as soon as his bunch of notables finally got off their butts. That would be the day, all right. Death and taxes would probably go by the boards too.

But the old guy had something else up his sleeve, something a bit more practical, if less spectacular.

"Yes, my friends," he said, his eyes glowing with the fervor you find in con men or crackpots, "study groups. All over this great city we have established clandestine study groups. For your benefit, my friends. So that you might further deepen your understanding, broaden your perspective. There, group leaders will answer each and every one of your questions. The courses will last six weeks. They are step two on the path of enlightenment. Step two, my friends, is more or less passive. But once you have successfully graduated, your active phase will commence. . . ."

The whole thing made me wonder. This Brotherhood business seemed to be just about out in the open. Either the cops had stopped caring or more Credits were changing hands than I'd figured.

Half the crowd, meanwhile, had gone home while the rest were lining up to get their study group data. I got mine from one of the flunkies too; no questions asked. Oh, brother!

I was about to call it a day myself. But the old guy had been bragging that his movement was full of big shots. I figured a bit of chitchat couldn't do much harm. I made my way through the crowd, trying to remember the geezer's name—a printed program hadn't been part of the package. A small group was gathered around my party; he was basking in the attention, nodding his head, showing his dentures. I could see how the old boy might enjoy being a leader.

I muscled my way to his side. "Excuse me, Mr.—?"

He glanced my way. "Not mister," the oldster said, "brother. Brother Nelson."

He held out a veined hand. I pumped it. "James Morgan," I said. "Fine speech, Brother Nelson."

"You really think so?"

"It should give everyone here something to think about."

"Indeed, that was my hope. There is so much still to be done for our mutant brothers."

I nodded. "That's what I want to talk to you about."

"Of course, of course, Mr. Morgan."

"Maybe some place a little bit out of the way?"

"I quite understand." Brother Nelson took me by the elbow, steered me to a quiet corner in the hall. "Now then," he said.

I figured the truth was probably as good as a lie in this case. And maybe a hell of a lot easier to get away with. I dug my credentials out of a pants pocket, showed them to Brother Nelson.

"I don't believe I understand," he said.

"Look," I said, "I won't beat around the bush. You mentioned something about men in high places."

"Yes, I did; but you must understand, Mr. Morgan, all that is classified material."

"That's not what I'm after."

"I'm afraid I still do not—"

I held up a hand. "Just give me a moment; it'll all come clear."

"You are really a Moon Base ambassador?"

"Uh-huh."

"Well—"

"Call this an unofficial visit."

"Still, for Moon Base to be concerned with the mutant cause, Mr. Morgan, why that is astonishing."

"You're telling me."

"Then why—?"

"Sorry, that just slipped out. Actually I haven't been at this ambassador game all that long. Listen, it's true enough Moon Base hasn't taken much of a hand in Earth-side squabbles. And, in fact, we aim to keep it that way. But there is a chance that indirectly we can be of some help to you."

"I see," Brother Nelson said, which was a lot more than I did. "We are, of course, always grateful for any assistance. But perhaps I am not the one you wish to speak to. Frankly, Mr. Morgan, there are those who possess far greater authority than I in this organization."

"Then you can pass my message on."

"Why yes, I'd be glad to do so."

"This is about Senator Scott Fulton."

Brother Nelson said, "Please, Mr. Morgan, I can disclose none of our supporters; did I not make that abundantly clear? I can neither verify nor deny—"

"Don't jump the gun," I told him, "you don't have to say anything."

"I do not?"

"Uh-uh. Just listen?"

"Well, I can certainly do that."

"Sure you can; just put your mind to it." I glanced around to make sure no one was giving us the ear. The crowd was still pretty dense. Folks were carrying on as if they were at a party. And why not? A lot of these birds looked as if they didn't get invited out very often. It seemed safe to continue. "We've had reports that Senator Scott Fulton's been seen in these parts, Brother Nelson. Now, that doesn't mean anything to us one way or the other; you understand?"

"No."

"Right. Let's put it this way. If you've got something going with Fulton, that's okay with us; in fact, we don't even want to know about it. And I hope no one else finds out until it's too late."

"My dear sir—"

"Just hang in there a second more, Brother Nelson, here comes the good part."

"I was beginning to wonder if there *was* one."

"You've got to have heart, brother. Now this I'm giving you is strictly off the record. But you look like a man who can keep a secret."

"You may count on me, Mr. Morgan."

"That's what I figured. You know Senator Fulton has always had a good word for Moon Base. Well, this time around, we're going to have a good word for him, too; we're getting behind the senator and giving it all we've got."

"I'm sure the senator will appreciate that."

"You bet. Maybe you can even get word to Fulton that Moon Base wants to talk with him, huh? Actually, we don't care how you do it. Just do it."

"Ah!"

"Now you've got it. We want to put the senator over the top, plain and simple. That's all we care about. We manage to swing that little play, and if you've got Fulton in your corner, you've got it made."

"But if he is *not* in our corner?"

"Then we've been misinformed. All you've got to do is check it out with your higher-ups."

"Top Brothers, Mr. Morgan."

"Uh-huh, that's what I meant. You've got nothing to lose by asking. See, I've told you the absolute truth and nothing bad has happened yet. It gives one confidence, right? Of course, nothing good's happened either. But that's in your hands now. I don't need a yes or no from you. You just look into the matter, that's all, and then let me know. I'll be moving around a lot so your best bet is to call our P.R. office; it's in the book. What do you say?"

"I will do as you ask, Mr. Morgan; but do not get your hopes up."

"I never get my hopes up, Brother Nelson."

The old guy went back to his duties, whatever those were, and I started wondering how to get out of this place. My job was done. I'd gotten the ball rolling. Maybe I'd stick Litkey on these birds. Then I could safely turn my attention to other matters. Provided I found some other matters. I caught sight of the big guy who'd been my welcoming committee and started for him.

A voice over a loud speaker said, "Nobody move!"

I stopped moving.

"All the exits are blocked," the voice continued.

I gave the exits a quick look-see. Sure enough, men were pouring out of the doors and tunnels, men in blue-black uniforms and peaked caps with lasers in their hands.

The voice said: "This is State Security. You are all under arrest."

The voice seemed to know what it was talking about.

CHAPTER 15

We wound our way up the street, darkness on all sides of us. But the procession itself was lit well enough. State Security saw to that. There were even more of them than of us. And there were plenty of us—all the suckers left in the hall who'd been eyeing the Brotherhood spectacle. The security boys had us marching in a long column, four abreast, in the center of the street. They had guns and glowers and they kept pace with us on either side. Vehicles both headed and followed up our march. We didn't have far to go, I knew that much. For its get-together the Brotherhood had chosen an old office building—empty at night—with a huge, unused sub-basement. The building was only eleven blocks from the Government Complex. And State Security headquarters. Very convenient.

I was the outside man in my group of four. A State Security cop walked by my side; his gun was drawn, but he wasn't paying much attention to anything. With all his colleagues around, he hardly had to. I could grab his gun and make a run for it. But there were better ways of committing suicide. Like beating myself over the head with a club or trying to strangle myself. Besides, I wasn't in the mood for committing suicide. Maybe later when the security boys got through with me. But not yet.

Since I'd ruled out force, that left guile. I didn't really think it was going to be much of an improvement over force. But at least I wouldn't get my head handed to me.

I turned toward my uniformed companion. He was big, heavy, with a full nose, thick lips, and square shoulders. "Officer," I said.

The cop just looked at me.

"You guys are making a mistake," I told him. "A bad one."

"Is that so?" he said in a gravelly voice. He didn't seem too impressed so far. But then, I'd just begun.

"Ever hear of Moon Base?"

"Uh-huh."

"Well, I'm the Moon Base ambassador."

The cop began to look interested. "No shit?"

"That's right and—"

"Can you beat that? The Moon Base rep a mutie lover." The cop spat.

"But that's my point, officer. I'm not."

"Right. You were just takin' in the sights down there."

"Look, I was on an undercover assignment."

"Sure you were."

"Can you get me someone in authority to speak to?"

"Don't you worry about that, friend; we got a whole crew waitin' to talk to you."

"But that's later."

"Not much later."

"Couldn't you sort of get someone over here now?"

"That's the trouble with you mutie lovers. Always in a rush. Tryin' to change everything overnight. Well, friend, your rushin' days are just about over. We got a swell place reserved for you mutie lovers. One you're gonna spend a lotta time in, a whole lot." The cop seemed pleased at the prospect.

"What's your name, officer?"

The cop shrugged. "Kipper."

"Well, listen, Kipper. I don't like muties any more than you do, less maybe. You can do me, State Security and yourself a big favor by getting your boss over here, pronto."

Kipper looked at me and grinned. "Why, friend?"

A good question. I hunted through my brain for something that might sound right. "Okay, Kipper," I said, "I'll tell you. Let's say I really *am* the Moon Base rep."

"Sure, why not?"

"Let's say that I really am working undercover."

"That's a hot one."

"You bet. Here's an even hotter one, Kipper; I've got your name, for one thing. And I've got diplomatic immunity for another. Put those two together and they spell trouble—for you, Kipper."

Kipper laughed. "And how's that, friend, you gonna accuse me, maybe, of bein' a mutie?"

"Perish the thought, Kipper; all I'm going to do is say my piece when I reach State Security. The news-lines will be waiting at HQ's gates. You know that. I'll be spotted for sure. It'll blow my mission to smithereens; Moon Base'll be up in arms. Of course, I'll get off because of good old diplomatic immunity. But someone'll have to take the fall for blowing my cover and I've got just the guy. Guess who?"

"You're fulla crap, friend," Kipper said, but he'd stopped smiling.

"Someone's got to take the blame, right? Someone who could've kept the lid on my mission; someone who knew the score, but wouldn't listen. The only someone around is you, Kipper!"

Kipper's lips were a tight line. "Look, friend, if you're askin' for trouble, you'll get plenty."

"I've already got plenty, thanks. What I'm trying to do is get rid of it. Here, feast your eyes on this." I dug my ambassadorial papers out of my pocket, handed them to the cop. Kipper flashed his glower on them; his lips moved as he silently scanned the two sheets of parchment. He glanced up at me, shook his head. "I don't know about this."

"Of course you don't. You're not supposed to. But it looks real, doesn't it?"

The cop nodded uncertainly.

"Notice especially the Moon Base seal in the upper left-hand corner. Impressive, eh? And hard as the dickens to fake."

"Look, friend, there's nothin' I can do about this."

"Didn't say there was, Officer Kipper. What you need is someone in authority, some big shot you can pass the buck to. That gets you home free, see? Why not pick someone you don't like. And put him in the hot seat? Then it's *his* baby, not yours. I'll only have good words to say about you, Officer Kipper."

Officer Kipper thought it over.

"It's better if you don't say *nothin'* about me at all," he said.

"I can live with that."

"It's a deal, friend, but I ain't gonna enjoy it."

Officer Kipper trotted off to find some big shot.

I'd done it, all right. But just what was it I'd done? Darned if I knew. I wasn't even sure I *had* diplomatic immunity. Maybe all I'd really managed was to put myself in the spotlight. Better now than later. Or was it? I looked around to see where we were. We'd covered five blocks, six to go.

And then maybe the third degree, or whatever they had in mind. I didn't even want to find out.

Presently, Officer Kipper came trotting back, a slender man in gray mustache and blue uniform by his side.

"I'm Major Lewis," he identified himself. "What's this about immunity?"

The arrestee next to me piped up, "I work for the electric company. That's a public utility. Shouldn't I get a break, too?"

"Shaddup, you," Officer Kipper said.

"Electricity serves everyone. I ain't no mutie lover. Honest-to-God. I just came down outta curiosity."

"You want a club across the kisser?" Officer Kipper asked, using an irrefutable argument.

The guy shut up.

Major Lewis glared at me. "Well?"

"You see my papers?" I asked.

The major waved them at me. "You mean these?"

"That's what I mean. They're not a dime a dozen, Major Lewis—"

"I know that."

I reached into my pocket. "And here's my Moon Base ID."

The Major squinted at it.

"That's my snapshot on the right. Good likeness, eh?"

"So?"

"So there's no way in the world I can take a powder, is there? You know who I am, who I work for."

"Get on with it," the major said.

"And you know I'm the Moon Base ambassador. Right?"

The major looked at my papers again. "Right," he said.

"So you might as well save both of us a lot of grief and believe me. I was on Moon Base business tonight."

"What kind of business?"

"The hush-hush kind. That figures, doesn't it? Moon Base doesn't give a hoot about muties, and never has. I've only been back on Earth-side a couple of days. They sent me down on a special errand, one that involved a stake-out in that basement tonight. If you pull me into headquarters with all those newshawks hanging around, it'll only be a matter of hours before I've made the news-lines. I'll get off in the end, but that kind of publicity will put a real crimp in my mission. You can check every word I say with my boss up on Moon Base. He wouldn't cover up for me or anyone else. You can always haul me in if my story doesn't hold up. But if you give me my walking papers now, we both spare ourselves a lot of grief, Major, and Moon Base is bound to be grateful. Me too, for that matter."

Major Lewis looked at me. "Right," he said.

"Right?" I said.

He handed me my ID, my papers. "You're right."

"I am?"

"No doubt about it."

"None?"

"Better get going, Mr. Ambassador, we're only two blocks from HQ."

"I'll be darned," I said, meaning every word of it. "Thanks, Major Lewis, I'll see that Moon Base hears of this."

The major touched his cap with two fingers, smiled under his mustache. "All part of the job, you know. Move fast now."

I didn't have to be told twice.

I stepped out of line, half expecting to be shot down in my tracks. Nothing happened. A few steps brought me to the sidewalk. No one was even looking my way. I stepped into a dark side street. The procession looked like a large snake crawling up the roadway.

I got out of there.

CHAPTER 16

I walked for a while. I wanted to think things over. Tonight's doings had shaken me. What I really couldn't figure was how I'd managed to talk my way out of it. I was good. But I didn't think I was *that* good. The whole thing didn't hang together right.

I kept glancing back over my shoulder, trying to make sure I wasn't being followed. The streets were dark, deserted. A small voice kept asking: Why bother to follow you, Morgan, when they could've had you under lock and key for the asking? Smart voice.

By now I was in a residential section. A few blocks off I saw the bright neon lights of a Service Strip. Shops, bars, entertainie marts—the works. I turned my feet in that direction.

What I needed was a view-phone. I had to alert Timins. If Lewis was on the level, my story would be checked and double-checked all the way to Moon Base itself. Timins had to have something ready for the chief to recite. I didn't want Fulton showing in it. Not till I tracked him down.

I was working up a couple of so-so yarns when I hit the crowds again. No view-phones in sight. I pushed through the crush and into a whoopy bar. I closed the door behind me and the ruckus out on the street was shut off as if someone had flicked a dial.

The bar was filled. A dim, quiet place, the voice of the holo in back blended with the murmur of chitchat that came from stools and tables. Suddenly I felt tired, as spent as last year's expense account. I needed a drink. Even if it didn't wake me up, I could use it. I had it coming.

I made my way to the end of the bar, climbed on an empty stool and ordered a double shot of joy-juice.

I sat there nursing my drink. The warmth spread through me, and after a while I started feeling better. Okay, Morgan, I told myself, you pulled off the stunt of the decade. Maybe century even. And for all you know, someone might actually turn up Fulton—unlikely as that seems. Then, all you'd have to do is the rest of the job.

The last part didn't seem all that simple, so I took another swig of my joy-juice and was starting to feel *very* good when my face came up on the holo.

I gazed at it, wondering vaguely why the handsome Amerikanar looked so familiar. I almost fell off the stool when the answer hit me.

I leaned forward to catch the voice-over: One James Morgan, it explained—a Moon Base astro—had been caught attending an illegal pro-mutie confab. Here the image switched to a street scene, one of the arrestees being marched along Government Complex. Familiar enough. I'd just left the place. And all those unhappy looking Joes headed for the lockup were my former companions.

The news-boys had obviously been waiting in droves, tipped off from the word go. And no wonder. This catch was a hot item. The cops responsible would want as much credit as they could get.

My image snapped back on the holo. It didn't quite resemble the present day, slightly over-fed, me. It'd been taken before I'd gone off to the Moon. I was thankful for small favors. But this one—all things considered— seemed to be *very* small.

The voice-over meanwhile was busy telling the world about my exploits. They were doozies all right. Somehow, long-time mutie-lover James Morgan had managed to smash his way through five armed guards—leaving them all crippled and helpless on the pavement—while he beat it into the dark, faceless city before any of the other two-hundred-odd State Security cops were even able to draw their guns. Oh, brother! The voice-over alerted all patriotic and right-minded citizens to be on the lookout for dangerous mutie-lover James Morgan. The cops had spread a dragnet throughout the city and predicted his arrest any second now, if not sooner.

Well, it was too late to kick myself and it wouldn't have done much good anyway, but now I knew why Major Lewis had been so accommodating. Or at least I thought I knew.

The whole farce with the major had been a setup, its sole aim to put me out of commission, to discredit me. And what could discredit me more than being a hunted mutie-lover?

The holo switched to a basketball game; the barkeep was eyeing my almost-finished drink. Only a matter of time before his gaze drifted up to my face and I was finished, too.

I dug a fistful of coins out of my pocket, left them next to my glass, made my way through the crowd and out the front door.

I was back on the street. I had finally become a celebrity. But hardly the way I'd expected. I went hunting for an outdoor view-phone in some nice dark spot. It took me a while, but I found one.

I was about to stick my rate-card in the slot when I had a thought. My card-input would register at Computer Central. And if my card number had been tagged for a tap, I'd have the Security boys here in jig time, breathing down my neck. I fished a couple of coins out of my pocket and used them.

The Moon Base P.R. office, I figured, was probably bugged already. Or would be soon. I was hoping they hadn't gotten around to the home phones of the personnel. The phone buzzed.

"Timins?" I said.

A wide-awake Timins stared from the viewer. "The mutie lover himself!"

"Now cut that out!" I said. "All that's a frame and you know it. Think your phone's tapped?"

"Relax, Morgan. We of the Moon Base P.R. office have our ways, too. I was expecting this call from you. After all, someone's got to bail you out."

"I don't need bailing out yet!"

"Just a figure of speech. Anyway, I had this phone checked over by one of our techs just moments ago. How's that for speed? The boy lives next door, fortunately. It's clean."

"You sure?"

"No, but he was."

"That's something."

"Not much. But I *have* managed to get the ball rolling on your behalf."

"You have?"

"All in a day's work, Morgan."

"Remind me to buy you two drinks, George."

"You're a spendthrift, James. I hope you stay out of jail long enough to keep that promise. Just to make certain I have put our lawyer on the case. Ever hear of J. Z. Fleetwood?"

"No."

"Well, he's on the case."

"Great! You couldn't hire someone famous?"

"Famous costs money. Fleetwood is just as good—almost. He'll either get you off, or reduce your sentence."

"I haven't got a sentence yet."

"Just taking all the eventualities into account."

"Don't jump the gun, Timins. I'm still in there fighting. Which reminds me, I didn't knock out those five cops either."

"Somehow I hadn't supposed you did. Anyone get knocked out, James?"

"Only the brilliance of my ploy. But it turned out to be a put-up job. Or that's the way it looks from here. What I did was, I talked two of the cops into letting me go."

"That is what you did?"

"Yeah. Besides getting caught. At the time I thought it was plenty."

"Did you at least get a line on Fulton?"

"Uh-uh. But I hoped to get word to him through the muties."

"A lot of good that will do now. You recall Ellie Fenwick, James?"

"Yeah. The doll in your office."

"Right." He gave me her address. "We keep a half dozen anonymous rate-cards made out to the company for special projects. Ellie has a couple. Consider yourself a special project, Morgan."

"I always have."

"You won't want to use your hotel anymore, either. Not with your face all over the tel-viser."

"I know, George, I figured that out all on my own."

"I'm sure you did. Perhaps you can spend the night at Ellie's. If you think it safe. We'll come up with something after that. If there *is* an after that."

"Thanks. There was a little guy next to me on line, before I made my getaway. Said he worked for the electric company. Have Fleetwood bail him out. He's a witness that I didn't bop anyone."

"That leaves the mutie-lover charge."

"Yeah, I know. How's this for an angle. Say I was trying to get something on Barnabus, because he's been so anti-Moon Base. Or get hold of Senator Tarken. He's supposed to be Fulton's stand-in. Have him use his clout to get me off the hook. He should be able to think of something. If not, maybe he and your Fleetwood can put their heads together."

"That'll be some sight, James. But I'll get on it right away."

"If things really get bad I can always tell the truth."

"Things *are* bad. And who's going to believe the truth?"

"Yeah. Look, I'd better get off the streets before they get too empty."

"So you had, James. I'm outfitting the office with view-phone scramblers; you should be able to call without fear of interception. Incidentally, I've tried to contact Captain Ryder."

"And?"

"You're not going to believe this."

"I'm just tired enough to believe anything, George."

"Ryder seems to be missing, too."

"Good God, it's an epidemic."

"I've called him a number of times."

"And?"

"Nothing."

"So?"

"He's usually around."

"Maybe he's off on a bender?"

"He'd have let me know."

"You sure?"

"Not really."

"That's nice. Any more revelations?"

"That's about it. Take care of yourself, James."

"I'll try."

"Night, James."

"Night, George."

CHAPTER 17

Ellie Fenwick was a good half-hour's trek from where I was. I didn't see any cabs scooting by. I started hiking, tried to keep to the shadows. Except for an occasional car, nothing and no one disturbed my solitude.

My new status as fugitive took a little getting used to. I'd hardly gotten it into my head that I was a real ambassador, and here I was hitting the skids. Was there no justice? Probably not.

I stood across the street from Ellie Fenwick's—a huge, multileveled structure—and tried to see if anyone was watching the joint. I'd have literally had to be all eyes along with a healthy dose of x-ray vision to spot *anyone;* especially if they didn't want to be spotted.

I gave it up and strolled across the street. After all, with a mouthpiece like J. Z. Fleetwood, what did I have to worry about?

Fenwick lived up on the eighty-sixth floor. I used the buzzer. The camera-eye gave me a good going over and the door clicked open. I took the chutes up.

Ellie Fenwick was waiting for me at her apartment door. "Hiya," she said, "you're now in Blissful Towers."

I went inside, closing the door behind us.

"It's really called Blissful Towers?" I asked.

"Just by the management. Take a load off your dogs, Mr. Ambassador."

"Thanks. I know you're taking a risk. And I appreciate it."

"Wow, it's an honor, no kidding."

I sat down on the couch while Ellie went off to fetch my new rate-card. The girl had a point: it probably *was* an honor. But there were honors and honors. And this one was too risky.

"Here," she said.

I examined the rate-card; it bore the inscription Moon Base, Inc. For the time being I was back in the chips. Give or take a chip. I shoved it into my pocket and sighed, "You wouldn't happen to have a snack handy, would you? I think I'm starting to run low on feed."

"Gee, sure." Ellie went off to the kitchen. I got up and went to a window. The city looked back at me, grim and impersonal, as though it couldn't care less. Not many windows were lit at this hour. But the good-time streets, far off, sent up a spray of colored lights. I looked down at the street below. An occasional car went by. Two pedestrians were out walking. Probably they had nothing to do with me. But until I found out just how widespread the hunt was, it wouldn't do to stick too close to home base. And Ellie Fenwick was home base. I rejoined her on the couch to put away some sandwiches.

"What is this?" I asked.

"Tuna fish."

"Up on the Moon this stuff was a luxury. Along with everything else."

"There must've been *something* good about being on the Moon, huh?"

"Sure. A couple of things. The money and looking forward to getting off the Moon."

"Our P.R. guys never said a thing about any of *that.*"

"How many of them've ever been up on the Moon?"

I finished off my repast with a bottle of beer and said, "I really don't know how to thank you. But I'll probably think of a way sooner or later. Unfortunately it looks like it's gotta be later. The truth is none of this is safe. And every once in a while you gotta go with the truth. Just to keep in practice."

"But I *feel* safe."

"Sure you do. But that feeling won't last long once you're pinched for harboring a fugitive."

"Golly."

"Yeah. My feelings exactly."

"So whatta we do?"

"Safety first. I scram."

"Now? At night?"

"When else? If the cops are working their way through Moon Base personnel, it's only a matter of time before they show up here."

"Gee. But where'll you go?"

I raised a finger. "That, my dear, it's better you don't know."

"But how you gonna get there?"

"You have some kind of vehicle handy?"

"A motorbike."

"Who would suspect the city's mutie lover galavanting around on a motorbike?"

"Yeah. Who?"

"No one, I hope. Maybe you can give me a lift—part way."

Ellie and I exchanged so-longs five blocks from my destination. She rode off into the night. I turned, began hoofing it.

The street was completely deserted. I didn't mind. I went along till I reached a twelve-story apartment building. In daylight the darn thing was painted a grayish green. But right now everything was a comforting black.

The time was 3 A.M. It took some leaning on the buzzer before I finally got my reply. The chutes lifted me to the sixth floor.

Tom Bossly—king of the airways journalists—clad in wrinkled white striped pajamas, answered my first knock. His sparse hair was uncombed. No drink or cigar was clutched in his mitt. He even forgot to leer at me.

"Jesus H. Christopher!"

"Not really," I said, "it's just the dim light in your hallway that makes you think so. That and my saintly nature, no doubt. Although, actually, I didn't know it showed so clearly."

"Good God, man, not in the hallway!" Bossly said.

"Don't worry," I said. "Anyone who's dumb enough to be out here at this hour is too dumb to recognize me."

I stepped in.

Bossly closed the door behind me, stood leaning on it. "I hope there's a reward out for you by now. Only that will compensate for this outrageous inconvenience."

"I'll be honest with you, Tom, I hear you've got some muties squirreled away here. We mutie lovers can't keep our hands off 'em, you know, and I've run short of my own supply."

Bossly padded across the room, dropped into an overstuffed easy chair. I pulled up an armchair for myself.

Bossly wiped his brow. "It just goes to show, Jim boy, you can know a guy all your life and still not know him."

"You haven't known me all your life, Tom."

"That's true. And don't think I'm not grateful. If I'd known you were a mutie lover I'd've turned you in long ago. What is it you like about them?"

I thought it over. "Their special features mostly. Where else can you get three heads on one body. It's a bargain."

"What *were* you doing with those people, Jim?"

"Trying to track down our missing senator, what else?"

"Come off it, lad."

"Yeah, it does sound kind of nutty, doesn't it?"

"Moronic is the word you're looking for."

"I suppose. But I had it on *very good* authority that there's some kind of tie-in."

"And?"

"Search me. I never got very far with my so-called investigator. If I didn't know any better I'd say the whole yarn was designed to nab me."

"Ah, but you *do* know better?"

I shrugged. "What do you think? Do I look crazy?"

"I'll pass on that one. And to what do I owe the dubious pleasure of your company?"

"I got lonely."

"Should've stayed with the Security boys, Jim. Lots of company there."

"Not *that* lonely. Besides, who would ever look for me here?"

"You'd better be right."

"Hmmmmmm. If I am, it'll be the first time. Look, Tom, I don't know why or who's behind it, but there was something very wrong with the way I became a fugitive."

"Such as?"

I filled Bossly in on my derring-do escape and how it hit the news-lines seconds after I beat it.

"They had you tossing around five guys?" Bossly asked.

"Want to feel my muscle?"

"*What* muscle?"

"Uh-huh. You're beginning to catch on. Maybe you should look into this one, huh? I didn't steer you wrong when it came to the senator, did I? Our P.R. office got me a lawyer, one J. Z. Fleetwood."

"Not *the* J. Z. Fleetwood, Jim boy?"

"Yeah, know anything about him?"

"Wellll, he was disbarred twice."

"That sounds about right. But is he any good?"

"Stinks."

I sighed. "That sounds about right too. Get hold of him. I've got him buttering up the witness to my innocence."

"Your mother?"

"This little guy from the electric company. There's a big story here somewhere. Look at all the wires that must've been pulled to set this up."

"I *like* big stories."

"That was my hope."

"Big stories make *me* big. Especially when I break them."

"A stretching machine would make you even bigger. Now aren't you glad I came here?"

"I'll let you know, if this pans out."

"Break this quick and you might even get me cleared."

"So, trying to save your hide again, and here I thought you were just out to get me a scoop."

"I was. You got an extra bed, maybe?"

"Better than that, James boy. I've got a whole guest room."

"I don't believe it. I've finally done something right today. Jeez. Lead on, Tom."

He led.

CHAPTER 18

The auto-cab let me off a couple of blocks from my target. It scooted away and I was left standing on a quiet residential block. One thirty-five P.M. A clear bright day with a couple of small, fluffy clouds and a very blue sky. The houses were one-and two-story types, each one with a lawn and some even with flowers and a few trees. The last tree I'd seen in the city was on a poster. There were some kids around, a guy watering his lawn, an elderly lady with a shopping bag, and a couple of women walking up the block. I took a deep breath. The air smelled a hell of a lot better than on Moon Base or in the city, even if it was coming through the phony mustache I'd glued over my upper lip. The mustache itched, but not half as much as the beard I'd stuck on my chin. The round spectacles I wore were made of plain glass; the world seemed neither better nor worse as I gazed through them. Their chief virtue—I hoped—was that they helped make me un-recognizable. Tom Bossly had trotted out at nine-thirty to hunt them up at a theatrical costume shop. Along with the snazzy black pinstriped vested suit I had on. A modest gray hat hid my hair line from view. And the attaché case I carried contained two jelly sandwiches wrapped in tin foil. I had no idea what kind of person I looked like—and didn't much care—as long as it wasn't a mutie-loving fugitive.

I started walking.

No one bothered to give me a second glance. My first success of the day. I wondered if there'd be any others.

I stopped in the middle of the block, checked my address. There it was, all right, the home of my old pal, Captain Charles Ryder.

I went up the walk, used the brass lion's-head knocker. I could hear it echoing through the house. I waited around a while; when nothing happened, I went over to the house on the right, rang the bell.

A middle-aged man answered my ring. He was in shirt sleeves, slacks and slippers.

"Sorry to bother you," I said.

"That's okay," the man said, "glad to get away for a minute from the job."

I nodded. Here was one of the many home-computer workers who filled the suburbs and residential sections of town. A direct line tied them to their employer's master computer. A lot of them did piece work. You could stay home twenty-four hours a day and not miss a moment's work. It didn't quite sound like peaches and cream.

I stuck out my hand. "Ted Brown," I said.

"Allerton," the man said, pumping my hand, "Ted Allerton. What can I do for you, Mr. Brown? Selling something? Taking a survey? I really don't have too much time. They can tell when the computer isn't working, you know."

"Yeah, I know. Actually I'm looking for your neighbor, Captain Ryder."

"Ryder?"

"Uh-huh."

"He's not home, huh?"

"Nope."

"That's funny, he's usually home. He's retired, you know."

"I know."

"Come to think about it, I haven't *seen* him in some time, I guess."

"How much time is that?"

"About a week, maybe, give or take a day."

"Ever happen before?"

Allerton shrugged a shoulder. "Can't say I know one way or another."

"How about visitors? Notice anything unusual?"

"Nothing unusual ever happens in this neighborhood, Mr. Brown. That's why we all live here."

"Thanks, Mr. Allerton, you've been a great help."

"Really?"

I thought it over. "Well, at least not a hindrance. 'By, now."

" 'By."

He closed the door. I went over to the house on the left. No one answered my ring. I went back to Ryder's place, used the knocker again. Wasted effort. I went to one of the windows, peeked in. If Ryder had hung himself, or was lying on the floor in a stupor, he wasn't doing it near that window.

I went around out back. Ryder had a garden, but he'd been neglecting it lately. A lot of the plants and flowers had gone to meet their maker. The rest looked like they were about ready to follow. Ryder, when I knew him, had been a stickler for detail; he wouldn't have forgotten to water his charges. But that had been a long time ago. Maybe Ryder had changed.

I looked around.

A six-foot picket fence gave me all the privacy I needed and then some. No one would notice my illegal act.

I went over to Ryder's back door. I had a long piece of wire with me, and while it had been a number of years since I'd picked anyone's lock, I was going to give it the old try now. I didn't have much to lose. With all the charges against me another would hardly matter. Besides, I didn't expect to get caught. On the other hand, who ever does?

Just for laughs I tried the door before giving it the business.

The door slowly swung in on silent hinges.

I stood there gaping at it as though it had burst into song and started to tap dance. So much for my criminal act. Luckily I still had a couple left. Like trespassing. I stuck my head into the house, and when nothing bad happened, the rest of me followed.

"Ryder?" I called. But not too loudly. There didn't seem to be much point to it. No one called back.

I gave the ground floor a quick once-over: kitchen, living room, dining room. No one was hiding under any tables. No stray evidence caught my eye. Everything seemed shipshape. Time to go through the drawers later. I went up the stairs. Ryder wasn't in the bed or under it. He wasn't camping in one of the closets either. There was a desk in his study, a minicomputer and a tel-viser. It looked like I had my work cut out for me if I planned to crack the computer code and see what, if anything, Ryder had filed away. I put it off for a while to finish my tour. Time is what I had lots of. There was only the cellar left. I hoped I didn't come across any bodies.

I went back downstairs, opened the cellar door and started down.

That's when the sound reached me.

It brought me up short. I stood there trying to figure out what the hell it was. It came from down below, somewhere in the cellar. Vaguely, it sounded like someone humming to himself. That didn't make much sense. For an instant I wondered if I ought to just turn tail and get out of there, let well enough alone. I hadn't come here in the expectation of finding anyone alive and kicking, just a clue or two that might lead me to the next clue. *That* certainly had seemed safe enough. But going down in the cellar, now that it was going vocal on me, didn't seem safe at all. Still, the sound could've been anything; although just what kind of anything, I couldn't for the life of me figure out.

I started down again, only this time much slower. Maybe if I took enough time the sound would go away.

I hit bottom. The cellar was divided into a number of rooms. The one I was in had a Ping-Pong table and a small tel-viser. The sound had stopped now. It hadn't come from this room. Where then? As if in answer the thing started up again. I listened closely. It could be human, all right. But something about the humming wasn't quite right. Very slowly I followed the sound into the next room and then into the one after that.

Captain Charles R. Ryder, U.S. Air Force, retired, the former astronaut and my old buddy, was seated on the floor. He hadn't picked the best room; this one housed a sink and the boiler. Ryder didn't seem to mind. He was busy playing with his toy helicopter and humming happily to himself. He had a pretty good growth of beard, maybe a week or more, black hair streaked with lots of gray. That's all he had. Charles Ryder was in his birthday suit, as stark naked as a butterfly. The floor was littered with apple cores, peach pits, banana peels, a half-eaten loaf of wheat bread. The stuff was beginning to smell.

"Charley," I said.

Charles Ryder stopped humming and looked up at me. He had a little trouble focusing but after a while he got the hang of it. A childish grin split his gaunt face. He held up his toy. He drooled out of the corner of his mouth.

"Charley, what's happened?"

"Ga, ga," Charles Ryder said.

"Don't you know me, Charles?"

But I'd lost his interest. He'd gone back to playing with his toy.

"Charley," I said, "listen to me, man!" But I had a feeling "man" wasn't quite the right word anymore.

Again Ryder looked up.

I leaned over him. "It's me, James Morgan. You remember, don't you? Jimmy?"

Ryder obviously liked the word Jimmy and tried to imitate my lip movements and say it. But it proved too tough for him. Some things are like that: too tough.

This business with Ryder was starting to be too tough for *me*. I hadn't come prepared for it. How could I? How could anyone?

Standing there I began to wonder how it had happened. On its own accord? Or with help? And what kind of help could possibly produce *this?* Maybe it was just temporary, I thought, not believing it for a moment.

"Charley," I said, "what have they done to you?"

"Ga," Charley said.

It didn't look as if I was going to have that intellectually stimulating chat I might have hoped for.

But if this wasn't my day, it sure as hell was a lot worse for Charley Ryder.

"Ellie," I said.

"Jim."

"Got the scramblers in yet?"

"Yep."

"How safe are they?"

"Seems okay."

"Seems. Right. Get Timins on the phone, too."

"Gotcha."

I held on.

"How goes it?" Timins asked.

"Don't ask."

"It can't be *that* bad, Morgan."

"Worse."

"But you've been a fugitive less than twenty-four hours."

"It's beginning to feel like a lifetime."

"What's happened?" Ellie asked.

"It's Ryder."

"Ryder?" Timins said. "What about Ryder?"

"I found him."

"And they said you were a washout."

"They knew what they were talking about."

"Where was he, James?"

"Here. In his house. He was here all along."

"He's dead?" Timins asked.

"Only in a manner of speaking."

"What *is* wrong with you?" Timins asked.

"Not *me,*" I said, "I'm fit as a fiddle. It's *him.*"

"Well, perhaps you can tell us what's wrong with *him.* I gather *something* is wrong."

"You got it right. He's off his rocker."

"Meaning what?"

"He's lost his marbles. Gone cuckoo. Became a loony."

"A loony?" Ellie said. "You're kidding."

"Wanna bet?" I said.

"You mean he's insane?" Timins said.

"That's what I mean."

"He's there now?"

"Uh-huh."

"Put him on."

I laughed. Good old Timins. "You don't believe me, do you, George?"

"It's not that, James."

"It's something else?"

"What do you *mean* by crazy, James?"

"Well, George, I mean that our chum, Captain Ryder, the guy who's been keeping our senator in line, is at this very moment seated in the basement of this house."

"Seated you say?"

"Uh-huh. On the floor."

"The floor."

"That's right."

"What's he doing there?"

"Playing with his toy helicopter, George. At least he still shows some loyalty to the Air Force."

"If this is some kind of joke, James, it is *not* terribly amusing."

"I can make better jokes than that, George."

"I suppose you can."

"Sure I can."

Timins said, "I'd still like to speak with him."

"Anyone ever tell you you're a terrible pain, George?"

"Why, yes I believe so."

"Just checking. He's naked, you know."

"Who is?"

"Ryder."

"Naked?"

"Uh-huh."

"How should I have known that?"

"You do now."

"*All* naked?" Ellie asked.

"As nude as a jaybird. They don't come any nuder, honey."

"Gee," Ellie said.

"Yeah. That's about the size of it. And all he says is ga."

"Ga?" Ellie said.

"Ga. It sounds okay from you, but not from him."

"This is awful," Timins said.

"That's what I've been trying to tell you."

"Are you sure he says nothing else?"

"Not to me he doesn't. And we're old pals."

"How is he otherwise?"

"Just dandy. He showed me his toy. Seemed real happy."

"Happy," Timins said.

"Yeah. Doesn't have a care in the world. I should be so lucky."

"How long has he been in this lamentable condition?"

"Who knows? A week or more, I'd guess."

"And he's still kicking around," Ellie said.

"It's warm down in the cellar. And he keeps raiding the fridge. He's crazy all right, but not crazy enough to starve to death. You've got to get him out of here, George."

"*I* have to get him out of there?"

"Well, you can't expect me to call the paddy wagon, can you? They'd put *me* in and have *him* sign the papers."

"Ah, I see your point."

"Sure you do. Don't go public on this, George, it's got to be kept quiet."

"Quiet."

"Now you've got it."

"Of course. But *why* does it have to be kept quiet?"

"Why not? It's embarrassing enough to have an astronaut go whacky without splashing it all over the news-lines."

"Well, yes . . ."

"Besides, we want to know *why* he's gone crackers."

Ellie said, "You think it might have something to do with Fulton?"

"Who thinks anything? We'll see what the shrinks say. Get hold of some private hospital. Have 'em pick Ryder up. I'll leave the door unlatched. Have 'em report back to us as soon as they figure out what his problem is."

"Yes, I suppose that *is* best," Timins said. "It's hard to believe that Ryder is actually insane."

"It's hard to believe we've had four coups in the last year, too. Or that Fulton's gone AWOL. Or that I've become public enemy number one. That's the hardest one of all to believe. Which reminds me, how's my mouthpiece doing? Have I been cleared yet?"

"Not quite."

"Uh-huh."

"But he's working on it. It's only a matter of time."

"What isn't? Another fifty years and it won't matter one way or the other."

"I think Fleetwood had a somewhat shorter period in mind."

"Let's hope."

"Jim?" Ellie said.

"Yeah?"

"There's a message for you."

"If it's from the cops, I definitely will not give myself up."

"It's from Senator Tarken."

"What does he want?"

"To see you. He sent a special courier; note's got his seal and signature and everything."

"Is he on our side?"

"He's against Hess and for Moon Base," Timins said. "At least up until now."

"Now is when it counts," I said.

"What are you going to do?" Timins wanted to know.

"See him, what else? At this stage of the game I can't turn down *any* offer. Anyway, Tarken's famous. He doesn't *need* to turn me in to get on the map. Or does he? Where, when and how do I meet him? Who knows, maybe he can tell me something important and I'll be able to wrap up this mess. Ha-ha. And they say *Ryder's* crazy!"

CHAPTER 19

It was just a house. You've seen one, you've seen them all. I'd been seeing it for ten minutes now.

I was down the block and across the street from the place, loitering in a doorway. When it came to loitering I could hold my own with the best. When it came to anything else, I wasn't so sure.

At least no one was paying any attention to me. But why should they? My disguise was still in place. And out here on the street no one could care less. It was once I got in that house that my real worries would begin. But as usual I was jumping the gun and worrying now.

I'd come an hour early for my visit with Tarken. Hardly brilliant strategy, but the best I could do on short notice. If he showed up with a truckload of State Security agents I'd know it. Of course, if they were *already* here and planted in the building, I was out of luck. I'd hate that. But then who wouldn't?

I waited another twenty minutes and started to get restless. It was too quiet, too peaceful, too dull. Tall buildings, elevated walks, air and ground traffic, served as a distant backdrop. Where I was, only small buildings and strolling pedestrians held sway. A nice, sleepy spot. I didn't want to be around if it was going to be spoiled by ugly Security cops.

Leaving my vantage point I walked down one block, over half a block, found an alley, climbed over a fence and there I was. Behind the six-story building I'd been watching.

I went to the service door, stepping around a number of trash cans, and tried the knob. No soap. Some overeager janitor had remembered to do his job. Two back doors open in one day would've been too much of a good thing anyway.

I got out my wire and started fiddling with the lock. It didn't take too long. I closed the door behind me and trotted up the back staircase making as little noise as possible. I stopped when I hit the fifth floor. Opening the fire door an inch, I peeked through at an empty corridor. Listening hard, I heard nothing.

I strolled down the hallway to 5C, put my ear to the door. If anyone was waiting for me in there, I couldn't hear it.

I tried the knob. Locked, naturally enough. I still had some time before the senator was due to show up. I figured a quick perusal of the territory couldn't do any harm. Maybe I'd even learn something.

I went to work with my wire again. A click and the lock snapped open. Child's play. I went on in. I wasn't in an office. Tarken had chosen someone's apartment for our get-together. A closer look at a couple of papers on the desk told me who's place this was: Tarken's own. Or more likely his hideaway. Things were starting to look better. I couldn't see Tarken using his own flat as a trap. Maybe everything was going to be all right after all.

I stepped into the bedroom and right away all my new-found cheer went out the window. Senator Tarken was stretched out on the bed. He wasn't going to be telling me or anyone anything. Someone had cut his throat from ear to ear. The bed was full of dried blood. I felt my stomach turning over like an idling engine. Any minute now, it would look for a way to crawl out of my torso and get away from here. My stomach had the right idea. Time to go. The cops couldn't prove that I'd done this, but could I prove that I hadn't? Could a mutie lover prove anything? I wasn't going to bet on it.

I stuck around long enough to frisk the joint, beginning with the living room and ending in the kitchen. I found nothing.

I made myself go to the body. There were worse things than searching a body—namely being one yourself. Somehow the thought didn't cheer me much. Gingerly I stuck a hand in one pocket, then in another. My fingers closed over a wallet. I slid it out, took it and myself into the next room.

I inspected my prize and that's when I found it.

"It" was a small square piece of paper. On it a diagram of a building. One of the rooms had an X penciled over it. And next to the X, an F. The F could've stood for lots of things. But I was willing to lay odds it stood for Fulton.

All I had to do was prove it.

CHAPTER 20

"What you got there, buster," Brian Litkey said, "is State Security headquarters."

The heavyset confidential investigator looked up from the piece of paper I'd handed him and smirked at me. It didn't take much to make the old gumshoe chipper. A broken arm or leg—as long as it wasn't his—would probably have him rolling on the floor, laughing to bust a gut.

"Say not," I said simply.

"I can say it, chump, but it won't make no difference. That's what you got."

"That's about the last thing I need."

"Easy enough to get in there." Litkey grinned widely. "Just let them nail you." Litkey laughed and slapped me on the back. There were times I felt that maybe Litkey wasn't a hundred percent on my side, Lord knows why. On the other hand, I figured that as long as Moon Base kept paying their bills, Litkey probably wouldn't turn me in. At least not right away. I took the diagram back from him, glared at it sourly.

"You sure about this?" I said.

"Sure, I'm sure. If you don't believe me, look it up in the City Almanac."

"That's where this comes from?"

"Uh-huh."

I sighed, got up, went to Litkey's ninth-floor window, looked down on Central and North streets. The pedestrians down below moved around as though they were actually going someplace. Which was a lot more than I seemed to be doing.

It was all slipping away. The damn job had me hanging on the ropes.

Only a matter of time before even innocent bystanders saw I was making a flop of it.

So far I'd been wrong on every score. An almost perfect record—for the other side. Instead of pulling down the big Credits—a just reward for an errand well done—I'd be lucky if I kept out of the hoosegow.

I was in over my head, no doubt about it. What chance did I have with the cops, army and Feds all stacked against me?

Fulton had to be my ace, my best bet for rounding up a winning combo. But I didn't even know if the senator was alive and kicking, let alone if he wanted in on the play.

But maybe I could find out.

All I'd have to do was break into State Security, scout around till I hunted up the senator and—provided he wasn't a cadaver—ask him.

Simple enough.

And the dumbest stunt I'd ever heard of. The mere thought of it was a sure sign I was losing my marbles, was going off the deep end . . .

On the other hand, this racing around town was a bust, and breaking and entering was at least something I knew about. It was something I was good at. And if my disguise was okay, maybe I had an even chance of pulling it off. Oh, brother! But I couldn't stand much more of this. At the rate I was going, this could take forever. And that was too long.

I turned to Litkey.

"I'm going in after him," I heard myself say.

"You're *what?*"

"Fulton. I'm getting him out."

Litkey laughed. "You got a screw loose, chump. For all you know, that F stands for Flummoxed; just what you'll be if Fulton ain't there."

"Yeah. But what if he *is* there. Think how grateful he'll be."

"Sure. You'll be able to keep him company in the pen."

"Uh-uh. I come all dressed up in a State Security outfit. And with enough hardware to open *any* lock. The senator and I will just take a walk."

"Didn't know you had all that stuff lyin' around, Morgan."

"I don't," I said, seating myself on his windowsill. "What this operation needs is someone smart and resourceful, with enough pull to round up the necessary items."

"Shit."

"Come on, Litkey, I've got an unlimited expense account."

"So what?"

"So I'm not asking *you* to break into State Security, am I?"

"Nah, you ain't."

"H-mmmm. I wonder *why* I'm not asking you."

"Because I won't do it. You really gone nuts, Morgan?"

"Look, Litkey, all I want is that you dig up the goods. I'll pay for it. Or rather, Moon Base will. You can *trust* Moon Base, Litkey. As long as there is one. And that, in the long run, is what we're trying to do, isn't it? See that there is one."

"Know something, Morgan?"

"What, Litkey?"

"I think I could stand it if there weren't no Moon Base."

"You could, eh?"

"Yeah."

"You always were pretty tough, Litkey."

"I figure I could get to sleep at night."

"I guess you could."

"It's the Moon I'd miss, buster; you're not figuring on doin' away with the Moon, are you?"

"The Moon stays, Litkey."

"That's good. Yeah. As for this other thing, I might be able to come up with what you need. Only it'll cost you plenty."

I got up off the windowsill, went back to the client's chair. "I knew I could count on you, Litkey; when the going gets rough, you're true-blue."

"Yeah, sure. That's me all right. Anything you say, sucker. By when do you need the stuff?"

"Tomorrow."

"Shit. Don't want much, do you. That'll cost you even more."

"Don't say, 'you' Litkey; always say 'them.' And them've got more than enough. At least they did the last time I looked."

"Yeah? Well, they got that much, maybe they got even more? I got a couple contacts at State Security. Say I nose around, find out if Fulton's really holed up in that joint."

"You can do that?"

"Sure. If the pay's right. Hey, Morgan, ain't you even gonna *ask* about those hoods I collared for you."

"Jeez, I almost forgot. Where've you got them?"

Litkey shrugged a beefy shoulder. "You gotta be kiddin'. What do I look like, a warden or somethin'? I let 'em go."

"You did?"

"I pumped 'em first, see? Fulton, he left orders to go after anyone poking around. And you got them pissed at you too, right? But now with everyone gunning for you, Morgan, they'll lay off."

"Great. With everyone gunning for me it hardly matters, does it?"

"It matters."

"Yeah?"

"Take it from me. Your two pals, buster, used to be in the rackets."

"I kind of guessed that myself, Litkey."

"Yeah. But they got a promotion. They're captains now."

"What kind of captains?"

"In Fulton's private army."

"His *what?*"

"He got a private army. Maybe he saw the handwritin' on the wall. You gonna make a coup, you need some kind of muscle. Hess had a piece of the army. And most of West's State Security boys. That's what put him over. All the big shots got some kind of muscle. Fulton's got himself about five generals, maybe a third of the capital cops, none of State Security, and two thousand goons."

"*Two thousand?* How come none of this made the news-lines?"

"Why should it?"

"It's news."

"Uh-uh. Not when all the heavyweights are roundin' up their teams. Then it's classified data, a one-way ticket to the clink for the lucky guy who blows the whistle, see?"

"Remind me not to blow the whistle."

"Shit. They got enough on you, chump, to put you away for keeps."

"I've got J. Z. Fleetwood on my side, Litkey."

"Then you're really sunk." Litkey handed me a sheet of paper. "Here's a list of some Fulton goons. Good luck, buster."

I folded it, put it in a pocket. "You got anything handy that shorts alarms, Litkey?"

"Yeah, I got a couple items."

"Mind if I borrow one?"

"Uh-uh. I'll put it on your bill."

"You're a pal, Litkey."

"Don't you believe it."

CHAPTER 21

The eat-o-mat was crowded. I punched out a full-course dinner, a mug of beer. The whole works came sliding down the food chute. I pocketed my rate-card, carried my tray over to a small empty corner table. I watched dusk rolling in over the city. Soon it would be dark.

My beard and mustache were holding up okay. Which was more than I was doing. This private armies business was the pits. The politicos had finally done it, gone off their rockers. With all those armies around, a plain solid citizen like myself hardly had a prayer. What I needed was a couple of regiments at my back. What I had was the Moon Base P.R. office, a few hired hands like Litkey and J. Z. Fleetwood and a stray pal or two. It didn't add up to much—probably because it wasn't.

By now it was pretty dark outside. I polished off a last slice of rye bread, finished my coffee and headed out into the night.

"Jesus H. Christopher!" Tom Bossly said. His mouth had dropped open and he was staring at me as if my face had broken out in yellow and purple spots, a sure sign of the plague. I closed his office door behind me.

"Not to worry," I assured him.

"It's bad enough you accost me in my domicile with half the city out hunting for you. But here where I work! Have you taken leave of your senses, Jim boy? Do you think you've become invisible? What have you done?"

"Nothing at all," I told him, pulling up a chair. "And yet I'm a wanted man. Is there no justice?"

"Not much," Bossly admitted.

"Yeah, I noticed. Look, Tom, my own mother wouldn't recognize me in this getup."

"It's not your mother I'm worried about."

"The cops won't tumble either. Remember this is actually *your* handiwork. And a good job you've done."

"Save the flattery. For God's sake, you couldn't wait till I got home?"

"Who could count on your getting home? If a story broke you'd be stuck here all night. You're working overtime as it is."

"Overtime's for the union, Jim. I'm management. And I *am* stuck here all night."

"See? So what's cooking?"

"Mutant Village, that's what. They're boiling over. Hess's been cracking down on mutie supporters. That little round-up you were part of was just a sample. The muties don't like it."

"I wasn't too keen on it myself. But what can the muties expect? A mutie's a mutie."

"They've got all kinds of expectations, Jim boy, from being allowed to join the Security forces to running one of their kind for chairman."

"Don't want much, do they?"

"Can you imagine a mutant party on the ballot?" Bossly leered at me. "Wellll, they're backing up their demands with a lot of rallies."

"Where? *Out here?*"

Bossly shook his head. "You nuts? That crazy they're not. It's all in the village."

"So?"

"So they've been hinting. If their demands aren't met the next rally's in Government Square."

"Very subtle hint."

"Subtle enough to keep me here tonight. Chairman Hess is supposed to come out with some kind of statement later."

"Okay, I've got something for you too. To fill in those long empty hours."

"Yeah?" Bossly plucked a half-smoked cigar out of his ashtray, lit up, inhaled.

"Something big. But there's one slight hitch. Story's too hot to handle, Tom."

Bossly waved away my reservations. "We get dozens like that every day. Never back down an inch. Power of the press. News-line alert's got the kick of a mule. No one messes with us, Jim boy. Let's have it."

"This story, Tom, it might be classified."

Bossly laughed. "What've you come up with, the number of warheads in the local silo?"

"Worse than that."

"What could be worse?" Bossly asked with real interest.

"Hess has got himself a private army."

"How about that?"

"Come on, Tom, I'm not kidding. He's got West, a bunch of generals and Lord knows what else."

"The chairmanship, that's what else."

"Fulton's got a similar setup. Maybe five generals and part of the capital cops, too."

Bossly blew smoke toward the ceiling. "No wonder Fulton's powdered out. If he's paying all those guys' wages, he must've gone stone cold broke years ago. His creditors probably chased him out of town."

I looked at Bossly in disgust. "I don't get it, Tom; here I'm handing you the biggest story of the decade maybe and all you can think of is to sit here and wisecrack. It's not like you, Tom."

Bossly shook his head. "The trouble with you, Jim, is that you've been sequestered on Moon Base too long."

"That's the trouble, eh?" I said with some skepticism.

"Yep. That and the silly costume I bought you. The beard and whiskers may make you look like a professor, but you're the same dumb yokel you always were."

I sighed. "Okay, you knew about it all along. Everyone in the news business knows about it. But nobody's talking worth a damn, let alone broadcasting this yarn because no one wants to end up in the slammer. How's that?"

"Just so-so, Jim boy."

"I got something wrong?"

"Just a bit. Franklin Kelly tried to air it. So did Rudy Jennings. And Martha Gail. They weren't the only ones."

"So what happened to them?"

"Search me, Jim. Maybe they *did* end up in a cell. Nobody knows. All I can tell you is that they're gone."

"Gone, eh?"

"That's it. Gone. I can see enlightenment beginning to penetrate. We of the media pride ourselves on the spread of enlightenment. You will also note another interesting point. I'm *here*, engaged in this fascinating chat with you, while my aforementioned colleagues are *not*. Probably they are not anywhere anymore. That's just an educated guess, mind you. But who would dare knock education? Follow?"

"Uh-huh."

"Good for you. Anything else I can do for you?"

"Uh-uh. You've done too much already. All this enlightenment is hard to take. A little more and I'll give up watching the news-lines altogether."

"It'll be a tough blow, Jim boy. But we'll no doubt keep on pitching anyway."

"Sure you will, Tom, especially when I give you my very last sure-fire angle. You see, there's still something I can do for you."

"Don't you ever give up?"

"Lots of times. Who doesn't? Have an eyeful." I gave him Litkey's list of hoods. "What do you think of *that?*"

"If these gentlemen are pals of yours, you've been keeping bad company," Bossly said.

"Not me, Senator Fulton."

"You trying to tell me Fulton's in the rackets?"

"What do you mean 'trying'?"

Bossly waved a hand. "Come off it, Jim, Fulton's loaded. He needs the rackets like I need an ulcer."

"We yokels don't like to tease the media so I'll come right out and tell you. Fulton's got those guys as part of his private army. Maybe two thousand strong. The payoff's got to be a whopper. *That* story you can break, right?"

"Yeah. If it checks out. Crooks are always fair game. Even if they're hooked up with a senator. Where'd you get this?"

"Brian Litkey, a private eye working for Moon Base. He's got the goods on Fulton. And the goods are all yours, free of charge. Just give him a ring."

"I don't get it, Jim; I thought your aim was to buddy up with Fulton."

"Sure. My bet is that Fulton's not the only one being palsy-walsy with the underworld. Nab one and you'll soon get wind of the others. Hess's got the State Security boys lined up solid behind him and who knows who else? If Fulton's mob connection goes public, it'll give Hess something to yak about. Fulton's got part of the capital cops sewed up. It'll be swell to see their flacks tangle with the State Security media boys. And that ought to bring the generals into it, too. They'll all be slinging mud at each other like crazy. All the cats'll be out of the bag and even the average Joe'll be able to figure out the score. It'll bust this town wide open. Moon Base'll end up smelling so pure and sweet, the politicos will be lining up in droves for our blessings. That's when we'll give Fulton the nod. By then he'll *really* need us. He'll be pushed right into our corner. Where else could he go? And at least Fulton *likes* Moon Base, always has. It's a lot safer to buy someone who's already sold on your product."

"But Fulton's a crook, you say."

"Sure. But so are the rest of them. The difference is that Fulton could be *our* crook. And that's one helluva difference."

CHAPTER 22

All this talk about crooks had, if nothing else, put me in the right frame of mind for what I had to do next. I left Bossly, hopped an auto-cab and was transported to the southwest business complex. It was only seven-thirty but it might have been midnight for all the people strolling about. Business packed up and went home for dinner promptly at four-thirty. I couldn't complain. So far, all my crimes had been imaginary ones, cooked up by the opposition—whoever *that* happened to be—to keep me on ice. Now I was actually going to do something bad. About time, too.

I walked over a couple of blocks. I had no trouble recognizing Henderson's six-story office building. The front door was locked tight. That was to be expected. I found an alleyway halfway around the block and followed it down to the back of the building. The back door was just as unbudgeable as the front. I didn't mind, I'd come prepared. The first thing I did was clamp Litkey's shorter on the knob.

It would short any alarm the management had hooked up, unlock the secrets of a computer, help crack a safe and maybe scramble eggs. If the crooks who used it weren't getting rich, the guys who manufactured it certainly were. And each year saw a new up-to-date model making the rounds. I used the shorter.

Next I got my wire out and gave the lock the old one-two. The lock went click. It always did.

I put my wire away, opened the door and, flash in hand, went on in. The stairs took me to the third floor.

I used my wire and shorter on the door of the Speedy Service Agency.

I didn't turn on the light in the waiting room or inner office. My pocket flash was enough. The minicomputer was on Henderson's desk. I used the shorter on it, overrode the code and punched out my name.

James Morgan was there all right in bold-typed letters on the small view screen. The report was given in a couple of paragraphs. Along with the name of the guy who'd ordered it.

Sweet and simple. And at least the guy wasn't an out-and-out stranger. I knew the name. What I didn't know was why Malcolm Lane—Moon Base's very own paid spook—would want to get me off the scene.

But maybe I could find out.

Clayton Towers was a skyscraper that actually lived up to its description. I wondered if the tenants on the top floor didn't go around in oxygen masks. Nearby, other towers reached for the sky too. I was on an island of overweening concrete. High above me part of the Moon peeked out from behind a cloud. I didn't feel homesick.

I pressed Malcolm Lane's downstairs buzzer, one on a panel of hundreds. No response. I still had my attaché case with me, although I'd polished off the jelly sandwiches long ago. I glanced over my shoulder. There was only the wind and a lot of empty sidewalk. Anyone watching from a window would figure I was just having trouble with my door key. I got the shorter and wire out again, went to work on the door.

I took the chutes up to the hundred and fifty-second floor. On my way I passed everything from five-story shopping marts and entertainie dens to public sex clubs. I had half a mind to stop off at the latter, but since that was the weak, silly half, I ignored it. At least for the time being.

I got off at Lane's floor, found his door. When the bell and my knuckles got me nowhere, I picked his lock.

The door opened on darkness. I stepped in, dug my flash out, closed the door behind me. I stood there staring at what was left of Malcolm Lane's flat. Oh, brother! My fingers fumbled for the light switch. I needed a better look.

Someone had taken the place apart piece by piece. The couch had been overturned and sliced open; stuffing was scattered around the room. Chairs were upset, drawers pulled open, the table overturned. The rug had been yanked off the floor and left in a heap in one corner. Shit.

I had a sudden hunch that I would find nothing of interest here. That someone had already made off with anything and everything. But like a lot of my hunches lately, this one was a bit off the mark. Because in the very next room I found what was left of Malcolm Lane himself.

"Another stiff?" Ellie Fenwick said. I was using a street corner view-phone.

"Yeah. I almost went through the floor. This Lane guy was one body too many. All this is happening around me and I don't even know why. Do *you* know why?"

"Uh-uh."

"Yeah. Neither of us knows why. How'd the Ryder thing go?"

"Restview Sanatorium sent out its wagon and took him away."

"Good old Restview. It's grown to a good-sized town, hasn't it?"

"City. Gee, you'd think with all that time on their hands, folks'd find better things to do than go crazy."

"Yeah. One would think. They come up with anything on Ryder yet?"

"They say he's got a bee in his bonnet."

"Uh-huh. Anything else?"

"They're still working on it."

"Right. Give Timins the what's what on Lane, eh? Ask him to buzz the chief, find out if he told Lane I was bound for Earth. Got that?"

"Sure."

"I'll be in touch. Gotta run."

I ran.

Still in disguise I checked into a seedy midtown hotel. I checked out the next morning. Nothing to it. The rest should be so easy.

CHAPTER 23

Frank Broderick was a short, very fat party, somewhere in his late sixties. His head was round, almost bald; his belly made a neat bulge under his striped, dark blue business suit. He removed his gold-rimmed spectacles and stared at me.

"What do you *mean,* you couldn't find me?"

"Scratch that," I said.

"I've been here, Mr. James, at this *very* desk for the last forty years."

"I'm sure."

"Now what is this about Senator Fulton?"

"As I said, Mr. Broderick, I represent Moon Base." I'd already flashed my badge at Broderick; it bore no name, but the lobbyist hadn't asked to see my ID. Why should he?

"You were one of the last persons to see the senator before his disappearance."

"I was?" The fat man seemed surprised.

"Uh-huh. We've been conducting our own hunt for Senator Fulton. We thought you might be of some help."

Broderick smacked his lips together. "I don't see *how.*"

"What was your visit about?"

"Environment Inc. wished to warn him."

"Warn him, eh?"

"About the trees."

"The trees?"

"In York Park."

"Yeah?"

"They are dying, Mr. James."

"Dying?"

"Quite right."

"And?"

"Funds *must* be allocated to save them."

"Funds. That's why you saw the senator?"

"Certainly."

"How did he take the news?"

"He was *very* upset, as you might imagine. But who wouldn't be?"

I called Ellie from a corner view-phone.

"Scrambler's on?"

"Golly, yes. All the time now."

"Get hold of the chief?"

"Sure thing. No one knew you were coming."

"No one?"

"Except one person."

"One."

"Malcolm Lane."

"Son of a gun."

Brian Litkey said, "Nice going, sucker."

"Yeah," I said, "I take it either something very good or very bad is about to happen. Why don't you just keep me in suspense for a couple of years?"

"Ha-ha," Litkey said.

I was back in his office, back in the client's chair, back looking out through his window at a lot of other windows looking back at me. I hated it.

"So—spill it already," I said. "You got news?"

"He's there, all right."

"There," I said.

Litkey nodded pleasantly. "In the State Security Building. Right where the X was on that little piece of paper you showed me. Like I said, nice going, sucker."

"You sure?"

"No."

"Thank God."

"But my tipster—one-a the guards, see?—tells me they got a guy there."

"Yeah?"

"And this guy looks like Fulton."

"There're probably hundreds of guys who look like Fulton. Thousands even."

"Ain't it the truth?"

I sighed. "But I bet this one really *is* Fulton, eh?"

Litkey nodded. "Who else? Look, chump, you can't live forever, right? But I got somethin' here that'll make this whole operation a cinch." Litkey waved a diagram at me. "What I got here, for only a couple extra thousand Credits—"

"Thousand!"

"Don't look a gift horse in the mouth, Morgan."

"Gift?"

"Sure, you know, don't you, that State Security's honeycombed with spotter eyes?"

"How should I know *that?*"

"You know now, buster, State Security gotta be secure, right? Well, this little diagram tells you where they got 'em stashed so you can avoid 'em."

"Avoid 'em."

"That's the ticket. And there're a couple restricted areas. Guards there. You'll want to skirt 'em."

"Skirt 'em."

"Now you're talkin'! And a couple doors set off alarms when you open 'em. You'll wanna pass 'em by."

"Pass 'em by."

"Righto. I think you got it, Morgan. About the changin' of the guard, you should know that, too. It's all here on this little piece of paper."

"Death warrant is more like it."

"Listen, buster, I didn't ask you to do this dumb thing, did I? Look, I even got you the key?"

"The key?"

"To room X. My pigeon lifted a duplicate."

"Some pigeon. Can this stoolie be trusted?"

"Shit. Who knows? But I used him before, see? And he played ball okay. He goes for the extra bread. But who don't?"

"That's nice. I bet he can't come up with some document giving me charge of Fulton, eh?"

"You said it, chump, he can't."

"Just asking."

"He does chores, not miracles, Morgan."

"Uh-huh. You dig up a uniform?"

"If I can get a key to their joint, you think I can't get their uniform?"

Litkey went off to a closet, came back with a nice spiffy black and gray State Security outfit. On a hanger, no less.

I looked at it glumly. "I figured the next time I saw one of those I'd be throwing stones at it, not wearing it."

"You live and you learn, buster."

Slowly I got my street clothes off, climbed into the hateful uniform. "How do I look?" I finally asked.

"It's you, Morgan!"

"Thanks. Makes a man want to club someone, wearing this thing."

"Six tonight's an okay time to show up at Security HQ. Shift change. Lotsa confusion. People goin' in and out the building. Just look like you know what you're doin'."

"I'm a goner already."

"Shit. A lotta those cops're even dumber than you, Morgan. How you figure on gettin' Fulton outta that joint?"

"I'm hoping it's not him. Then I can just go away."

"Good luck, buster."

"What a mess."

CHAPTER 24

I spent the rest of the day loafing in Tom Bossly's flat.

At twenty to six I went back out on the street. I felt like a clown. The uniform Litkey had given me fit okay, but I didn't fit the uniform, nohow. I was breaking out into a cold sweat. At least there were no crimes in progress where I was. I could just see myself coming to the aid of some elderly victim and having the shit beat out of me.

I wondered whether State Security cops tended to traffic and if I could be drafted to work some street corner. It didn't seem likely. Trouble was, I didn't know what *was* likely. I'd neglected to bone up. The whole thing had seemed pretty simple until I'd actually put on the uniform. Now nothing seemed simple.

I flagged an auto-cab, got in and told it State Security Building. The cab took off and I cringed back into a corner. I'd never seen uniformed cops riding a cab before. But that didn't necessarily mean it wasn't done. I wondered if the computerized machine I was in would mind if I lay down on its floor. Probably I'd just be calling attention to myself. I didn't want to do that. By now I didn't want to do anything.

A glance out the window told me we were approaching my destination. Stepping out of a cab in full view of a bunch of State Security gents didn't seem like an exactly brilliant move. If I was going to survive this dumb scheme every move I made had to be nothing short of brilliant.

"Stop here," I croaked at the cab.

"We still have three blocks to go," the cabbie voice intoned.

"Gotta stretch a leg," I explained. *You miserable heap of junk,* I added to myself.

The cab screeched to a halt. I fished my Moon Base rate-card out of a pocket.

The cabbie voice intoned: "State Security agents ride free."

"So they do," I chuckled, feeling myself turn beet red. I stumbled out the door and all but ran down the block. Another minute and I would've no doubt confessed everything to the stupid machine. The word fiasco began to light up in my brain like a neon sign. Get a grip on yourself, Morgan, I told myself sternly. What's to worry? All you're doing is going into the dreaded State Security HQ. It's not as though you were the Most Wanted on their list. You're probably no higher than third or fourth.

But just as I'd decided it was definitely time to backtrack a bit and think things over—maybe for a year or two—I rounded a corner, and there I was, in full view of my colleagues, all done up in their neat black and gray uniforms. Just like me.

I had enough presence of mind to slow down, stick my chest out, pull my stomach in and look like I knew what I was doing. Actually, it could have been a lot worse. I'd hit six o'clock right on the button. The shift was changing. Cops were pouring out of the building and others were streaming in. Chances were that if I'd shown up in diapers, no one would've noticed. I got caught up in a wave of new arrivals and let myself be carried along into the building.

The wave broke up around me, everyone heading in their own direction. I knew I had a direction, too, but just at the moment I couldn't for the life of me remember what it was. I looked around for someplace to hide. No dice. I continued down a long hallway with a lot of uniformed guys. The last thing I needed was to end up odd man out in some kind of formation. I spied a doorway up ahead. Anything was better than this. I pulled even with the door, grasped the knob, and stepped through. No one stopped me. I was on a staircase. For the time being I had it all to myself. I got out the floor plan Litkey had given me and took a look-see.

No doubt about it, I'd been going in the wrong direction, heading right when I should have been angling left. Good thing I'd stopped. Now everything was clear, except, maybe what I should do about it.

I studied the floor plan some more.

I could take these stairs up two flights, double back to a section marked B, go down one flight to avoid a spotter eye, go up two more flights to dodge a checkpoint and the rest would all be clear sailing. Unless someone asked me where I was going. That would blow it, all right. But so would camping here on the staircase all night.

I knew that I'd had a simpler way of reaching Fulton when I'd first checked over the diagram. But now I couldn't find it. Sweat was dripping into my eyes and I was having trouble seeing the stupid piece of paper.

Wiping my brow, I looked again. Things began to make more sense. I'd used the wrong door. State Security had three entranceways and the one I'd wanted was located in the west wing of the building. I'd come through the south door. And boloxed up my whole plan! At least I hadn't charged through the northern door, which was where they brought criminals. "Time enough for that," I told myself.

Slowly I started up the staircase.

I opened the door leading to the second floor landing, peeked out. A hallway very much like the one on the first floor. It wasn't empty. Three guys dressed just like me were walking down the hall. I waited till they'd rounded a corner, then stepped out. From behind closed doors I heard all kinds of commotion: voices, the rattle of auto-mat typewriters, what sounded like someone getting the crap beaten out of them. I didn't stop to investigate. After all, what could I do, call the cops? These *were* the cops. On the other hand, all I might've been hearing was some training film on the use of the blackjack and thumbscrew. No need to jump to conclusions. I didn't want to get myself worked up. If I started taking things personally, it would only interfere with my cool objective judgment—whatever was left of it.

A door opened; a chubby man in a gray business suit looked out. "You there," he said.

I was the only "you there" in sight. I opened my mouth to say something smart, but all I could get out were little gagging noises. I knew the thing to do was run for my life, but my legs wouldn't move. Right away, I decided to confess *before* they broke my head open; why make trouble?

The man thrust a brown folder at me. "Would you run this down to C section?"

I took the folder.

"Thanks," the man said.

I was alone again in the hallway. Cautiously I looked around for some nice safe place to pass out. Since there wasn't any, I kept walking.

If I was going to duck the spotter eyes, checkpoints, and other menaces that lay ahead on this floor, I had to find a staircase soon. But did I really have to duck them? The folder I was carting had a nice official C stamped on it. Which probably meant I could get through section B unmolested. I looked around. No one was watching. I got my diagram out and gave it the once-over. Room X, where they had Fulton, was almost next to section C. A short flight of stairs going up would have me knocking on his door. The thing to do then was march straight ahead. Now. Before I changed my mind.

The State Security Building is pretty big. During the next eight minutes I hoofed through multidesk offices, map rooms, computer rooms, weapons control, something called disaster projections and a place that sold soft drinks. I passed three spotter eyes. I kept the C on my folder prominently displayed. No alarms went off. No one even gave me a second glance. The guys at the checkpoints just nodded. I nodded back. It began to look as though I might come out of this alive, after all, just barely.

Section C came and went. The folder would do me no more good, I was on my own again. I left it in a waste can, found a staircase and headed up.

The second floor had been a beehive of activity, the third was something else. I saw no one and heard nothing. Even the lights seemed dimmer up here. I didn't like it. Was this floor unused? Was room X somewhere else?

Was the dumb diagram playing me for a sucker? One thing was for sure: I couldn't hide in the crowd here; I was the only crowd there was. Time to get a move on, Morgan. I consulted my diagram again.

I moved.

I had counted the doors twice just to make sure I was doing the right thing. The right thing—as usual—was being evasive as hell. No one had bothered to put numbers on these doors. Not even a small X, like on my diagram.

I glanced around again in both directions. Safe enough. I put my ear to the door. If Fulton was inside that room, he was being very quiet about it.

I got the shorter out, clamped it on the door knob. The gismo had worked like a charm the last few times I'd tried it. But this was State Security territory. And if the security boys couldn't come up with a pick-proof lock, it was time to round up a new team.

On the other hand this wasn't the jail section. It was only a room. And one that was darn tough to reach. So maybe the gismo would still be okay. Maybe.

I flipped it on. No bells went off.

I got the key out of another pocket. It shook in my fingers. Stupid key. I put it in the lock and turned.

There was a small, satisfying *click*.

Still no bells, alarms, armed sentries.

Very slowly I pushed open the door.

He was lying on a cot. He was dressed in gray pants and a white open-neck shirt. He was about five-foot five. The top of his dome was bald, sun-tanned; a fringe of curly white hair grew around it. His nose was large, lips determined, jaw firm, just like on his campaign posters. He had a potbelly and it sagged over his belt buckle—not like his campaign posters at all. His eyes were blue—but I couldn't tell from looking at him because his eyelids were closed. He was asleep.

I'd found Senator Fulton.

CHAPTER 25

I stood looking down at the old galoot, wondering if he had been worth all this effort. No contest. *Nothing* was worth all this effort.

Actually, I'd been half hoping the senator would be somewhere else. A real live senator to whisk through this building presented a number of problems. Like how to get out alive. There was a problem, all right. And if I didn't get the senator out alive, I doubted if he'd be grateful.

"Senator," I said, "oh, Senator."

Senator Scott Fulton opened an eye. "Can't you leave me in peace?" he asked.

"Senator," I said, "I've come to save you."

The senator yawned. "A likely story. I didn't become top-ranking member of the Budget Committee by buying twaddle like that, boy." He sat up. "All you uniformed thugs are alike," he said bitterly. "Well, you won't get me to talk. And when I get out of here, I'll see you all in hell. And not a red cent for State Security, either."

"That last item'll get them. Want you to talk, eh?"

"They think I'm planning a coup."

"And are you?"

"Mum's the word."

"Boy, no wonder they've got you bottled up here. What's wrong with you guys? Is *everyone* trying to make a coup?"

"If you're interested, boy, I can give you some snappy tips."

"I'm sure you can, Senator. And what I should've done is stayed on the Moon. Brother! Anyway, I'm here to save you. No kidding. My name's James Morgan and I'm the new Moon Base ambassador."

"Moon Base? Why, I've been the staunchest supporter of Moon Base."

"So you have. And that's why I'm here. One good turn deserves another, right? By the way, are we safe having this little chat or are some guards likely to come busting in?"

"It is evening?"

"Yep."

"They never disturb me during the night."

"Very considerate."

"And you really are Moon Base, young man?"

"The very personification, give or take a little."

"I didn't know Moon Base really *cared.*"

"Cared is putting it mildly. It's giving them conniptions."

"But how did you find me, boy?"

"Blind luck. And lots of money; mostly the latter."

"That's all?"

"It's not enough? Actually, your colleague, Senator Tarken, got wind of your whereabouts. And tipped us."

"Jeff? He did that? For me?"

"Yeah. May he rest in peace. Uh-huh, he got himself bumped off, I'm afraid. In the line of duty, it seems."

Fulton's mouth fell open. "Oh, no!"

"Sorry about that. Hate to break it to you so suddenly, sir. But I figured you'd want to know what we're up against."

"Jeff Tarken and I were friends." Senator Fulton drew himself to his full height, which all things considered, wasn't so high. "Will Moon Base give me *full* support, Morgan?"

"That's what I've been trying to tell you, Senator. We're set to go down the line with you. One hundred percent. Why stint?"

"You'll do that officially?"

"Our P.R. office is all yours, Senator."

"Thank you, my boy."

"Aw, it's nothing, Senator. Especially if we don't get out of here."

"Then lead on."

"I was afraid you were never going to say that. Know anything about the guard setup out there?"

"I have only been out of this room a few times. For interrogation."

"And?"

"Well, they do not keep a guard at my door."

"I noticed."

"Or down the hall."

"Uh-huh."

"Or anywhere else that I could see."

"Good. Just checking. So all we've got to do is get by the other two floors and out one of the doors. *ALL,*" I sighed.

"Will that be hard?"

"It won't be child's play. Better stick in your shirt front, comb your hair."

"What in the world does that have to do with anything?"

"Plenty. We've got to look respectable. Even the goons in here admire respectability."

"I have always been the epitome of respectability," the senator said.

"You're a credit to your family, sir. Now, let's see if we can walk out of here and down two flights of stairs; that's the easy part."

"There's more?"

"Yeah. Like always."

"And it is . . . ?"

"The tough part. We gotta get you past a lot of offices, guys walking in the hallways, stuff like that. And we've got to do it without shooting. Because there are more of them than us."

"You have a plan?"

"Yeah. Prayer. A stiff upper lip. And lots of luck. Ready?"

"Ready."

"Right. Let's go."

We went.

"Actually," I said, as we hustled down the empty hallway, "we just might get away with it. After all, how many of these goons know you're here? The big shots would want to keep it quiet. So no one will do a double take if they spot you."

"But I *am* well known."

"Sure. And that's all to the good. They'll either figure you're here because you're buddied-up with the top brass. Or they won't believe you're you. Not in these surroundings, anyway."

"Ah, I begin to see. I think."

"Sure you do. Either way, with me as your official-looking escort, we ought to get by, look like we belong. That's the name of the game."

We got to the staircase, started down. We never reached the second floor. A voice through a loudspeaker said, "Stay where you are."

"Oh-oh," I said.

"We have armed men covering all exits," the loudspeaker voice continued. The voice didn't sound friendly at all.

I cast a sideways glance at my companion. He was taking our little setback in stride. At least he hadn't started to cry. Which, in about a second maybe, was more than they'd be able to say about me.

"Drop your gun to the ground, and put your hands over your head," the voice suggested.

"Don't worry," I told Fulton, out of a corner of my mouth. "We're not licked yet." Although if we weren't licked, I wasn't sure what the hell we *were.* I decided to withhold this information from the senator for the time being. I didn't want him demoralized. So far, he hadn't said a word or made a move. Scared shitless, no doubt. He wasn't the only one.

"You have until the count of three," the voice explained. "Then we kill you." That voice was starting to get on my nerves.

"Don't believe them," I whispered to Fulton. "They're bluffing. They wouldn't dare lay a finger on you. On the other hand, maybe we *should* do what they want. What do you think?" I put an arm on the senator's shoulder. Very slowly, without even glancing in my direction, the senator began to topple over. "Jeez," I thought, "he's fainted."

"One," the voice said.

The senator hit the stairs. It sounded like someone knocking over a tin trash can.

"Senator," I said.

"Two," the voice said.

The senator's head detached itself from his body. Wires stuck out of the neck; I could see gears and bolts and other hardware inside the head.

"Three," the voice said.

The senator's head began to bounce down the stairs.

There wasn't time to drop my gun, which was still hanging in its holster on my belt. So I just raised my hands. Slowly.

I didn't want the nice voice to mistake my gesture for resistance.

The senator had just lost his head. I didn't intend to lose mine.

CHAPTER 26

General Manning West was a tall, thin guy with high cheekbones, a straight nose, a pencil-line mustache, shiny black hair slicked back over a large head. His black and gray uniform was just like mine, only better tailored. I sat in his office, minus my gun, and wondered if I had a chance diving through his window. It didn't seem likely since his window was on the twenty-first floor. That left the door and the three armed guards in the hallway. Not to mention the general himself, who was seated across the desk smiling at me. I'd seen faces on iodine bottles with nicer smiles. I decided to forget a spectacular getaway for the time being and concentrate on begging for mercy. Or anything else that might fit the bill.

"Caught you red-handed, didn't we?" The general smiled again. He had even white teeth and a surprising bass voice.

I shrugged, "At what? Kidnapping a robot? You'll never make it stick."

"What about impersonating an officer? Entering restricted areas? Or—if you wish—conspiring with the mutants, assaulting security agents while escaping, that whole can of worms?"

"Uh-uh," I said, "the latter junk is just junk and I'll be able to prove it in court. Maybe you've got a case with the other stuff. But why bother? What have I done to you?"

"Nothing yet."

"There you are," I said, "so why mess around? Moon Base will come down heavy on my side. I'm their ambassador, you know."

"Of course I know. That, in fact, is why you are here, Mr. Morgan."

"That's why?"

"Certainly. To make quite sure you do nothing."

"I've got you worried, eh? Little me? I can't believe it."

"Not *you,* Mr. Morgan, but rather what you represent, the prestige of Moon Base. We hope to neutralize that by neutralizing you."

"I don't know if I'd like that."

"They rarely do."

"Look—I can be bought off."

"We thought so. But you turned down our very generous offer."

"I did?"

"Oh, yes. The one we made through Mr. Henderson. The Speedy Service Agency. And after we went to the trouble of supplying Mr. Henderson with your dossier. You *really* have been a pain in the ass, Mr. Morgan."

"That was *you?*"

"Who else?"

"Malcolm Lane, for one."

West grinned. "We *did* use his name, didn't we?"

"Oh, brother."

"Call it muddying the waters."

"How about calling it murder, too?"

"Heavens, no." West looked genuinely offended. He waved a hand. "We have such *fine* facilities here—really extraordinary, wouldn't you say? We would hardly waste them by dispatching a suspect in his domicile."

"Suspect?"

"To State Security, Mr. Morgan, *all* men are suspect. You really don't understand how *anything* works, do you?"

"Don't worry, I'm learning fast."

"Next we tried to discredit you, turn you into a fugitive. We hoped that you would see reason, curtail your activities. But to no avail."

"No avail," I said sadly. "That was my mistake, all right."

"It certainly was, Mr. Morgan. You were more trouble to us as a fugitive than an ambassador."

"Is it too late to say I'm sorry?"

"Much too late."

"That's what I figured."

"What you couldn't know, Mr. Morgan, was the great confusion existing behind the scenes. All the various factions were busy trying to gain some advantage. Why, I myself—and the forces I lead—have changed sides twice in the last forty-eight hours. Under those fluid conditions, it seemed best to either buy you outright or put you in cold storage."

"Sounds a bit chilly."

"A South Sea island can hardly be described as *chilly,* Mr. Morgan. We felt that a time *might* come when a modicum of Moon Base assistance *would* be in order. But I do believe that moment has past. I feel we can do handily *without* Moon Base. One less compromise to make, so to speak. And you *were* proving to be a terrible, unpredictable nuisance. So we had to round you up, Mr. Morgan."

"I can see that."

"We knew, of course, you were seeking the senator."

"It wasn't a secret."

"And we appreciate that."

I sighed. "Glad to oblige."

"So we made a decision to, as it were, set you up."

"Nice not to be neglected."

"It wasn't easy."

"Good things rarely are."

"But not *all* that hard either. We *do* have the resources."

"I'm sure."

"We utilized them and sent out the word."

"The word."

"To many. Tarken was one of those, naturally."

"Tarken," I pointed out, "was Fulton's man. How'd you get him to cooperate—bash his head in?"

"Hardly necessary, Mr. Morgan."

"Had the goods on him, eh?"

"Such cynicism, Mr. Morgan, tsk, tsk. Senator Tarken thought he had come into possession of *legitimate* information."

"Shows how much *he* knew."

"But our information *was* quite persuasive. Senator Tarken bought that map from a reliable source."

"One of your stooges, West?"

"Oh, no, a *real* informer, Mr. Morgan. He too thought he was getting the genuine article."

"Have you no shame?"

"Obviously not. And you *are* here, aren't you?"

"In the flesh, unfortunately. So what happened to Tarken?"

"No doubt he had enemies. So many do."

"You really claim you had nothing to do with his killing?"

"My dear Mr. Morgan, *we* do not claim anything."

"You don't?"

"We do not *have* to claim anything, now do we? After all, Mr. Morgan, we *are* the authorities."

"And a law unto yourselves, eh, General?"

West shrugged. "It wasn't always that way. But so it has become."

"So it has."

"And there's more where that came from."

"I'm sure."

"Yes, Mr. Morgan, things are changing."

"I can hardly wait. You had that robot all dolled up to look like Fulton. Why?"

"For you, Mr. Morgan. To flush you out. Much simpler than having hundreds of agents hunting you, staking out your old haunts, trying to anticipate your moves. This is a time of crises, Mr. Morgan; we can put our manpower to better use. We decided to have *you* come to *us*. The Fulton robot was seen by many in the building. Of course, we had no way of knowing if you would check that. But we thought it best to cover all contingencies."

"One thing I don't get."

"Please."

"How come you didn't pick me up when I hit the third floor? You let me shlep around, till I got to your robot."

"Why not, Mr. Morgan?"

"Why yes?"

"We wished the two of you to converse."

"The robot was getting lonely?"

"We wondered what Moon Base *actually* wanted with the senator. The *strength* of the commitment, so to speak. We felt we knew, but we wanted to be sure. And now we *are.*"

I sat there staring gloomily at the general.

"So what are your plans for me?" I asked.

"They are simple in the extreme."

"Simple."

"We put you on ice."

"Ice."

"And you stay that way."

"Stay."

"For as long as necessary."

"That long?"

"Maybe longer, Mr. Morgan."

CHAPTER 27

The office wing of the State Security Building had been no pip. But it was a pleasure palace next to the prison section. And then some.

Everything was made of metal—walls, floors and doors. If you didn't have the key or combination, only dynamite or a blowtorch could get you out. I didn't have any of these items. I didn't have much hope, either.

I was in an eight by ten cell. A bunk bed and toilet were my only company. The door was made of solid metal with only a peephole to break the monotony. Unfortunately, all I could see through the peephole was another metal door and peephole across the aisle.

Some prisons have bars on the doors, cell mates, and all kinds of other amenities. Some prisons are more like home than home. Not here, though. Maybe in another wing, but I doubted it. What I'd seen on the way to my cell was strictly solitary confinement. State Security took no chances. Maybe the state was better off. *I* sure wasn't.

My second day in solitary was like my first. I got three square meals a day and a sullen turnkey.

"Nice day," I said.

"Shut up," he said. I followed his advice; he seemed to know what he was talking about.

Otherwise I was left to my own devices, which, at the moment, didn't add up to a hill of beans. They hadn't even taken all of my uniform away, only the jacket. They just let me sit. I was becoming a nonperson. And there was nothing I could do about it.

I had tapped on both walls of my cell. Just like it said to do in the entertainies. But if anyone was holed up on either side of me, they weren't bothering to tap back. Maybe they'd lost heart. I was beginning to see why.

I paced up and down trying to figure the angles. But there didn't seem to be any. Brian Litkey was the one guy in the whole world who knew what I was up to. And I hadn't even said I'd check back with him. What I should've done was clue in Timins. But at the time, I'd figured the less he knew the better. On the other hand what could Timins have done, alert J. Z. Fleetwood?

I knew it wouldn't take Litkey long to size up the situation. But then what? I couldn't see him mounting a rescue operation, no matter what. Litkey was out for the dough. The best I might expect from him was maybe letting Moon Base in on the secret. Which would put it right back in Timins' lap with old J. Z. Fleetwood waiting in the wings. Any way I sliced it, I was out of luck. And maybe out for the count.

That night I dreamed a dream:

The things were out to get me. I wasn't sure what things but they were rotten to the core. I ran up the block. Nighttime. Only a few streetlamps lit my way. I kept looking back but the things were always out of sight, lost in the murky blackness. Around me, tall, lightless buildings loomed. There were no sounds, not even my running feet. The streets were deserted. But I knew the things were gaining on me. My progress was slow because I always seemed to be running uphill. Then the lights began to snap on in the buildings. I tried to run harder. Somehow I knew the things were in the buildings. If they looked out the windows they would see me. Faces began to appear in the windows. Senator Scott Fulton leaned far out, shouted something. I saw Senator Tarken, eyes wide and staring. Malcolm Lane, a bloodless cadaver, smiling and winking. "Don't run!" Malcolm Lane screamed. General West joined the chorus. I glimpsed Brian Litkey, Timins, the distorted face of Captain Charles Ryder. Then I was running down a dark alley. The voices were gone. But I knew I had made a terrible mistake. I looked around for some exit, but there was none. The things began crawling out of the walls. I saw them now. The things were muties, triple-headed, double bodies, with arms like tentacles, with feet like a centipede. And they were all coming for me. I began to scream.

A hand roughly shook my shoulder.

I opened my eyes slowly, not sure where I was. At least I was out of that alley. Then I remembered. Right away my store of good cheer vanished. A voice was saying, "Shut up."

I raised my eyes. A tall, thin man was bending over me, gripping my shoulder.

The turnkey? Had my screams awakened the prisoners, some of the guards? Had someone complained? What a way to start off my new career as inmate. I wasn't going to apologize though. If they didn't like it, they could chuck me out.

The cell door, I saw, was open. Some men were gathered around it. "Jeez," I thought, "I must've roused the whole prison!"

Again I looked up at the man standing by my cot. The light was dim. But the guy seemed vaguely familiar. A long horselike face, very large ears, black hair combed straight back and large brown eyes under heavy brows. I sat up to get a better view.

And almost shit in my pants.

The guy was Malcolm Lane!

CHAPTER 28

Obviously I was still caught up in my nightmare. Any second now the things would come back and I'd be running down the alley again. In a way it would almost be an improvement over the cell. And the corpse of Malcolm Lane that had popped up for some chitchat. I closed my eyes and opened them, hoping that the rotten scene would somehow change. No such luck.

I gazed up at my new companion. "Tell me you're not Malcolm Lane."

"That would be lying," he said.

"I'm dead?" I asked.

"Goodness, no."

"*You're* dead?"

"I'm alive, too."

"So who's the dead guy who looked like you?"

"Why, a cadaver we had stored and made up *especially* for the occasion. To be *utterly* truthful, I left that little decoy as a lark. To befuddle anyone who might come hunting for me. And apparently many did. No one even called the undertaker. Or examined the *corpus delicti* carefully. Very sad, really."

I nodded thoughtfully; a small light was beginning to dawn. "Okay, I can almost buy that. So tell me: You going to be my new cell mate?"

"You don't even have an *old* cell mate."

"They caught you?"

"They wouldn't know how."

"And I take it you're not one of them?"

"That's all I need," Lane said. "To be one of those horrid persons."

"Then your being here can have only *one* explanation."

"It's *not* selling insurance. All things considered, you'd make a very poor risk."

"You're right about that," I admitted. "So you're here to spring me, eh?

Any second, pal, I'm going to wake up and you'll turn into a wisp of smoke. I think I'm still in shock. Who're your sidekicks, by the way?" I nodded at the men at the door. They were just standing there.

"Members of the Liberty Committee. Not unlike myself."

"You free prisoners?"

"You're the first one."

"You have other functions?"

"A few."

"Maybe you'd better tell me *later.*"

"Later would be ducky."

"Ducky, eh? You really figure we can get out of here?"

"We got *in,* didn't we?"

"Sure. So did I. That's the easy part."

"Well, we'll know soon enough, won't we?"

"Uh-huh. I suppose there's a good reason we're just sitting here calmly chewing the rag like this, instead of running hysterically for our lives. There's gotta be a good reason, otherwise we're goners. Tell me there's a good reason."

Lane shrugged. "Why rush? Who needs the excitement?"

"After two days in this cell I can use the excitement."

"Well, if you want to leave, you'd better dress for the occasion."

"I put on tie and tails?"

"Just the jacket."

One of the guys from the doorway brought over a jacket. I got up and tried it on.

"A bit tight," I said. "I'm glad you fellas don't know everything."

"But we do," Lane said. "Button it."

"Nothing like being back in uniform," I said. "Makes a man feel wanted."

"You'll be wanted, all right. In about twenty minutes. By all the authorities in town. Come on."

We went.

In all there were eight of us, each clad in the garb of State Security cops. I didn't think we'd fool anyone. Once we hit a check post, spotter eye or any of the other fancy doodads that filled the building, the fat would be in the fire. Along with us.

We were on the thirteenth floor of the jailhouse. Bad luck in anyone's book. I said to Lane, "Look. One thing we don't want is shooting. Shooting can lead to permanent injury, maiming, disfigurement, crippling, not to mention death. So if it looks like there's gonna be shooting, I think we should give up. Better a live prisoner than a dead escapee, eh? After all, I got J. Z. Fleetwood, that legal eagle, on my side; didn't know that, huh? Well, it's a fact. So maybe I can get out of here on the up-and-up. On the other hand, maybe not. Still, it's a chance. But going out of here in a wooden box is no chance at all. So the point I wanna bring across is: if you guys wanna get killed, that's okay by me. But if there's any shooting, I'm jumping ship, see?"

"What *is* wrong with you, Morgan?" Lane asked.

"I'm raving."

We had been traipsing down a long corridor, closed cells on either side of us. So far we had met no one.

"If it wasn't for you guys, it'd really be lonesome out here, ha-ha," I said.

"Keep quiet, man!" Lane said.

"Yes, sir," I said. I'd sure come a long way these last few days of solitary. All of it downhill.

We stopped in front of a closed chute. Lane stretched out a hand, pressed the button.

"Uh-uh," I said. "You sure you want to do that? Wouldn't the stairs be a better bet? I mean, less crowded, if nothing else."

Lane said, "We took the chutes up, we can take them down. Don't worry."

"What do you mean, don't worry? How else can I fill the long, endless seconds as they slide by?"

I looked around at the other six guys. None of them had said a word yet.

"Cat got their tongues?" I asked Lane.

One of the guys looked at me mournfully. "Listen, bud," he said, "we're too *scared* to talk."

"There is *always* a pessimist in the crowd," Lane said.

"Yeah. But six of them?"

The chute door opened.

We stepped in, were whisked down.

Lane said, "Should we meet anyone just allow me to do the talking."

"You can count on it," I said.

We hit bottom.

Eight of us stepped out. Right into the middle of a mob scene.

Outside—I saw through a window—was the dead of night. But in here, milling, churning armed security guards filled the lobby from one end to another. There were men—and even women here too—in plain clothes, carrying bulletin boards, computer printouts, maps. The noise was deafening.

We started pushing our way through the crush.

I whispered to Lane, "The troops are really out tonight, huh?"

Lane nodded.

"Someone tip them to my imminent escape? I didn't know I was that important."

"You're not."

"So what gives?"

"Mutant Village is starting to fuss."

"Hmmmmm, must be quite a fuss, eh?"

"Morgan, *do* you have to chatter so?"

"Why not? Everyone else is. We don't want to look different, do we?"

"There are times," Lane said, "when I begin to regret this mission."

"I can believe it. Which reminds me. Why *have* you gone on this mission, Lane? There must be better ways to spend the night."

"Any way is better."

"So?"

"Just part of this dreadful job, Morgan."

"For the base?"

"Who else?"

"For money?"

"What else?"

"The base ordered me sprung?"

"No, Morgan. I just went and did it."

"Shows initiative, all right."

"Lucky you, Morgan."

"I guess."

"*Now* I bill them."

"Very businesslike."

"And then, Morgan, I retire."

"Big bill, no doubt."

"The biggest."

"Think they'll pay?"

"Always have, Morgan. You *are* worth it, aren't you?"

"Every blessed Credit," I said with feeling.

"So hush up now; here comes the tricky part."

"I thought *this* was the tricky part."

We had reached the edge of the crowd. A loudspeaker had started blaring away giving some kind of instructions. As long as they weren't about me, I wasn't going to complain. I followed Lane and his pals down a corridor. Up ahead a couple of cops stood at a wide doorway. We had left most of the hubbub and all of the crowd behind us.

We reined up at the door.

"Hey," a heavyset guard said. "Where you think you're going? Building's on alert." The guy had his hand on his holster.

"We've got orders," Lane said.

"Yeah? Let's see 'em."

The other guard just stared at us stonily. If I'd ever wanted a job in security, I changed my mind right then. The only friendly security guy I'd met so far was General West, and I couldn't stand him.

Lane rummaged in a pocket, came up with a sheet of paper. The guard glanced at it, shook his head. "Uh-uh, buddy, can't you read? Small print says 'orders superseded in the event of an alert.' "

"And this is an alert," Lane said.

"Right, buddy. You need the colonel's stamp on this thing if you want to get out."

"You learn something new every day," Lane said. He and the other six guys jumped the two guards. I stood by and watched them. Nice to have someone else doing my dirty work for a change. The bout was short and sweet, if not exactly fair. Nothing like seven guys fighting for their lives to speed things up.

"Let's go," Lane said.

No one had to be told twice. We stepped over the guards, piled through the door.

"Now we're in trouble," Lane said.

"Only now?"

Behind us an alarm began to shriek.

"Spotter eye probably took in the whole thing," Lane said.

"So what do we do?"

"Run, what else?"

"That," I said, breaking into a trot, "I already figured out for myself."

CHAPTER 29

"That way!" Lane shouted.

That way turned out to be straight down the block and not around some safe corner. For an instant I thought of going off on my own. But misery loves company. And the chance of getting a bullet in the back was sure as hell making me miserable. I followed Lane and his crew. He'd gotten me this far, maybe he'd get me the rest of the way. Unlikely as that seemed.

One glance over my shoulder told me more than I wanted to know:

Lights were snapping on in the State Security Building, armed men were pouring through the front doors; sirens, alarms, whistles and horns were competing to see which could screech the loudest. No one had made such a fuss over me since I'd won the Boy Scout of the Month Award.

"Lane!" I shouted, working my legs for all they were worth.

"Yesss?" He was huffing and puffing about a foot ahead of me. The other six guys were doing better than both of us, racing up the block as though they were bent on breaking the three-minute mile.

"What makes you think," I panted, "that we can outrun bullets and lasers?"

"This," Lane said. "Now," he said.

"Now *what?*" I said.

One of the guys up front reached into his pocket, did something. Behind me the street went BOOM!

I looked back.

The bottom half of the State Security Building was swallowed up by thick black smoke. Along with the guards who'd been chasing us. The smoke began to climb up the building and roll after us down the street. I felt my knees begin to buckle.

"You blew up the place?" I asked in a voice I hardly recognized. I could already see myself as the World's Most Wanted Man—only not to shower kisses on. Odds had it I'd be tagged as the guy responsible for the blast, for the death of hundreds of men. Who'd ever believe I had nothing to do with it?

"Don't you worry," Lane said.

"Why not, for Christ's sake?"

"Because it's merely smoke, not fire."

"Not," I said.

"Now you've got it. Not that I would have minded blowing them up. Only it's too hard. And not the right time."

"Damn straight. The time is when I'm not around."

"We turn at this corner, Morgan."

"Not a moment too soon."

"Not tired?"

"Nothing that a wheelchair wouldn't fix."

"Two days of enforced idleness should have given you plenty of pep."

"Two days in the slammer turned me into an old man."

Around the corner three cars were waiting for us. Nobody bothered exchanging so-longs. We tumbled in and took off like nobody's business. Lane and I had a car to ourselves; he drove. The other cars soon went off on their own. Lane headed out of the city. Slowly I began to unwind, to settle down. After a while I almost felt halfway human. "Lane," I said.

"Yes?"

"The chief told you I was coming to Earth, didn't he?"

"Of course. I *am* his principal agent here."

"And you tipped West, eh?"

"Don't be asinine."

"You deny it?"

"Certainly."

"Then how did West find out? Tell me that. The guy even had my picture snapped when I got off the shuttle."

Lane shrugged a shoulder. "How in the world should *I* know?"

How indeed.

We rode in silence. Behind us the tall buildings, spiraling walks, high drives, seemed to grow smaller, became part of another distant world. We sped through a residential section: small two- and three-story houses lined the wide streets. Up ahead red lights glowed in the center of the street.

"Oh-oh," I said.

"Roadblock," Lane said.

"Fast work," I said.

"May not be for us. A lot *has* been happening, you know."

We swerved onto a side street, turned a number of corners. Again our headlights pointed north. We roared down a different highway. This time no one blocked our progress.

I didn't bother to ask where we were going. For the time being I couldn't have cared less. As long as it was far away from State Security, I was satisfied.

"So," Valerie Loring said, "you've had a busy night, haven't you."

"Yeah, you might say that."

"Sit down. And help yourself."

I wasn't about to argue. I plunked down on the kitchen chair and went to work on the food and drink. Nothing like a little freedom to do wonders for a guy's appetite—even at three in the morning. But I couldn't help wondering just how free I was.

I was on an estate far out in the country. The nearest highway was at least a mile off. The last part of the journey had been over a gravel road.

"Thanks for the chow," I told Melissa Sussman's coworker. Valerie had decked out her petite figure in jeans and a flannel shirt. Her black hair was braided in two pigtails. She smiled at me.

"You've earned it," she said.

"Yeah. Sitting in a cell is hard work."

"You did your best."

"Uh-huh." I poured myself a last shot. I was starting to feel like my old self again. But my old self had been no world-beater either. "You know all about it?"

"Malcolm Lane told me."

"You two pals?"

The girl shook her head. "Just met."

"Very convenient."

Valerie smiled. "Through Dr. Sussman." She seated herself, facing me across the small table.

"Sussman and Lane are buddies?"

"I don't really know. You'll have to ask her."

I grinned. "What I'm trying to figure out is what I'm doing here."

"Got it. Well, Melissa called."

"When?"

"A couple of days ago."

"Uh-huh."

"Said I would be visited by a man."

"Lane."

"Right. And that I could trust him."

"Do you?"

"Why not?" Lane said from the doorway.

"Why yes?" I asked.

"Trustworthy, sincere, noble," Lane said, "and the very person who won you your freedom."

"Have a bite, Mr. Lane?" Valerie asked.

"Indeed, yes." Lane pulled up a chair. "It *is* really quite simple," he said.

"Nothing's simple anymore," I said.

"This is. Like you, I work for Moon Base. Dr. Sussman supports the project. Along with many other scientists. When we discovered through *internal* sources that you had been apprehended, we decided first, to rescue you, and secondly, to hide you in a *very* safe place."

Valerie said, "Who would think of looking here? It was Melissa's idea."

"Nice idea," I said. "Very cozy."

"It will be," Lane said, "for you."

"But dangerous for Valerie. What if I'm caught?"

"You won't be," Lane said.

"I'm not worried," Valerie said.

"I'm glad someone isn't," I said.

"Just don't surface," Lane said, "until I get you cleared."

"You're going to do that? For me?"

"I'll try."

"I hardly deserve it."

"Certainly. But who's to know?"

Bright sunlight shone through my window. I rolled over, sat up in bed. The fact that I had a bed meant that I wasn't in the clink. Now all I had to do was figure out where the hell I was. After a moment it came to me. I sank back against my pillow. And grinned. I was all right. I wondered how long that was going to last.

Lane—before taking off—had provided me with a simple leisure getup to romp in. As someone who's always supported leisure, I was grateful. I broke out the clean underwear and socks; tried on the dark gray slacks, blue sports shirt and gray wide-collared zipper jacket. Not bad. They went okay with the shiny black State Security boots I'd left standing by the side of the bed. I washed up in the bathroom and climbed into my new duds.

Brunch was waiting for me when I got downstairs. The kitchen clock said eleven-fifteen.

"Hi," Valerie greeted me. She had on purple jeans, a yellow blouse. Her black hair hung loose, flipped as she moved her head.

"Morning." I smiled back, seated myself and took a swig of orange juice. "Day off?"

Valerie shrugged. "I'm not tied to the lab."

"Don't need the Credits, huh?" I buttered a slice of toast, poured myself a cup of coffee. Sheer luxury.

"I can take it or leave it," she said.

"I'm sure. I could get used to a place like this myself without any strain."

"Then maybe I've got bad news for you."

"So soon?"

"Melissa called. She'd like to see you. In the city. She said it was *very* urgent."

"Tell her Lane is carrying the ball just now?"

"I did."

"And?"

"She wants *you.*"

"Must be my dynamic personality. I used to have one before I got pinched. Why can't she come here?"

"I think she wants to show you something."

"Yeah?"

"In the lab."

"You *think?* I bit into a piece of sausage, followed it up with a forkful of eggs. "I thought you two were pretty thick."

"We're friends, of course. And coworkers. But we each have our own projects, Jim. Only a couple overlap."

"So it could be anything?"

Valerie nodded.

I said, "This is a hell of a time for me to go waltzing back to the city. After last night's fracas I'll be the talk of the town."

"Not quite."

"Something *else's* happened?"

"I'm afraid so."

I pushed away my plate. Luckily it was already empty. "Go on, tell me, I can take it. Whatever it was. *I think.*"

We sat in Valerie's study and watched the tel-viser. I'd taken along an extra cup of coffee to help ward off the dull spots. Only there weren't any. The coffee grew cold as I sat staring wide-eyed at the high jinks depicted in the three-dimensional circle. During the night while I'd been snoozing away, the city had gone haywire.

The muties were on a rampage, had come pouring out of their village and taken over whole sections of town. The regular army, State Security forces and local cops were shooting it out with them, trying to hold them in check. So far the results had been only a stand-off. Other forces seemed to be involved, too, maybe mutie supporters, maybe some private units controlled by parties unknown. The voice-over didn't know and officials weren't saying. Chairman Hess had called an emergency session of Congress; he had also asked for calm and order. Fat chance. To make matters worse, the muties seemed to have a destination in mind: Computer Central. Most of the city, in one way or another, was hooked up to Computer Central. Chaos would have a field day if the computer works went on the blink. And the whole city would probably go down the chutes. Of course *getting* to Central was no cinch. Even under ordinary conditions the site was heavily guarded. Now it would become a fortress, surrounded by tons of hardware and hundreds of fighting men. The muties didn't stand a chance.

So why wasn't I reassured?

People's Counsel Barnabus had taken to the airways, too, but instead of calling for calm, he'd torn into the government.

My name, at least, didn't come up once. Neither did Senator Fulton's. Yesterday's headlines had been trampled under the muties. I took my loss of fame in stride. No one would bother me in the city now. Except maybe a stray bullet. There seemed to be plenty of those.

CHAPTER 30

I borrowed Valerie's mini-scooter. For ten whole hours I had felt safe, a rare feeling lately. I hoped it would last, at least for part of my trip. I was heading back to the real world.

Green fields were on both sides of me as I zoomed along the highway. A blue sky overhead. I relaxed and let time slide by. Traffic was light for most of my jaunt; it began to bunch up as I neared the city.

I left the highway for some side roads. When those got too crowded I took to the fields. By now traffic was packed solid and all but standing still.

I used the back streets to get me where I was going. Roadblocks were set up along the way. I lugged the scooter through back alleys, hoisted it over fences. I heard shooting, shouts from somewhere. Nothing near at hand. That was okay with me.

I could see the white towers of the Science Fed Complex in the distance. I chained the scooter to a lamppost, said my prayers, took off on foot. Twice I ducked the soldiers by going through the front door of a building and out the back. I still kept to the side streets. The Science Complex itself, I saw, was untouched by the fracas. The government forces had managed to hold the muties at bay, so far. I wished them luck.

The Federation HQ was at Science Square. It was crowded with pedestrians hiking from one building to another. Business as usual. I was glad to see it. No one stopped me when I walked through the wide HQ doors.

I took the chutes up to the twenty-sixth floor. I heard voices and smelled smoke at the same time. The corridor curved so I couldn't see what was what. But the voices—a lot of them—were coming from the direction of Sussman's lab. Maybe one of her projects had caught fire? Whatever it was, a crowd meant I wouldn't be a stand-out. I decided to go take in the sights.

The crowd was larger than I thought. I recognized this bunch, all right. The network had sent out their news-alert crews, hand-held cameras and all. The guy standing at Sussman's door was being interviewed. I ignored him. The door, and what lay beyond it, claimed my attention completely.

The door was lying on the floor, a charred and broken collection of boards and splinters. The door frame was blackened. The walls inside

Sussman's office were black too, and whatever furniture and equipment was in there had been reduced to rubble. I stared at the mess. My stare didn't bring enlightenment.

I turned to the small, skinny guy standing next to me, whispered, "What happened?"

"Just what you see," he whispered back in a thin, reedy voice.

"Something blow up, huh?"

"Yep."

"Anything left in there?"

"Not to speak of."

"Too bad. Anyone hurt?"

"Only the doc."

"You mean Dr. *Sussman?*"

"Her office, ain't it?"

I asked, "Hurt bad?"

"What do *you* think, mister?"

"Bad."

"To smithereens."

"That's bad, all right."

"Can't get any badder. They'll be scraping her off the floor and ceiling, soon's the meat wagon gets here."

"The meat wagon."

"Yeah. It's kinda busy right now, what with all the fuss and everything."

"I imagine. She blow herself up?"

"Had help, according to that fella up there."

I looked at the 'fella up there' holding down the spotlight. "He's what?"

"State Security spokesman."

"No shit."

"I wouldn't shit you, mister."

I moved my head a couple of inches so it was directly behind the guy in front of me. I didn't want this spokesman to have too clear a view. He had enough on his mind without being bothered by Morgan the Felon.

"What kind of help?"

"The kind you wouldn't want, mister."

"Inept?"

"Worse than that."

"What could be worse?"

"That spokesman fella, he says looks like someone planted a bomb."

"Yeah," I admitted, "that would be worse."

"Sure."

"But why couldn't it've been something she was working on, an experiment gone wrong? How does this guy know so soon it was a bomb?"

"Fella says she wasn't working on anything that could blow up like that."

"No, huh?"

"Says it hadda be a bomb."

"But who'd do a terrible thing like that?"

"Search me. Maybe she kinda rubbed someone the wrong way."

"Maybe. You a newsman?"

"Accounting office next door. Blast damn near knocked my dentures out."

"Hear or see anything before that?"

"Nope. Try to mind my own business."

"Smart move."

"The smartest."

Back outside I retrieved the scooter, climbed aboard and scooted away. The sounds of combat grew closer.

All I needed was to get caught in the middle of some dumb shoot-out with muties. I decided to keep to the side streets.

Not much happened for the first ten minutes. I had the place to myself. Citizens were wisely sticking close to home. Probably the only wise thing that had happened in the city in twenty-four hours.

Then I heard the sound.

It came from somewhere to the right of me, rising over the houses, maybe five or ten blocks away. That sound—whatever it was—didn't belong on those streets.

I slowed, tried to make sense out of it. Nothing doing.

I kicked the scooter back into high gear, turned left.

I rode by tightly shuttered windows, deserted streets. The sound got bigger, if not better, as I drew closer. By now I had begun to figure out what it was. But not why it was.

I turned a corner.

They were marching six abreast, their voices raised in a gigantic roar. Men. Women. Children. What looked to be thousands of them. I saw no muties but that didn't mean beans. Placards waved over the marchers' heads:

SAVE THE MUTANTS. DEATH TO TYRANTS. ONWARD TO COMPUTER CENTRAL.

The stupids were out in full force.

It didn't figure at all, no way, no how. There simply *couldn't* be this many mutant supporters. And they were headed for Computer Central.

I backtracked, gunned the scooter down the block which ran parallel to the marchers. Computer Central. Oh, brother. Lasers and cannons would be strung out around the complex. Not to mention machine guns, rifles, pistols, bayonets, and the good old billy club.

I had to see whose brainchild this stunt was, which dumdum was running the show.

I'd reached an empty intersection, one well ahead of the procession. Turning, I scooted up the block, pulled to a halt.

I didn't have long to wait.

They came. The whole loony procession. And at their head, People's Counsel Barnabus.

Right off the bat he lost my vote. I wondered if he'd even have enough sense to duck when the shooting started. I had my doubts.

I knew there was nothing I could do here, no way to turn this suicide squad around.

I rode out of there.

Again, I whizzed along toward the Leisure Guild. The whole world was coming apart at the seams. And no one seemed to give a damn. A fine how-do-you-do!

A couple of additions to the landscape greeted me as I approached my goal.

Swerving into an alley between two large buildings, I dismounted, went back to the sidewalk, took stock of the situation. It wasn't too hot.

Tanks were blocking the gates, troops in full military regalia backed them up.

I climbed on my scooter and put-putted back a couple of blocks till I found a view-phone. Pulling up, I used it.

I had some trouble getting by the flunkies but after a while Harley Stokes was on the line. Longish blond hair neatly combed, tapered chin well-shaved, hazel eyes under heavy lids clear and forthright. As usual, Stokes was showing no signs of wear and tear. A disgusting trait, if ever there was one.

"I don't believe it," he said.

"Yeah," I admitted, "still alive and kicking. Especially kicking."

"Just goes to show," Stokes said, "what a rotten police force we have."

"I'll write my senator. If there's still one left after all this. Look, Harley, I've got to see you now."

"So what's stopping you, old man?"

"About a thousand armed troops and a bunch of tanks."

"Ah!"

"Well, don't just stand there, do something!"

"I'm not standing, I'm sitting. Besides, I couldn't get rid of those troops even if I tried."

"Hell, I know that, Harley."

"Then why are you pestering me?"

"Jeez. You've got the brainpower of a two-year-old today, don't you?"

"True enough. I'm bushed. Why, I nearly forgot to get my monthly kickback from the theater owners."

"Say, you *are* in a bad way."

"Didn't I just say so?"

"Harley, you still got your official limo?"

"The limousine? I have about five at last count. Government's very generous."

"Harley, you almost *are* the government."

"Sure. But almost isn't good enough."

"I couldn't agree more. In fact, that's precisely what I want to see you about."

"It is?"

"Uh-huh. Why don't you send one of your limos out to fetch me. I'm at Third and Belmont. I trust your limos can still come and go as they please."

"Your trust is well founded."

"That's what I figured."

"Sit tight, Jim."

"You'll do it, huh?"

"Need you ask?"

"Just checking, pal."

"My car's all but on its way."

"Good. The driver will recognize me by my hollowed eye and desperate look. Besides, I'm the only one here."

"Let's hope he doesn't recognize you too well."

"Big deal. The way things are going there won't be any authorities left to give him his reward. As my buddy and former jailer General West said, 'things are changing.' "

"The old boy's got a point."

"Yeah. But not changing the right way."

I sat back in the cushioned limo and held my breath. The uniformed chauffeur up front didn't bat an eye, stared straight ahead and drove by a phalanx of troops. Two of them snapped to attention and smartly saluted. Illusion had triumphed again over reality. Good old illusion.

CHAPTER 31

Stokes grinned at me as I ambled in. He seemed even more at ease now than on the view-phone. He was dressed in a simple blue suede suit, cream shirt, black boots. A walking endorsement of the good life. Too bad the good life looked as though it was going under for the third time. I sank into an easy chair, sighed. "The whole system's going to pot."

"You're telling me, old chum?" Stokes said. "You don't know the half of it. Drink?"

"Uh-uh. The half I *do* know is bad enough. Guess what Barnabus is up to."

Stokes leaned back in his chair behind the wide desk, smiled pleasantly. "Haven't the foggiest. The man's a crackpot anyway, but no doubt harmless."

"Yeah. Don't bet on it. I caught sight of him on the way down here, Harley."

"Oh?"

"Your harmless crackpot was heading up a parade."

"A parade? Now? In the middle of all this?"

"Yeah. Seemed to be having the time of his life. This parade wasn't just a parade, Harley. It was kind of special."

"You *are* going to tell me, I take it?"

"Sure. There were maybe five, ten thousand mutie lovers at his heels."

Stokes sat up straight, squinted at me, "That's certainly special, in fact it's virtually impossible."

"Yeah. I know. You know. But someone isn't telling the marchers. The muties haven't got that kind of drawing power."

"And never will."

"Uh-huh. I'm glad that's settled. They were screaming their heads off, too. Very committed. And guess where they were going?"

"The city mental asylum?"

"No such luck."

"I'm almost afraid to ask, old chap."

"Would you believe Computer Central?"

"No, I wouldn't. Now that you mention it."

"They'll make mincemeat of 'em , Harley; Barnabus is leading his sheep to the slaughter. It's screwy."

Stokes sighed, shook his head. "My tale is hardly more edifying. But I'd better give it to you, anyway. State Security."

"What about 'em?"

"West has joined the mayhem."

"So?"

"Against the capital police."

"Oh, brother. Who's side's he on?"

"His own, it looks like."

"He always was ambitious."

"Seems everyone is, Jim; they're all tossing their hats in the ring."

I got to my feet, perched on Stokes's desk. "We've got to do something, Harley. It's a madhouse out there. What we need now is a faction for sanity and reason."

"You're not suggesting *us,* are you, old man?"

"Who else? I figure since there aren't any better qualified candidates, we're stuck with the job."

"You're about the only one who'd say that, of course."

"Maybe. But so what? If *you* say so, we've got a team."

Harley raised an eyebrow. "Just *what* is this team supposed to do, Jim? We're too old for tennis. And a two-man army wouldn't get very far."

"Aw, come on, Harley, use your head. You and your outfit are tops. You're the guys who dish out the nation's entertainies. You're all over the tel-viser. You're in clubs and theaters. You've got an in with all the networks. Listen, we can push our own candidate—come up with a general or two for muscle—and put him over."

"Hmmmmm," Harley said, "I can see *my* role, I suppose. But where do *you* come in, old buddy?"

"Glad you asked." I stood up, leaned on the desk. "In all this, Harley, Moon Base is the only faction that comes out clean. With West running wild, the charges against me will seem like so much hooey, a put-up job. No one's going to take them seriously now. I can get Moon Base behind you, Harley. You'll need that to be legit. My guess is it'll go over big. The public'll buy it, hook, line and sinker: Moon Base and the Leisure Guild, teamed up for reason, sanity and moderation. What a ticket! All we gotta do then is go out and ring in some support. Maybe the Science guild for a starter. They should jump at the chance—their boss, Melissa Sussman, was knocked off this morning. They're part of the fracas, like it or not. And if they aim to come out of this with a whole skin, they'd better join the winning side. Namely us."

"I see."

"Sure you do. The astros come mainly from the Air Force. They've been with Moon Base from the word go. And I don't think they're going to let us down now. With the Air Force falling into line, some of the army and cops are bound to come over. Who knows how many? What with the factions at each other's throats, gunning each other down in the streets, a coalition like ours could make a clean sweep of it."

I went back to my chair, seated myself, crossed one leg over the other, and said, "Well?"

"I hate to admit it, old bean, but you may actually be on to something."

"Not may, *am.*"

"So let's say I agree. Who do we get for a front man?"

"Fulton, maybe. If he ever turns up and is willing. But anyone else will do. In a pinch there's always us."

"*Us.* That's really scraping the barrel, old buddy."

"Don't knock yourself, Harley. Who could be better? Me, maybe. But we're a team. So it's all for one and one for all. Namely two in our case. Us."

"You're suggesting that I use our networks to make us heros?"

"What do you mean 'make us'? Didn't I come all the way from Moon Base to pull the fat out of the fire? Aren't you the guy who gives the masses what they want? Who could be *more* heroic? That's our angle."

"Actually that's not so bad."

"Glad you finally noticed."

"If nothing else we could probably hold our own."

"Sure."

"And we *do* go back a long way."

"Ah, the good old days."

"So there's *trust* between us, Jim."

"At least," I said, "we've never double-crossed each other. Yet. We can stick together long enough to see this through, Harley. What do you say?"

"I say what you say."

"Shows sense," I admitted.

Stokes got to his feet.

"Come on, Jim."

"We're going someplace?"

Stokes nodded "We're going to push the panic button."

"Didn't know you had one."

"It's we now, partner. Sure we got one. Trade secret, of course."

I followed him out of the office, down a long corridor. We stepped into the chutes, were whisked down to the sub-basement. Again I followed Stokes. The luxurious settings were gone down here. The walls were made of concrete. Dim light bulbs glowed from the ceiling. Our footsteps echoed along the winding corridor. Dampness seemed to hang in the air. The place smelled musty and unused. "Where the hell *are* we?" I asked.

"The inner sanctum."

"No kidding? I'd never have guessed."

"Couple of vaults down here. Only it's not public knowledge. Officially they don't even exist, old man."

"Why the hush-hush?"

"It's where we keep the illegal items. *Everyone's* got something illegal. *Ours* is just bigger and better. Much better."

"I'm impressed, partner."

"Thought you might be. I've been saving this for a rainy day, so to speak. When worse comes to worst."

"And?"

"It's come."

Stokes fiddled with the dials; the large metal door slid open, closed after we stepped inside. Shelves lined the walls. Rows of hardware, all shapes and sizes, filled the shelves. Bright reddish lights glowed overhead. A wooden table and two benches stood in the center of the room. There were no other furnishings.

"Homey, isn't it?" I said.

"The Ritz it ain't, but it does serve its purpose. Which is more than can be said for some, old chap."

"Don't rub it in."

"Not you, partner; we're exempt."

"Glad to hear it. So what gives with this vault?"

"Well, Jim, you know, of course, that we've got a whole flock of scientists on our payroll, not to mention technicians and floor sweeps. We even have some help from the Science Fed. Why not? Man can't live by bread alone."

"A depressing notion, if ever there was one."

Stokes began rummaging on the shelves.

"Not everything our boys come up with is *suitable* for the public. Some of these gadgets are actually dangerous. Ah, here it is." Stokes held a small flat squarish object in the palm of his hand. It didn't look like much of anything. But then neither did I. "Got to program it," he said.

I followed Stokes down another corridor. It was getting to be a habit. We entered a room which was all computer from floor to ceiling. Stokes slipped his prize into a slot.

"Very illegal, this," he said.

"It has a name?"

"The Benny."

"That tells me a lot."

"Named after its inventor, the late, lamented Dr. Joseph Benny, Ph.D."

"No shit?"

"It creates illusions. Most lifelike. Actual concrete images, you know."

"How could I know that?"

"You do now. I've taken the liberty of programming your Benny, old bean."

"That's real nice of you, Harley."

"What are friends for?"

"This program, it includes song and dance?"

"No such luck. I've given you programs A and L."

"What happened to all the letters in between?"

"You won't be needing them. Besides, to activate the image, you must have the code. Just a little built-in safety device. Got these two little code books for you. But if I programmed the whole works you'd need a sack to carry all those booklets. Or a couple of porters. Not very practical if you're out there fronting for us and perhaps end up running for your life."

"Not practical at all."

"So all you get is two: A and L. That is: political leaders and armed forces. One for persuasion, the other for illusory force. They should both come in handy considering your mission."

"I volunteered for a mission?"

"Hardly, old man. You already had it. *I'm* the one who volunteered. Remember?"

"Oh, yeah, so you did."

"You've got a silver tongue, Jim."

"I'd trade it in for a one-way ticket to Moon Base, any day."

"All in good time. Listen, punch out the code and you've got an army behind you or even General West by your side."

"Pretty cute. General West, yet! Can this army shoot anyone?"

"You have to do that yourself, Jim."

"Then what good is it?"

Harley grinned. "Keeps the opposition busy while you're shooting them."

"Well, that's something."

"The images have some substance. Backed up electrically. But they couldn't really hit someone."

"I suppose I gotta do that, too?"

"Right you are. You do the talking, by the way. Try not to move your lips too much. But don't worry, the rubes'll think it's the image. Anyway, they usually do. Very deceptive. The Benny is really a transmitter. The work goes on right here in this very room. That's why I had these steel doors put up. Don't want anyone creeping around. I'm the only one who has the combination. So everything's perfectly safe."

"Perfectly," I said, "except me."

"Can't have everything, now can we, old thing?"

"Perish the thought. How do I get these images of yours to move?"

"You talk to them."

"They understand?"

"This computer here does. There's a mike in your Benny. It'll broadcast your commands back to the computer. The computer will give the orders. Your Benny will translate them into electric impulses. Everything clear now?"

"Everything except why I suggested this operation. You know, Harley, this might not be the brightest idea after all."

"Too late to back out now, old bean, what would the neighbors say?"

CHAPTER 32

I loitered on a side street near the Capitol building and looked up "arresting officers" in the code book. I punched out the code on my Benny. Armed uniformed guards sprang up on all sides of me. They didn't look a bit friendly, either. I punched "wipe out" and made them go away. The "honor guard" I conjured up next suited me a lot better. They were sturdy-looking types who stood at attention respectfully and even saluted when I asked them to. What more could I want, except maybe a couple of *live* soldiers, with a bayonet or two, on my side?

Taking a deep breath, I told my phantom crew to tag along. They didn't object. Smartly we stepped out onto the main avenue and headed for the Capitol building. We were almost there when I had a sudden afterthought that made me want to about-face and dash back to the safety of my side street. I'd figured that an honor guard would get me by the capital guards. But why should it? I carried no pass, had no document to back me up. Two to one there'd be a squabble. And in a squabble my spooky cohorts would be worse than useless.

Frantically I started thumbing through the code book. This safety device business would be my undoing yet! We were just hitting the wide, concrete stairs when I produced Major General Howard Riggs out of thin air. He was chief of the air force and we'd even met once, at a Moon Base dinner. I felt more comfortable materializing someone I knew.

The guards snapped to attention like steel springs. They didn't even notice that I was yesterday's Most Wanted Suspect. They were too busy staring straight ahead. We marched past them like we owned the joint. I was beginning to get a new respect for this Benny gadget.

I decided to keep my forces with me—especially General Riggs—they seemed to inspire a certain reverence in the ranks that could come in handy.

I went directly to Hess's office. The last time we chatted, he'd come down on the side of a Moon Base alliance. Nothing in that, of course. But now that things were topsy-turvy, he might want to make peace for real. Or he might not. To find out, I'd have to ask him. A flesh-and-blood Hess —the chairman, no less—was worth a couple of Fultons waiting in the wings.

Besides, I didn't know if he *was* waiting.

I expected some trouble in getting to the chairman, what with the crises and all. Guess again. The waiting room was empty, not even a guard on duty. No one was at the desk in the outer office. I opened a connecting door and entered the boss's private domain.

Sunlight shone through the window, splashed across desk and chair. Hess was nowhere in sight.

A thought of Hess out leading the troops flashed through my mind. Somehow he didn't seem the type.

I left my honor guard at the door, facing the outer office. If someone came barging in, they'd bump into General Riggs, figuratively speaking, of course. It would give them pause. I hoped.

I went over to Hess's desk. The desk drawers were locked. A desk-top computer told me nothing. Without the code word or shorter the thing was as speechless as a concrete brick. A single sheet of paper on Hess's desk told me more. A briefing session of some sort was being held this very hour in auditorium 9—wherever that was. And the chairman's name was listed along with a whole lot of others. Pay dirt, of sorts. If there was one thing I wanted, it was to be briefed.

I knew what I had to do. First I sent my honor guard back to limbo. They'd served their purpose in getting me in here. But from now on, they'd only call attention to me, something a man of my basic modesty could do without.

Next I told Riggs to put his arm around my shoulder as if we were buddy-buddy.

Together we strutted down the hall. The first guy we came to told us how to get to auditorium 9. He seemed proud to be asked. My admiration for the Benny was growing by leaps and bounds.

The sentry at the door snapped to attention. We went in to get our briefing.

The room was thick with cigar, cigarette and pipe smoke; a gas mask would've helped plenty.

A lot of men, mostly in uniform, stood with their backs to us. Another group sat up front on folding chairs. Hess and a man I recognized as General Stuart Noring held center stage. The general was talking, gesturing toward a view screen. On it was the image of General Manning West.

"What we face," General Noring was saying, "is a full-scale insurrection."

I sighed, glad to get confirmation of what, by now, every school kid probably knew. A little more of this and I'd lose my faith in the military.

A little more is what I got:

West and his State Security forces, Noring continued to explain, had gone up against everyone else in a bold-faced power grab and since "everyone else" had their hands full, West was holding his own.

The mutants, meanwhile, fully armed, along with a bunch of empty-handed sympathizers, were busy laying siege to the master computer. If the master computer went, the city would grind to a halt. So far, army units added by the capital police were holding them off. Noring didn't believe West would lend them a hand. He wasn't so sure about Malcolm Lane.

I stood there staring at the face which had popped up on the view screen. I blinked my eyes but the stupid image wouldn't go away. It was Lane, all right, the guy who'd sprung me from the pen and was pulling down a hefty Moon Base fee for his efforts.

This Lane, Noring said, was marching on the city at the head of an army. Noring didn't know his name even and kept referring to him as the Unknown Leader. Some leader. I'd had Lane down as an out-and-out hustler. And I wasn't ready to change my tune even now. I was sure of that. That's about all I was sure of.

At least I had company in my state of confusion.

Noring didn't know the score, either, wasn't sure whose army this was, or what it wanted.

Hess, at this point, interrupted the general. He didn't look happy at all. But neither did anyone else, as far as I could see. He waved a sheaf of papers at the crowd, told them that Intelligence reported three men, identical in appearance to this Unknown Leader, commanding separate forces in various strategic areas throughout the East Coast.

I felt my mouth drop open again. I was feeling as stupid as I must've looked.

Four Lanes? Oh boy. *One* was bad enough!

Did they *all* work for Moon Base? Or was there still just *one* Lane? A con artist who'd gotten his hands on a Benny?

But why in the world would he want to do something as silly as that?

I wondered if I ought to tell this crew the name of their Unknown

Leader. Only I knew I'd hate myself in the morning. I wasn't ready to become a stoolie—not yet, at least. And besides, if Lane turned out to be shooting square with me, was *really* working for the Base, I'd never hear the end of it.

I'd heard enough, too much, in fact, for my peace of mind. I took my phantom General Riggs out in the hall, before the real Riggs got wind of us, and beat it.

CHAPTER 33

"Good grief," Stokes said.

"Yeah," I said, "the pilgrim returns."

"So soon?"

I pulled up a chair, sat down heavily, wiped my brow with a damp palm. "This is proving to be *not* one of my better days, partner."

"What happened, old chum, did your Benny go on the blink or something?"

"The 'or somethings' have it. The Benny worked okay. That's about all that worked. Harley, you don't know what's going on out there."

"Oh, I think I have a fairly good idea."

"Like hell."

"Well, let's have it, Jim; it can't be all that bad."

"It's worse. Listen, the whole system's out of whack. The muties are trying to knock off the master computer. A bunch of pro-muties have come out of nowhere to join 'em. General West wants to be emperor or something. The other generals are out gunning for each other—"

"What's got into you, old man, that's not news. I told you some of that myself."

"Sure you did."

"So?"

"So this, wise guy: did you know that *four* armies are out there zeroing in on the city?"

"Four armies?"

"Uh-huh, you didn't know! See? Who knows *what* armies? But General Noring's got their boss pegged, all right. It's—now get this—the Unknown Leader!"

"The *who?*"

"Yeah. Intelligence seems to've fouled up on this one. But *I* haven't."

Stokes sat back in his chair. "Nice someone's on the ball. Especially when it's us."

"You bet. We've got an inside track, old buddy. The guy's Malcolm Lane. So there."

"Ah?" Stokes said with feeling.

I grinned. "Not exactly a household name, is it? This Lane is a Moon Base agent—"

"Well! That's great—isn't it?"

"That's just part of the story. There are *four* of him, Harley. And each one's at the head of a separate army."

"What in heaven's name, Jim, are you blabbering about?"

"Just quoting General Noring."

"What is he—drunk?"

"Seemed perfectly sober to me. Hess and all the other generals—the ones who aren't out sabotaging the government—are buying it lock, stock and barrel."

"I don't actually understand."

"Either do I."

"And this Lane works for Moon Base?"

"At least one of him does. Or used to. Whatever his game is, he didn't let me in on it. Look, Harley, is there any chance someone's run off with a Benny?"

Stokes shook his head. "Forget that. Every one is absolutely accounted for."

"How about someone coming up with their *own* Benny?"

"Highly unlikely."

"But not impossible?"

Stokes shrugged. "If our boy could invent the Benny, I suppose someone else could too. But it'd take a bit of doing. Know how much money, time and effort we put into that project? The Leisure Guild went all out. But a private outfit?"

"How about the Science Fed, Harley?"

Stokes wasn't as quick to answer this time. "Wellll, sure, if they put their minds to it . . ."

"Uh-huh."

"You believe this Lane has one?"

"Could be. Having used your little product myself, I figure that just *might* be how Lane multiplied himself. But what I can't figure out is *why?*"

"He has to have a reason, old bean? Everyone else is losing *their* marbles, why shouldn't *he?*"

"Yeah, true enough."

Stokes's view-phone lit up.

"Stokes here." He listened intently, nodded, said, "Okay," and hung up.

Stokes sat behind his desk staring at the wall.

"Yeah," I said, "that wall's sure a lulu. Although you wouldn't know it to look at it."

"Huh?"

"Wake up, Harley. What's wrong?"

"We're under attack."

"Tell me something new."

"Take a squint out the window, Jim."

I got up, went to the window. We were up high enough to see most of the surrounding terrain. I got an eyeful, all right; more than I'd bargained for.

Down below, the good and bad guys were going at it tooth and nail, right at our doorstep. At least that's what I guessed. The opposing forces were so bunched together, it was hard to tell who was what.

"West's boys taken on the army?" I asked.

Stokes rummaged in a desk drawer, came up with a pair of binoculars.

"See for yourself," he said.

I took the binoculars. I saw.

Only one guy had two heads. And only a couple were over ten feet tall. A lot of torsos were sporting more than the usual assortment of limbs. And some bodies looked a couple of yards wide, but maybe my eyes were playing tricks on me.

"Looks like the muties have landed," I said. I went back to my seat.

"That's not all they're up to," Stokes said. "They're storming the master computer, too. Right now, this very instant. And taking a crack at the Senate building while they're at it."

"Very energetic."

"Very."

"Didn't know there were that many around who knew how to aim a gun."

"There aren't. The muties seem to have about ten thousand helpers. Your citizens' parade has turned into a makeshift army. At least that was the report I just received. Sheer numbers is doing the job."

"This gets worse and worse, doesn't it, Harley? What's West up to?"

"Heading for the hills if he knows what's good for him."

"I hate to say it, he probably doesn't know what's good for him. We've got to do something."

"Such as?"

"I'd fill you in, Harley, but you're too simple-minded to grasp the beauty of my scheme. But I'll give you a hint. It's not even dangerous; almost."

"Sure," Harley said. "Almost."

"Can't have everything," I explained.

CHAPTER 34

We ran up the block.

I held the gas-rifle. Harley was behind me, carried the heavy artillery, a long-nosed laser gun. If it came to bumping someone off, I was more than ready to let Harley turn the trick—provided the maniacs loose on the streets let me.

Sounds of combat came at us from all angles: machine guns, grenades, pistols, rifles. The only items missing were cannons and fighter planes—an oversight I figured would soon be corrected. There were plenty of screams, too, an on-the-spot endorsement of the weapons' efficiency.

"Where to?" I yelled at Stokes.

"Left, at the corner!"

I didn't have to be told twice. I put on a burst of speed.

We rounded the corner.

There were three of them. One was at least nine feet tall. His hands looked as big as shovels. He opened his mouth. I saw crooked yellow teeth. He growled at us, a deep bass rumble. The guy at his heels was a dwarf, his head as large as a beach ball. He made up for his size, though; he had a tommy gun. The third was a girl. She had three arms.

I almost pissed in my pants!

But not before I let off a blast from the gas-rifle. Stokes and I nose-dived to the pavement.

The street instantly became a dense, fluffy cloud. I couldn't see a thing. But neither could the muties.

Overhead, machine gun fire tore through the air.

Stokes and I crawled out into the street.

"You couldn't build the damn station any closer?" I complained.

"You're lucky it's not out in the city," Stokes whispered. "Only three more blocks."

"Only," I pointed out.

I glanced over my shoulder. The muties were advancing out of the smoke. I let loose another blast of the gas-gun, yelled, "Right!"

Stokes got the message. We dived right as another burst from the tommy gun raked the ground where we'd been a second ago.

We climbed to our feet and sprinted around the corner.

"Where's a good place to hide?" I asked.

"There isn't any. Maybe we should go the long way. It seems safer."

"I'll buy that."

We detoured an extra block, trying to make up for lost time by pumping our legs in double-time—a noble but wasted effort. We ended up walking the last block. It was all I could do to keep from sitting down on the sidewalk.

The street, fortunately, was empty.

From east and west, the clamor of bloodletting grew louder, more frenzied.

Relay Station One lay dead ahead, a white stone twenty-story building with a huge antenna on its roof.

We barged through the front door in a sudden spurt of energy.

The pair of muties had their backs to us. One was spraying the long marble corridor with automatic rifle fire. The other had a hand-laser, was burning a hole through an obviously locked door.

The guy with the rifle was only four feet tall, but wide as a truck.

His pal turned out to be a lady. I didn't have time to find out what made her unique. I was busy with the truck.

My humane instincts had prompted me to whack him over the noodle with my trusty gas-rifle. An error. His bean was as tough as a boulder. He turned, gun in hand, a look of real displeasure on his face. I drove the butt of my rifle into his Adam's apple.

He made a choking sound.

I kicked him in the guts.

He doubled over.

I slugged him across the neck with my rifle.

He fell down.

Stooping, I grabbed his auto-rifle, looked around to see how Harley was doing. An altruist to the end, Harley hadn't used his weapon at all. He was down on the floor grappling with the mutie girl. The end looked like it wasn't far off either. I could see now what made his girl special. She had no nose at all. But that was hardly noticeable due to her mouth. Almost a foot wide, this mouth sprouted inch-long fangs. Her hands were hairy claws with razor-sharp nails. She was giving old Harley the works.

I decided to put off being hysterical for a moment or two, jumped over to the struggling pair, and began swinging the heavy auto-rifle like a club.

After a while the she-thing fell off Harley. Slowly he began climbing to his feet. He looked as though he was more than ready for early retirement.

I heard a sound behind me.

One glance was all I needed. The truck mutie was back on his feet.

He didn't have a weapon.

He didn't need one.

His hands would do the job just as well.

His teeth were bared in a grimace. His eyes glared at me. He didn't look one bit friendly.

He lunged at me.

I cut loose with the auto-rifle.

He screamed once, blood streaming from his chest like a small fountain.

He tumbled to the ground.

I didn't waste any sympathy on him.

"Jesus," Harley said. I knew what he meant.

The door the truck man had been using for target practice cautiously slid open. A lone white-faced man in technician's blue stuck his head out.

"Gee, boss," he said to Harley.

"You can say that again," Harley said.

"You all right?" I asked Stokes.

"No, but neither is anyone else."

Down the corridor other figures began to appear. None of them looked too jaunty.

"Someone bar the door," I shouted.

I tossed my auto-rifle to the first guy who didn't look like he was ready to keel over, said, "Take cover behind the staircase, shoot anything that comes through that door and doesn't look human. Don't ask questions. Just do it. You'll be glad later. Is there a back door to this place?"

The guy nodded.

Stokes had stripped the she-thing of her hand-laser. He gave it to the blue-clad tech. "Guard the back!"

The tech trotted off down the corridor.

He didn't get very far.

Two apparitions rounded the bend before him. They had six arms between them. All the hands held guns.

The guns roared.

I used the smoke-gun.

Harley and the other guy opened up with their weapons.

Smoke filled the corridor, rolling billows of it. There was only white smoke.

I grabbed Harley by an elbow, dragged him away.

"Let go!" he complained. "You crazy?"

"Probably; but this ain't the time for the soldier routine. Let's not forget what we came for, Harley. For God's sakes!"

"Came for . . ."

"That's the spirit."

We crawled into the chutes; they took us up to the top floor.

I stuck a handy chair between the sliding doors making the chutes inoperable.

Stokes bolted the door which led to the stairway.

"That won't hold them long," he said.

"Maybe our boys in the lobby will."

"Want to wager a bet?"

"Uh-uh."

We raced up the hallway, toward the broadcast chamber, locking doors behind us as we went.

"Perhaps this will slow them up," Stokes said.

"Something better."

In the chamber we bolted one final door and got busy.

"Know how to work this damned thing?"

Stokes was already at the control board. "Used to do this for a living, old boy. The hand never forgets its skill, I think."

"You don't sound confident," I complained.

"They seem to have added a couple of knobs to this board since my day."

"Your day?"

"Ages ago. But the old brain will find a way."

"The old brain better, before the bad guys get here and bash it in."

Stokes turned a number of dials. "Aha," he said.

"You don't say," I said. I was all but shaking hand and foot. My clothing was soaked with sweat as though I was wearing damp sheets instead of shirt and slacks.

"I think we're getting it," Stokes said.

"He *thinks,*" I said.

"Easy," Stokes said. "I'm going to try the monitor."

His hand reached out, flicked a red switch. Static, then utter silence came out of the speakers. Stokes thumbed a green switch. The giant view screen over the control board lit up. It was milky white, perfectly blank.

"Is that good or bad?" I asked Stokes.

"We've cleared the main channel. I've used emergency override," Stokes said.

"It certainly is an emergency," I said.

Stokes was busy pushing more knobs. His fingers danced over the control panel. "Knew I'd get the hang of it, old bean."

"So, can we start already?"

"A second. I'm blanking out the minor channels. We're not merely going to put on the best show on the Eastern Seaboard. We are going to put on the *only* show. How's that, Jim?"

"I knew there was some reason I had you along."

Stokes glanced at the view screen. It remained unchanged. He nodded jauntily.

"It's ready," he said.

"Okay," I said. *"You* ready, too?"

Stokes nodded.

We both used our respective Bennys.

Senator Scott Fulton stood before the cameras, drawn up to his full height, namely, five-foot five. With both Bennys working in sync, the senator looked solid enough. Our stunt, being electrically produced, was a natural for tel-viser screens. Only the voice might give us away. But who would notice? I did the talking. My chat with the Fulton robot had put me in good stead for a reasonable imitation.

"My fellow countrymen," I said. Fulton's lips moved, and the words seemed to be his. My speech was picked up by the Benny mikes, transmitted to the master computer, and sent back—lickety-split—to the Fulton image. I tipped my hat, mentally, to the wonders of technology, which had produced this miracle, but hadn't quite known how to keep the boobies from running amok. I continued my spiel: "In this moment of dire crisis, I come before you to ask each and every one of you for your help. There are dark forces loose in the land. Insurrection, riot and general lawlessness run rampant, threaten not only our cherished democratic institutions, but the very existence of the state . . ."

Somewhere far off in the building I heard raised voices, a crashing noise like someone breaking down a door. I exchanged glances with Harley. The opposition was moving in for the kill. Whatever the senator said next would have to be short and sweet, if Stokes and I hoped to get out with whole skins.

"The master computer is under siege! The halls of government are ready to crumble! I need not tell you where I stand; you all know that." I almost blushed. I hoped someone out there knew where the senator stood. Outside of his support of Moon Base, I didn't have a clue.

"I urge you to rally in support of democracy, to join forces with me in defense of law and order. Arm yourselves, my friends. March under my banner to save the government, to push back the minions of darkness . . ."

The voices and banging had grown louder, closer. The opposition had hit our floor. It was time to make a run for it.

I turned to Harley. "So where should the forces rally?" I whispered.

"Government Square."

"Government Square," I said in the senator's voice. "Meet me in Government Square at the stroke of five.

"God bless you all."

We switched off our Bennys, doused the tel-viser.

"Is there a back way out of here?"

"Yes."

We ran for it.

The fighting had grown since our leave-taking. And that had only been a half-hour ago. Machine guns, rifles, and cannons were having a field day.

"This place isn't safe for man or beast," Stokes pointed out.

"I wouldn't even want to be a building here," I admitted.

Stokes took a deserted side street, then trotted down a back alley. I followed. The alley led to a garbage disposal dump. We made our way around the garbage to a small door in an otherwise solid wall. We went through. And there we were, back in the outside world.

"Not half bad," Harley said. "Citizens seem to be in short supply here. Rather nice of them, I'd say."

"Yeah. And we're alive."

"For now."

"Go on, encourage me some more."

The block ahead of us looked safe enough. We kept moving.

"I hope we're not going to use the Bennys again, old boy. It'll be a wee bit more tricky in Government Square, what with a hundred thousand people in touching distance; you know?"

"Yeah, I know. You figure we'll raise that many?"

"Maybe more."

"Only one thing to do. We need a stand-in for Fulton. Someone who can take charge of a mob and make it into a fighting force. Or at least *look* like he can."

Harley thought it over. "How about General Markstein?"

"You trust him?"

"Can we trust *anyone?* He's come out for the senator before. Why shouldn't he now?"

"Yeah, why? Don't answer that. Sure, let's give the general a break and put him on the winning side. Think you can reach him?"

"I'll give it a whirl, old bean."

"Tell him the senator's out buttonholing help. And hand-picked Markstein for this vital mission. That should hold him."

"If he hasn't teamed up with someone else."

"Yeah. But if he has, we can always pick us another boy. Can't we?"

Stokes shrugged. "Markstein's right. He commands a lot of loyalty among the local troops. It'll take two generals to fill in for Markstein."

"We got them?"

"Probably. And a lot more where they came from. Only it'll be harder as we work our way down the line."

"So who said this was going to be easy? Can I borrow your laser?"

"Sure. Gone blood-simple, old buddy?"

"Nuts. Some of those clowns are dangerous. Or haven't you noticed?"

"I've noticed."

"Well, I'm off to scout the territory. And I'll feel better with a laser."

"What territory?"

"I'll let you know as soon as I find it."

The Tarken villa was ringed by a high stone wall. Someone—probably the senator himself—had thoughtfully put pointed metal spikes on top of the wall.

I decided not to climb over.

I looked behind me. There were only the woods, the sound of birds and small animals. Overhead the sky was blue, peaceful. The villa was miles away from the city. The senator had done all right for himself. But as a certified cadaver now, he wasn't apt to enjoy much of it anymore.

I used the laser, burned away the lock on the gate, went through. No bells rang. No one ran out with a shotgun to ask me my business. I liked that. I wasn't sure just *what* my business was. But if Tarken wasn't in the know, why had someone gone to the trouble of doing him in? A simple question. And one I hoped to answer sooner or later. Sooner if things worked out.

The house—a four-story job—was locked tight. Shutters closed. Both front and back doors unbudgeable.

I used the laser again, burned off the hinges of a shutter, broke the window behind it, reached in, released the catch, raised the window and climbed in.

Poor Tarken was hardly cold in his grave but already his home smelled musty and disused as if it had stood vacant for months. I suppressed a shudder and got busy.

It took me almost an hour to reach the small study on the top floor. It was in the rear of the house, overlooking the back garden.

I found nothing in the small gray filing cabinet. I had better luck in the bottom desk drawer once I got it open.

I sat at Tarken's desk and looked over my find, a single sheet of paper. It was headed "Ed-Out Takeover," a snappy title if there ever was one. Twenty-two relay stations were listed. Five were checked off. Presumably, they were taken over.

Ed-Out transmissions—as the official government printout explained—

provided unconscious education. Checks and balances from all factions kept Ed-Out neutral.

But if the relay stations were being monkeyed with, the whole system was in hot water. And everyone else along with it.

CHAPTER 35

My scooter put-putted down the wide expressway. Empty fields, grazing cattle, trees, gray-blue mountains in the distance and a sparse flow of vehicles. No military convoys in sight. But that meant nothing. The troops would be pouring in from all parts of the country, converging on the capital, choosing up sides. The government was up for grabs. And this business with Ed-Out only made it worse.

Whoever was trying to take over Ed-Out was going for broke. But who was it? Tarken himself? Or someone the senator had stumbled across? And how far had they gotten? Was the whole system rigged now, or still only part?

A neat bunch of questions, all right, as if I didn't have enough on my mind already.

If Hess was behind the scheme, I might as well toss in the sponge. Bad enough he had a slew of generals behind him. But with all those potential viewers? I wondered how many million that would be. Enough, probably. More than enough. *Given the time.* That was the catch, of course. It took a while to make a True Believer through Ed-Out. Only I didn't know how long, how many transmissions were needed. Maybe I still had some time on my side; a little, at least, until the new converts got their act together. Manpower meant a lot in this. The really heavy stuff—atomics, poison gases, disintegrator rays—would be held back in the arsenals. No one wanted to bust up the prize. At least not yet.

I had to get back to town, huddle with Stokes. But I still had one more visit to make.

No one answered my ring at Melissa Sussman's house. It was smaller than Tarken's—a two-story frame cottage—but just as secluded. And only a little closer to town. The windows weren't even locked. I lifted one gingerly and climbed over the sill.

Unlike Tarken's, this place still looked lived in. Roses, only a bit wilted, filled an antique vase on the living room table. Dust hadn't managed to invade the interior yet. Frilly curtains, brightly colored furniture, a lot of knickknacks, small pillows, and assorted doodads made me want to settle down in the padded easy chair and take it easy. The only item missing was the hostess. That kind of put a crimp in things.

I started giving the place a good going over. I wasn't an expert but at least I brought a lot of enthusiasm to the job. I began on the top floor since that was where Tarken had stashed his little secret. With a bit of luck, history might repeat itself, I figured.

It didn't.

I worked my way downstairs slowly, methodically. Nothing happened till I got to the basement. I was beginning to think my one-man expedition a dud. I nosed around a woodpile, a boiler, a Ping-Pong table. I tried a door over in the north wall. It opened.

Melissa Sussman stood before me. But a Melissa Sussman at least nine feet tall. A voice—Sussman's—boomed out in the otherwise empty room, all but shook my teeth loose.

"If you have reached this point," Sussman's voice roared, while the nine-foot figure—done up in a lab uniform—glared in my direction, "then this is indeed an emergency."

Indeed, I thought.

"I am either indisposed, or worse!"

The understatement of the year, I thought.

"There is terrible danger," the Sussman image bellowed. "Know this: Ed-Out is in jeopardy. There are forces at work who wish to subvert the system. If they succeed, civilization as we know it will cease to exist! Check the relay stations. Beware of tampering. Beware!"

The image snapped off.

I stood there in the small room and thought, *Beware!* The open door was behind me. I looked at the four concrete walls. I stepped back, closed and opened the door again.

The image was back.

"If you have reached this point . . ." the image told me.

"Yeah, beware," I said.

And bowed out of the basement.

I left the scooter parked on a side street. Night was beginning to slip over the city. A long day—with no end in sight. I could hear small arms fire off in the distance. But not too much of it. Maybe the night had put a damper on the shoot-out.

I didn't head for the Leisure Guild Complex. It was too much in the limelight. Stokes had decided to use his home as a base of operations. I got there some fifteen minutes later.

"How're we doing?" I asked.

"Just about holding our own. You eaten yet?"

"Darned if it didn't slip my mind. Must be all the fun I was having."

We went into the kitchen and Harley fixed me some ham on rye. We each took a bottle of beer. We ate in the living room. Harley, in rolled-up shirt sleeves and slippers, filled me in on the day's doings:

Markstein hadn't wasted much time falling in line, had joined ranks with Fulton, the Leisure Guild and Moon Base. The Big Four. Markstein figured it for a good deal. He'd gotten some of his pals on the general staff to do likewise. His forces had taken on the muties and driven them from the city. They were holed-up in Mutant Village. At least for now.

"So what's the beef?" I asked. "Looks like we're winning hands down."

"Looks can be deceiving, old chum."

I took a swallow of beer, settled back in my chair. We were on the eightieth floor of a residential complex, one reserved for big shots, which Stokes was. Unless, of course, he came out the loser in the current fracas. Then he'd end up in a seedy flat on the edge of town called Has-Been Row. Except that Stokes had probably put aside a tidy sum during his years at the helm. I decided to save my worries for myself, a far more worthy candidate. Outside, the stars twinkled peacefully through Harley's window. Which just went to show how much they knew.

"So, what's the pitch?" I asked.

"Hess and his boys have declared war on Markstein. And Hess has a lot of boys. At the moment it's a stalemate. But tomorrow the feathers ought to fly."

"Where's West in all this?"

"Regrouping. Just pray he doesn't team up with Hess."

"How about the Lanes?"

"Haven't been able to check up on that one yet. But it *does* seem a bit hard to swallow."

"Hess didn't think so."

Stokes shrugged. "In any case, he hasn't hit town yet."

"Not he, *them,*" I pointed out. "Well, if you think you've got troubles, listen to this." I gave him my up-to-the-minute report. "The Big Four won't last long, partner, if Hess gets a couple of million citizens gunning for us. This Ed-Out takeover, if it's really going on, is even worse than a Hess-West alliance. Who knows, maybe some two-bit nut is doing the dirty work, not a classy dictator like Hess & Co.? Then we'd all be in the soup. The question is: how do we check out these relay stations? Tarken neglected to list their address."

"Don't look at me," Stokes said, "that data isn't Leisure Guild, it's Ed-Out and strictly classified."

"Meaning what?"

"The watchdog committee knows where those stations are. So does their executive secretary, Parsons. And probably some of the techs."

"Can we get to them?"

"Parsons was appointed by Hess. He isn't likely to be cooperative. The committee's all over the map, Jim. It'll take time to track them down."

"Didn't Sussman have something to do with Ed-Out?"

Stokes admitted it.

"So let's call Valerie Loring, why don't we?"

CHAPTER 36

"This way," Valerie said.

She was dressed for night duty in black slacks and jacket. Stokes's blue and my dark gray weren't bad either. It was once we hit a lit area that the trouble would begin. Stokes and I stepped out of the shadows, followed her up the block.

The Science Complex loomed before us. So did the soldiers.

"Maybe my badge will get us through," Valerie said.

"At this hour?" Stokes said.

"Make out whose troops those are?" I wanted to know.

"Looks like city police," Stokes said.

"Who's their boss?"

"Commissioner Garcheck."

"Too high up."

"How about Chief Inspector Bass, old chap?"

"Yeah. Sounds about right. Let's hope he's not one of the guys up ahead."

"What in the world are you two talking about?" Valerie asked.

"Better tell her," I said.

Harley told her.

"Oh, yes," she said, "the Bennys."

Harley stared at her.

"Tut-tut," I said. "Some top secret."

"After all," Valerie said, "Dr. Sussman *was* president of the Science Fed. But I've never seen one in action."

"You're about to," I said.

The four figures who walked up to the checkpoint included Chief Inspector Bass. After doing a double take, the cops on duty all but fell on their knees. No one bothered to ask us who we were. Anyone with the chief was aces with the cops. We passed on through.

Valerie took us into the Admin Building. The chutes took us skyward. We got off at the hundred and ninth floor. The place was dark, deserted. An exit sign glowed dimly down the hall.

"Toward the sign," Valerie said.

"Certainly know your way around," Harley said.

"That was my job," Valerie said. "One of them, anyhow."

We entered an office. Valerie marched to the safe, worked the combination. The heavy door swung open. She rummaged in a drawer, pulled out a bunch of papers.

"The relay stations, gentlemen," Valerie said.

"What do you know," Stokes said. "And no one even shot at us."

"The evening's still young," I reminded him.

We used Stokes's official limo, Stokes at the wheel, Valerie and I next to him up front. Our mode of transportation had its advantages. The official gold seal of the Leisure Guild decorated both doors, bought us a measure of respect. Roadblocks parted for us, armed guards waved us through. Nobody was mad at the Leisure Guild—not yet, anyway. The Big Four alliance, so far, hadn't made the news-lines. I wondered how long it would take.

Stokes said, "Hell of a way to spend a night, old boy."

"Beats sitting in a cell, or working on a chain gang," I pointed out. "Both distinct possibilities if we ball this up."

"For my part, gentlemen," Valerie said, "I'm simply thrilled to be part of this glorious adventure. We're not going to be killed, are we?"

"Don't ask *me,*" said Stokes, "ask *him.*"

"How should I know," I complained.

"Well," Valerie said, "what *do* you plan to do if some relay station *has* been tampered with."

"Fix it," I said.

"And if there are people there?"

"Fix them, too."

Not much was doing at the first three relay stations we hit. A quick look-see gave us few insights into possible rigging. An expert was needed, only Valerie didn't fit the bill: no Ed-Out training. I began to wonder if the trip would turn up anything after all. I got my answer at the fourth station.

The stations were mostly out in the countryside; ditto for this one. A handy clump of trees helped give us and our car cover. Peering through the darkness we saw lights, movement, activity.

"Perhaps it's merely the clean-up crew?" Stokes suggested.

"Yeah. Working the night shift. That gets 'em time and a half. Except mechs handle that stint. And hardly need the overtime."

"Who are they?" Valerie asked.

"To answer that I'd need super vision. I guess we'd better climb out and get closer. They may not be friendly, so try not to get caught. Not making noise would be one way to do that."

"Are you addressing *me?*" Valerie asked coldly.

"No, me. I'm trying to cheer me up by sounding positive. So far, no dice."

"Onward, folks," Harley said, climbing out.

Onward it was.

There were some guys in uniform loitering around the relay station, I saw from my perch behind a clump of shrubbery; all had automatic weapons which were mostly slung over shoulders or otherwise left untended. The guys were dressed in the spiffy black and gray garb of General Manning West's State Security cops.

"Well," Harley whispered. "Now we know."

"Know what?" Valerie asked.

"Who the opposition is, who's been subverting Ed-Out."

"Yeah," I said, "but that's no scoop. West was never Mr. Nice-Guy. And for all we know these babies are here on their own."

"Don't bet your bottom Credit on it, old chap."

I looked where Harley was pointing. Through a large circular window on the ground floor I caught sight of the man in question, General West himself, chatting away with a fat fellow in striped overalls. A number of other characters in overalls were hard at work in the background.

"Techs," Valerie said.

"Busy as beavers," Stokes said.

"This is an outrage," Valerie said.

"You're telling me?" I said. "It's not even fair."

"Let's shoot them," Valerie said.

"They're more likely to shoot us," I pointed out.

"Just kidding," Valerie giggled. She was obviously suffering from advanced shock. She wasn't the only one.

"You don't want to tangle with West," Stokes said. "That's a job for the military."

"Smart thinking," I said. "Too bad I left my uniform home."

"Not you, Jim; you're too old and feeble. I meant Markstein."

"He's even older," I said.

"But he has loads of help," Harley said.

"Let's shoot them ourselves," Valerie said.

"Girl's got spirit," I said.

"She's kidding again," Stokes said.

"Laugh a minute," Valerie said. "So what are you two planning to do?"

"This way," Stokes said.

We followed him back to the car.

"Watch," Stokes said.

"He's going to do tricks?" Valerie asked.

"Valerie," I said, "how come you're so frisky?"

"It's my true nature," Valerie said. "Besides, this beats sitting in a lab all day."

"She's enjoying this," I told Stokes.

"Takes all kinds, old buddy." Stokes picked up his car view-phone receiver, punched out some co-ords.

A face appeared on the view screen, one sporting a military cap.

Stokes identified himself, asked for General Markstein. It didn't take the general long to get on the line.

Stokes didn't waste words. "I'm near one of the Ed-Out relay stations, General. West is here, rewiring the place. He has some troops with him."

"How many?" Markstein barked.

"Around twenty on the outside; perhaps more in the station itself."

"How do I get there?" Markstein demanded.

Stokes told him.

"Don't let him get away," Markstein hollered.

The view screen went blank.

"He'll be here in a jiffy," Stokes said.

"Doesn't let any grass grow under his feet, does he," I said.

"A real go-getter," Stokes agreed.

Valerie said, "You think West had a hand in Melissa's death?"

"Well, he *is* a candidate for the slot."

"Then someone should *really* shoot him, don't you think?"

"Fine with me," I said.

"You wouldn't catch me complaining either," Stokes told her.

We didn't have long to wait. Maybe about twenty-five minutes.

The troops arrived in style. First the copters, then the cycles, followed by trucks full of armed troops and a half-dozen jeeps holding the brass. A couple of speed tanks brought up the rear. No one fired a shot. The Security cops, it seemed, weren't in the mood for a pitched battle.

Markstein joined us behind our bush, where we were busy watching developments. For once developments left nothing to be desired.

"The army way," Markstein said, "sweet and simple."

Markstein was a short, somewhat stout, powerfully built man with a roundish face, gray crew cut and immaculate uniform. A lot of ribbons and medals were pinned on his chest. Tough on the cleaners, no doubt.

Stokes introduced us to the general.

"Moon Base, eh?" the general said. "Aren't you the mutie lover who made all those headlines?"

I probably blushed in the darkness, but who could see it?

Stokes spoke for me:

"Just propaganda, General. A State Security plot to discredit Moon Base."

"So that's it," the general said.

"Surprised you remembered, General," I put in. "Fame is so fleeting."

Stokes dug an elbow in my ribs. Markstein ignored my remark. Valerie got his attention.

"Don't hold with women scientists," he said with simple eloquence. Valerie lost his attention. So did we. Easy come, easy go. The general went marching off toward the relay station.

I sighed. "The Big Four, eh?"

Valerie said, "That's the best you could do, Mr. Stokes?"

Harley shrugged. "Given enough time, I could have joined the army and become a general myself. Under the circumstances this *was* the best I could do. Markstein has the troops behind him."

"Yeah, but will he put them behind us?"

"Why not, old bean? Generals know their place."

"Sure. But do we?"

The three of us followed Markstein into the relay station.

West was trying to stare down Markstein; it looked like quite a job.

"Hi," I said to West, waving cheerily. "Imagine bumping into *you* here. Gads, what a small world! Just yesterday I was enjoying your hospitality. And now you can enjoy mine."

West just looked at me. He didn't seem to appreciate my words of greeting. For that matter, neither did Markstein.

"General West here," he said, "is the army's charge, sir. And he will be given all due privileges that position entails."

"And a small cell, too, I hope."

"You will have to let me handle this, sir," Markstein said, "in the way I see fit."

I nodded. This was no time to take on the brass. At least I'd gotten a "sir" out of him.

Valerie had other ideas. "This man," she said, "may be responsible for the death of Dr. Melissa Sussman. He should be investigated. And if there's the least bit of evidence, put on trial."

West spoke for the first time; his voice was icy. "By whom?"

"Do you deny tampering with Ed-Out?" Stokes said.

West frowned. "What of it?"

"It's against the law," I pointed out.

"What law?" West asked.

"There'll be law soon enough," Stokes said.

"I didn't know the Leisure Guild was about to take over the courts," West sneered.

"The Leisure Guild has joined with the Science Federation, Moon Base and General Markstein here to restore law and order," Harley said. "And by God, we're going to do it!"

"I was *already* at the point of restoring law and order," West said. "Your intervention, General Markstein, is setting back the cause."

"This clown thinks he *is* law and order," I said.

West ignored me; his argument was with Markstein. "We've known each other a long time, General. Our positions aren't too far apart on what's right for this country."

"This is different, General," Markstein said.

"But why? I really fail to comprehend your actions, General."

Markstein actually looked ruffled; quite a trick, too.

"What in the world," West asked, "are you doing with these *persons?*"

These persons, namely us, exchanged glances. I was beginning to think it'd've been a darn sight better if Stokes *had* gone to general school. Good things are worth waiting for. What was happening now wasn't a good thing.

Harley jumped into the breach. "It's not just us, West. We speak in the name of Senator Fulton."

"That's right, Manning," Markstein said. "Manning," no less. Next thing you knew they'd be holding hands.

"Indeed?" West said.

"Uh-huh," I said. "We're working directly under Senator Fulton. It's his aim to bring democracy back to this land. You might call us the Fulton Coalition, West. No more coups, pal. No more imprisonment without trial. No more raids without a warrant. Tough luck, eh? But don't sweat it, you won't even have to get used to these annoying laws. Where you're going, there'll be a whole new different set of rules."

"General Markstein will be a witness at your trial," Stokes said. "And so will his troops. You can't meddle with Ed-Out and hope to get away with it."

West raised an eyebrow. "I suppose your Senator Fulton would object?"

"Darn tootin'," I said.

"You *believe* that, General?" West asked Markstein.

"Well . . ."

"Rubbish," West said.

"Put him under arrest," Harley said.

"In Senator Fulton's name, of course?" West said.

"Exactly," Stokes said.

"Where *is* your senator, Mr. Stokes?"

"Working to rid society of creeps like you," I said.

Harley nodded, watching Markstein.

West raised his voice. "Is that what you're doing, Scott?"

"Great balls of fire!" a voice bellowed from behind a closed door to our right. "I've heard enough!"

The door flew open.

I had no trouble recognizing the small, chubby figure who stood before us in a towering rage.

We'd found Senator Scott Fulton. Or more properly speaking, he'd found *us*.

CHAPTER 37

The senator gave us the eye.

"Stupid meddlers," he said.

I repressed an urge to look behind me, just to make sure he didn't have somebody else in mind.

General West was smiling. Markstein seemed stupefied. I looked at Harley, he looked at me. We'd obviously mislaid our script.

"Senator," I said, "you may have been misinformed. I'm James Morgan, Moon Base ambassador. I'm here to throw Moon Base support completely behind you."

Fulton shook a finger at me. "You're here to upset the apple cart, that's what. But you won't get away with it! And you, Stokes. What the devil did you do? Hire some actor to impersonate me on the tel-viser? That's the last phony illusion you'll ever engineer!"

General West chuckled. Markstein seemed to be pulling himself to attention. "It's *I* who have been misinformed," he said. "They told me they spoke in your name, sir."

"Poppycock," Fulton snapped. "West here speaks in my name."

"West?" I said.

Manning West gave me a half bow. He seemed to be enjoying himself. I'm glad someone was.

Valerie said, "Senator, West has been using Ed-Out for his own ends."

West actually began to laugh. I figured I knew what the joke was—and who it was on.

"Not his, *mine,*" Fulton explained.

"*Ours,*" West added smoothly. "The senator and I have been working together for some time, you know. Oh, we've had our little spats. We were even at odds at times. Moon Base support then would have been important to either one of us; in fact, that was a consideration in keeping Mr. Morgan here at hand rather than under the ground. But we've managed to patch up our differences, as you can see."

The senator nodded. "We have come up with a *grand* design."

I said, "A real beauty, I bet."

"You scoff! But have you taken notice, young man, of the halls of diversion, the gratification palaces, the endless drivel on the tel-viser? Who does the work now? Machines! Computers and robots. While mankind grows soft and sluggish. Decline is everywhere. One need but look. It is high time for a change. Time for a leader—a man among men—to bring his people out of the wilderness."

"A guy just like you, eh, Senator?"

West said, "Senator Fulton is loved and respected by all. He is ideally suited for this selfless mission."

The senator beamed. "It was *I* who shorted the regular Ed-Out transmissions."

"But *why?*" Stokes asked.

"Bah! To bring on the revolution, you numbskull! What else?"

"What else?" I asked Stokes.

"We have been feeding an urge to revolt into the system." West shrugged. "Unfortunately, our signal is still somewhat erratic. So far we have been aiming them experimentally at selected areas, with only, shall we say, limited results. Even so, I do believe we have some reason to be proud. Wouldn't you say?"

"Not especially," I said.

"Very shortsighted of you," West said.

"We are the future," Senator Fulton said.

"I'm entirely on your side, Senator," General Markstein said, glaring at us.

"If you're so convinced the future's yours, Senator, why didn't you put it to the vote?" I asked.

"What vote? You really believe Hess was about to hold elections?"

"Maybe not. But this revolt of yours has everyone gunning for everyone else. And not even knowing why. Hell, a gang of muties is all set to knock over the master computer. There'll be nothing left when this is over."

"So much the better," Fulton said. "We'll start anew. Won't we, Manning?"

"Oh, yes," West purred. "Brand new."

"And you figured old bloodsucker West here as your best bet for building this new order?"

"We will pick up the pieces of the old," Fulton intoned, "and make something better."

"Oh, brother," I said.

"Much better," West grinned.

I turned to Stokes. "Say something."

"I'm speechless," Harley said.

"Well, I'm not," Valerie said. "This is ridiculous! The 'loved and respected' Senator Fulton, acting like some sort of Caesar! You should be ashamed of yourself. I have every reason to believe, Senator, that General West was responsible for Dr. Sussman's murder! What do you say to *that?*"

"Bah! That's what I say."

"Man of few words," I said.

"Quiet, you!" Markstein roared.

"Big Four," I grumbled to Stokes.

"This jerk may have been my mistake, old boy, but look what *you* came up with."

I looked at the small, bald-headed, pot-bellied senator. I sighed.

"Doesn't it mean anything to you that General West is a possible killer?" Valerie demanded.

"You mean this Sussman woman?"

"Dr. Melissa Sussman, president of the Science Federation," Valerie said, "blown up in her office."

"And you think Manning had something to do with *that?*" the senator asked.

"I do."

"Forget it," Fulton said. "You've got the wrong man, my dear."

"What do you mean?" Valerie demanded.

"It's quite simple," the senator said. "I'm the one who had Dr. Sussman eliminated."

It was not a heartening moment. I was beginning to think that between this guy and his robot version the robot won hands down; the robot had shown a lot more human traits.

"Sussman," Fulton said, "was an obstacle to progress. Take my word

for it; she had no sense of social responsibility. That lady—somehow—
found out that I was cutting in on the Ed-Out broadcasts. She wouldn't
listen to reason. She was going to tell the world. The world wasn't ready
for that kind of news. Believe me, it could have sunk the whole project."

"So you killed her?" I said.

"You would have done the same," Fulton said. "And if not, you're
fools."

I said, "You put the chill on Tarken too, I bet?"

"Of course."

"Why?"

"He was going to talk."

"Yeah?"

"About me. And Ed-Out. To *you.*"

Markstein looked at us sternly. "You three are under arrest!"

Arrest was something we could do without. We still had a card up our
sleeves. I glanced at Stokes, nodded. Stokes nodded back. Smart Stokes. If
these birds thought we were going to fold up without a fight they had
another guess coming.

We both used our Bennys.

Cops and sailors filled the room.

The figures were all spooks, but it would take a moment till our hosts
caught on.

I grabbed Valerie's hand and ran. Stokes ran with us.

Too much opposition barred the way to the outside door. We'd be rub-
bing shoulders with them if we tried to push through.

Only our phantoms and a couple of guys stood between us and the
interior of the relay station.

We headed in.

A burly trooper grabbed me by the shoulder.

I swung my laser down on his head.

He let go.

Markstein moved to stop me. I punched him in the nose. Markstein sat
down on the floor.

By now Stokes and Valerie were ahead of me. I hurried to catch up.

Behind me there were shouts, even screams, the sound of a gun going
off.

I ignored it all.

I ran through bodies with as much substance as smoke, a milling crew of
cops and sailors, rolling their eyes, brandishing their weapons, mumbling
voiceless curses. I was glad this bunch was only make-believe. Two to one,
they'd have turned on us too.

Stokes and Valerie ran through a door. I followed at their heels,
slammed the door shut behind us.

We were in a long, empty hallway. The floor and walls were made of stone. Small barred windows were set high in the walls near the ceiling.

I said, "What happens to our shades when we leave the room, they hang around?"

"Are you kidding?" Stokes asked. "They vanish."

"Then we'd better too, partner."

Our feet echoed over the hard stone as we made tracks. Dim light bulbs glowed feebly overhead. Behind us we heard the door burst open.

"Damn!" Stokes said.

He knew what he was talking about.

We turned a corner.

Two doors faced us.

We took the right one.

This corridor was darker, narrower, wound its way downward.

"I don't know about you boys," Valerie said, "but we scientists prefer to ride."

"Me, too," I said. "If I'd known it was going to be this tough, I'd've worked out more in the gym. In fact, I wouldn't've even come."

We rounded a second turn.

"Where *are* you gentlemen taking me?" Valerie asked.

"Out," Stokes said. "I think."

"Where's that?" I asked.

"Wherever they've put the back door, old bean."

"*What* back door?" I demanded.

"Aw, come on, Jim; there must be a back door."

Behind us more tumult, feet pounding on stone.

I flattened myself in a shadowy recess, waiting for our pursuers to catch up.

The first couple came into sight.

I used the Benny, projected an image of Senator Scott Fulton racing to meet them. "The other door, you fools; they went that way!"

The uniformed Security cops gaped, turned on their heels and dashed off in the other direction. By the time they figured out their mistake, we'd be gone. Maybe. At least it would give us a breather. We could use any edge we could get.

I went after my two companions.

Another door stood open before me. A stairway led down into semi-darkness.

"Stokes," I called.

"Come on," his voice called from below. "And close that door!"

I followed orders, clattered down the stairs, rejoined my two friends.

"Shhh," Stokes whispered.

"Someone asleep?" I asked.

"Just you," he said. "Listen."

I listened.

Voices came from behind a closed door across the hallway, murmuring voices.

"What do you think?" I asked.

"We join them," Stokes said, "what else?"

"But not alone," I said. "General West?"

"Sounds about right," Stokes said.

"I think we should go hide," Valerie said.

"They'd only find us," I said.

"And you wouldn't like it," Stokes said.

"I don't like it now," Valerie said.

"Let's go," Stokes said.

We went.

The four guys looked up when we stepped into their private domain. They glanced at us for an instant, but it was the sight of General West that asked for and claimed their full attention. By the time they noticed that both Stokes and I were holding guns it was too late to do anything but sit very still. They did.

The room was a circular affair. Tel-visers were part of control panels which lined the walls. Images busily competed for viewers on these screens.

It took me only a second to become an avid viewer myself.

The screens were all showing military movement of some kind: tanks and trucks on the go. The trucks were full of soldiers in battle dress. Jeeps convoying the brass rode along at strategic points. Copters, hover crafts and jets flew overhead. On some screens tall mountains formed the backdrop. Others showed flat desert land. A third set sported skyscrapers. No mystery here: army maneuvers taking place in various parts of the country.

What wasn't so simple to explain were the three Malcolm Lanes.

Two were in jeeps, the third was on a truck. All three were in uniform. Except none of the uniforms were exactly alike. A long G.I. trench coat. A field jacket. An open-necked shirt.

Three Lanes. All the same, yet all different. Just what the doctor ordered.

I wondered what had happened to the fourth one?

"You there," I said to one of the guys.

"Me?"

He was a short guy in his fifties with thick glasses and graying hair.

"Uh-huh."

A fat guy asked, "Where's the general?"

"He went away."

"What're the guns for?"

Stokes said, "To make sure we get to ask the questions."

"Who are you guys?" I asked.

"Techs," the little guy said.

"What goes on here?"

"What business is it of yours?" a slim guy spoke up.

"This gun," I explained patiently, "makes it our business. Don't you guys know anything?"

The little guy said, "We're keeping tabs on the Lanes."

That made sense. Of a sort.

"Tell me about the Lanes," I prompted.

"We're running out of time," Valerie said.

"We ran out a long time ago," I said. "If we don't know the score, how can we tell if we're winning the game?"

"Don't worry," Valerie said, "we're not winning."

"The Lanes," the little guy said, "are headin' up these three armies, see?"

"Heading up?"

"Like generals. And we're keeping tabs on 'em."

"Where are these armies bound for?" Stokes asked.

"Here."

"The relay station?" I asked.

"The city."

"What happened to the fourth Lane?" I asked.

"What fourth Lane?"

"See," I said to Stokes, "they don't know everything."

"Thank God," Valerie said.

"Either do we," Stokes said.

"How do you do it?" I asked the little guy.

"Do what?"

"Watch them."

"Spy-eyes."

"Figures," I said, "whatever *that* means."

"We use them, too," Stokes said.

"That's nice."

"You gentlemen," Stokes said, "work for Ed-Out?"

"We useta," the fat guy said.

"But no more," the skinny guy said.

The fourth tech, a tall man with red hair, spoke up. "That's right."

"Most enlightening," Stokes said. "I think."

"So who *do* you work for?" I asked.

"General West," the little guy said.

"Can't catch old West napping," I said to Stokes. "Can you?"

"Not like *us,* old bean," Stokes said.

"How soon before the Lanes get here?" I asked.

"A day or two," the little guy said, "by land; a couple hours by air."

"If we don't do something soon," Valerie said, "it won't matter a smidgen to *us.*"

"We *are* doing something," I said. "But we can add to that something. Guys, I want you guys to take off your pants, shirts and jackets."

"What are you, mister," the little guy asked, "a pervert?"

"What we are," I explained, "are deranged, psychopathic killers. But on a whim we've decided to let you four live. If you don't hurry we may change our minds."

They hurried.

We left them tied hand and foot in a back room. But not before we'd asked directions. We returned to the hallway dressed in tech uniforms. Valerie wore a cap over her long hair.

"This won't fool a child," she said.

"It won't have to," I said. "All it has to do is fool West and his cronies."

"I think it's time for company again," Stokes said.

I agreed with him.

We used our Bennys. Four other techs joined us. Not quite a crowd but enough maybe to divert suspicion.

"Which way did the little guy say was out?" I asked.

"Left, three doors down, right along the corridor till we hit section B. Use the first door and follow your nose."

"You believe him?"

"Hardly matters, old chum, since we don't have any better plan. But for the record, yes, I believe him."

"So do I," I said. "Just checking."

We followed the little guy's directions. A map would've come in handy. This relay station was a little smaller than the Central City space-port. But not much.

About halfway to our destination, we heard the shooting. It came from the floor above us and to the left. Shooting was all right as long as it wasn't at us.

We pulled to a halt.

"What do you think?" Stokes asked.

"Maybe they're killing each other," Valerie said.

"Falling out among thieves?" I asked. "It's possible, I suppose."

"More likely, they've mistaken someone for us," Stokes said.

"What's up above?" I asked.

"Well," Valerie said, "this is the outside wall we've been following, so upstairs must be the windows facing out. It doesn't take a scientist to figure *that* out, gentlemen."

"Only someone with a working brain," I said. "Mine's gone east."

"That's the Atlantic Ocean, old chap," Stokes said.

"Anyplace is better than here," I said, "with a few possible exceptions. Maybe we ought to find out what the shooting's about and who's doing it?"

"You think help has shown up?" Valerie asked.

"The only leader on our side was Markstein," Stokes said.

"Yeah. And I just punched him in the nose."

"Maybe he had a change of heart?" Valerie said.

"He already had," Stokes said. "Unfortunately, it was about us."

"We probably don't want to camp here," I pointed out.

"Probably not," Valerie agreed.

We got going again. We didn't get very far.

Halfway up a staircase, sounds reached us. Men heading down, a lot of them. About the last thing we needed was that much company. We turned tail, retraced our steps on the double.

We were back where we'd just been a moment ago. The footsteps were still coming our way.

"What we need," I said, "is a full-fledged hero."

"No one like that here," Valerie said.

"How about someone willing to give his all for the old cause?" Stokes asked.

"Don't look at me," I said.

We started running. Our retreat was rapidly turning into a rout. At least they hadn't caught us. Yet. Increased gunfire from outside accompanied our racing feet.

Before we could round the bend which would make us invisible for another thirty seconds, the bad guys showed up.

Markstein was in the lead. For an old duffer he wasn't doing half bad. Probably the military training. The trouble was, I'd had the training too and was only half his age.

The troops were at his heels.

"There they are!" Markstein bellowed.

"Turncoat," I yelled back at him.

I used the Benny.

The corridor filled up with commandos. Markstein kept coming. So did his men. They ran right through my make-believe bunch. The general had caught on. So much for make-believe.

"We shoot it out?" Stokes yelled.

"Hell, no. What if they shoot back?"

Something went BOOM!

The floor shook.

"Jeez," I said.

"Take heart," Valerie said, clutching my arm in a steel-like grip. "At least that wasn't aimed at us."

"Leggo," I said, "you're breaking my arm."

Again the BOOM sounded.

The relay station seemed to jump as if trying to duck enemy fire.

"Someone means business," Stokes said.

"They're going to do us in along with the rest of these creeps," I yelled.

"Who's they?" Valerie said.

"Could be anyone," I said.

Yet another BOOM.

A long crack appeared in the wall above us.

"Get back!" Stokes yelled.

We jumped, scrambled for cover.

The wall seemed to heave a great sigh. And fell in on itself.

Debris showered down at our feet in a wild spray.

Most of the wall followed it.

We hadn't made it to outside. But outside had made it to us.

Cool air mingled with clouds of dust. The darkness was lit up by far-off stars and close-up searchlights. Troops were visible behind the glare.

"Will you look at that," Stokes coughed.

"Doggone," I said.

"Another army," Valerie said.

"Yeah. Whatever *that* is."

We crouched behind a hunk of wall. Our pursuers had lost interest in us, were exchanging potshots with the newcomers.

"Never a dull moment, eh?" I said.

"Our partnership," Stokes said to me, "looked so good on paper."

"You boys should have stuck to paper," Valerie said.

The firepower was beginning to pick up. Our cover left something to be desired.

"Darned if I know which side to shoot at," I complained.

"Both probably, old buddy."

Valerie said, "If we stay very low and crawl for it, we can reach that side corridor and get away from all this."

"I wouldn't mind," I admitted.

"Well, we'd better get a move on," Valerie said, "before they blow this whole place up."

"I wasn't really comfortable here anyway," I said.

We started crawling.

The falling wall acted as shield. What with all the dust and shooting no one seemed to take notice. That was fine by me. I didn't mind if someone else got all the attention. Why hog it?

"Give up," a voice from outside called through a bullhorn.

"Who the hell are you?" a voice from inside called back. Smart question.

"Malcolm Lane."

"What do you know?" Stokes said.

"He didn't say which Malcolm Lane," I said.

"Keep crawling," Valerie said.

We kept.

After a while we rounded a corner. Behind us both sides were busy seeing how many people they could kill. Here were all the earmarks of a first-class war, a bona fide preview of things to come. Three other Lane armies were rolling toward Central City. There'd be no shortage of combatants once they arrived.

"Hold on," Stokes said. He was looking over his shoulder at the fracas. We all paused to look.

"Nothing like a front-line seat to the latest war games," I said. "Too bad it's not a game."

"What I'm trying to figure out," Stokes said, "is who they are."

"Think they may be spooks?"

Stokes shook his head. "Those are real weapons, old man."

The three of us lay on our stomachs, peering down the corridor toward outside. Our view was limited. What with darkness, searchlights and exploding shells, we weren't exactly getting an eyeful.

"Nuts," Stokes said.

"If we remain here long enough," Valerie said, "those men out there will end up stepping on us."

"Provided Markstein's men don't step on them," Stokes said.

"She's right. We gotta get a move on."

"Just one peek," Stokes said, crawling off.

"There goes a brave nut," I said, "but if he gets nailed, I'm not going back for the body."

"What's so important about who they are, anyway?" Valerie demanded.

"Nice to know who's shooting at you."

"Why?"

"So you can shoot 'em when they least expect it. Figures, right?"

Harley came crawling back fast.

"Well?"

"Must hustle," Stokes said. "Think they're making their move."

We hustled; no one had to tell us twice.

Behind us all hell was busy breaking loose.

We turned another corner, got up and ran for it.

"Just people out there," Stokes said.

"What were you expecting?" I asked. "Monkeys?"

"I don't know, marines maybe. Or sailors. Perhaps even a police detachment. Who knows? But most of those people, old pal, were in street clothes."

"What's wrong with that?" Valerie asked.

"Ever hear of Lane before you met him?"

"No."

"Either has anyone else."

"Oh."

"Exactly."

We headed up a flight of stairs, hit the first floor. We didn't bother skulking along; it was way past that point. We entered at a gallop. No one was there to notice. We made it to the front door with no mishaps. Opening it was another matter.

"They're out in back and over to the right," I said. *"I think."*

"They were the last time we looked," Stokes admitted. "At least *some* of them."

Valerie went to a window, peered out. "Make that all of them out back. Coast's clear."

I turned the knob, stepped out into the night. No one shot at me. The three of us dashed across the clearing into the woods. Our car was parked where we'd left it. We piled in, pulled out of there. I pressed the pedal down to the floorboards. We made time.

"So here's this man," Stokes said, "who pops out of nowhere."

"Four of him," I added.

"Yep. And overnight rounds up four armies. Mostly civilians, too. *How does he do it? How?"*

I certainly didn't know. I kept my mouth shut. We sped down the highway.

Valerie cleared her throat. "Gentlemen, I have just thought of something."

"I'm glad someone has, I was starting to get worried."

"Well, Harley started me thinking. It wouldn't have occurred to me if he hadn't asked, 'How does he do it?' "

"Lane, you mean?" Stokes said.

"Lane. How does he get this following?"

"Charisma?" I asked.

"You're not going to believe this," she said.

"If I can believe in four Lanes, I can believe in anything," I said.

"Well, there's just a chance that I *know* how he does it."

"Know," I said.

"How?" Stokes said.

"I can't be sure," Valerie said.

"Of course," I said. "Who can?"

"But I just *may* actually know."

"You were right," I said, "I'm not going to believe it."

"Well, if that's the case, I guess I'll just have to show you."

"This theory of yours," I said, "it can be *shown?*"

"Like an object?" Stokes said.

"Sure."

"Jeez," I said.

CHAPTER 38

I followed Valerie's directions.

We skirted the city, rode toward the countryside again. I'd been getting an eyeful of the rural scene lately, but I wasn't about to complain. The urban scene had lost a lot of its kicks since the G.I.s landed.

A highway took us to a tar road. After a while the tar turned to gravel. A narrow dirt road, which ran through a patch of woods, finished off our journey.

We pulled up in front of a dark two-story building. It was made of brick and looked as if it belonged somewhere back in the city.

"The guy who built this out here was slightly batty," I said.

"Not a guy, Jim," Valerie said.

"An it?"

"Melissa Sussman."

"No kidding? Had queer taste, eh?"

"Wait till you see the inside," Valerie said.

We left the car.

"I don't have the key," Valerie said.

Stokes shrugged, reached for his laser. The double locks didn't last long. Stokes sighed. "She isn't going to mind."

We went into the house. Some house. It was full of hardware: pipes, machines, wires, dials, gauges. The walls were lined with computers.

"Cozy little nook," I said.

"This," said Valerie, "is where Melissa Sussman did her *real* work."

"Didn't the lady believe in rest?" Stokes asked.

"Not everyone," I told Stokes, "thinks leisure is life's chief goal."

"They *don't?*" Stokes said. "Well, that's their problem, old man."

"What's upstairs?" I asked, "more of the same?"

Valerie nodded. "Melissa was very dedicated."

"What did she do when she got tired," I asked, "pull up a machine and grab forty winks?"

"She didn't come here when she was tired," Valerie said.

"Smart move," Stokes said.

"So what the hell *is* this," I said, "and *what* are we doing here?"

"Well, you wanted to know how Lane got all those people on his side."

"That's what I wanted to know," I admitted.

Valerie waved her arm. "This is the only way I could think of."

"This," I said.

"Precisely," Valerie said. "You know, of course, that Dr. Sussman was instrumental in the development of Ed-Out?"

"Who doesn't know that?" I said.

"And it's suppressed successor, Neo-Ed-Out."

"Subliminal indoctrination," Harley said. "We're well rid of it."

"It was hardly foolproof, gentlemen. It took ages to get the job done. And then the job could get undone overnight."

"Some job," I said.

"Dr. Sussman thought that sooner or later, Neo-Ed-Out would be revived. And that's why she did what she did. In secret. Except that Malcolm Lane may have found out somehow. Or worked along similar lines and developed his own."

"Stupidity must've set in early. I don't understand a word you're saying," I complained.

"Super Ed-Out. A system of *total* control."

"Well?" I asked Stokes.

We were seated on a workbench up on the second floor. It had taken us a good hour to go through the place, hunting Sussman's notes on the project. We'd finally found them in a cardboard container, under a sink, in the cellar.

Stokes said, "Very complex."

All three of us had been going through the stack of pages.

I turned to Valerie. "Any luck?"

"Luck has nothing to do with it. It's all a matter of training, Jim."

"And?"

"My training stops short of knowing how to hook this system into the Ed-Out broadcasts."

I said, "How do we know this thing even works? Has it ever been tested?"

"Not that I know of," Valerie said, "but I don't really know very much. Dr. Sussman ran the project all by herself."

I looked around at the equipment. "How did she bankroll all this?"

"Are you kidding?" Stokes said. "The president of the Science Fed? Come now."

"Yeah. I suppose. So what do we do?"

"Jim, I'm willing to bet on Melissa any day," Valerie said. "Super Ed-Out is going to work."

"So all we've got to do is hook it up," I said. "All. Good thing we've got an expert here."

"Expert executive," Stokes said. "It's been a while since I've fiddled with the controls, old boy."

"So?"

"So, let's see if we can find a view-phone here and I'll demonstrate what an executive can do."

Chester Wheems was a small, skinny bird with a balding head and sparse mustache. He was a vice-president of the Leisure Guild and its top technician. He'd brought along five helpers and a thirty-man security force; they wouldn't do much good if we had to take on an army, but they were a darn sight better than the stuff which came out of our Bennys.

At my suggestion, Wheems had brought along some eats. Valerie, Harley and I snacked at a workbench while Wheems and his crew tried to decipher Sussman's notes.

After a while, Valerie left us to work with Wheems.

"Nothing like having our own scientist along," I said.

"Our own army would be a bit better," Stokes said.

He was right, too.

A couple of hours slid by before Valerie and Wheems got back to us. I used the time to stretch out on the workbench and doze. It had been a rough day, and by the looks of it, one that would probably go on forever.

Valerie shook me by the shoulder.

"We've done it," she said.

I sat bolt upright, wide awake.

"You have?"

"We've figured out how much we don't know."

"That's what I was afraid of," I groaned.

"It will not be easy, Mr. Morgan; oh dear me, no," Wheems said.

"It won't, eh?"

"But," Wheems added, "it is certainly within the realm of possibility."

"Glad to hear it," I said. "Now, what are we talking about?"

"Why, installing Dr. Sussman's Augmenter in headquarters, of course."

"Oh, of course," I said.

"How long will it take?" Stokes asked.

"If all goes well?" Wheems asked.

"Let's work on that unlikely assumption," Stokes said.

"Perhaps five to eight hours."

"What happens if things don't exactly fit into place?" I asked.

"It could take months."

"Figure on months," I told Stokes.

We used the side roads to get back to the city. I wasn't taking any chances. Despite the escort, we traveled with our lights out.

Wheems had dismantled the Augmenter and we'd stashed it in pieces in the back seats and trunks of four of our cars.

Stokes was at the wheel, Valerie between us.

"This is the way I see it," I said. "Lane somehow got his hands on Sussman's brainchild—don't ask me how—and used it to convince folks to sign up on his side, whatever that is. So all we've got to do is use the same dingus to unconvince them. And while we're at it, everyone else too. Simple as pie, eh? There's got to be a catch somewhere, right? So tell me where I went wrong?"

"Well," Stokes said, "for one thing, old chum, Wheems may not be able to hook the damn thing up."

"I'm not even going to think about that. He's a pro, isn't he? So he'll think of something. Next."

"Jim," Valerie said.

I didn't like the sound of that "Jim."

"You know something I don't?" I asked her.

"At *least* a few things."

"Acknowledged. Anything specific, like about this Augmenter?"

"I was going over Melissa's notes, Jim, and as far as I can see it's *never* been tested."

"Big deal. Lane had to test it to do his stuff, no? So it's tested."

"Perhaps. But what if he used some other method of persuasion? What if we're wrong?"

"So we'll test it ourselves. We'll use it on some of those soldier boys and see if they salute."

"It *could* be dangerous."

"Dangerous, shmangerous; that's the name of the game. When you put on that old uniform and start pointing guns at people, that's when you become fair game."

"No, Jim—"

I held up my hand, cutting her short.

"Yeah, I know what you're going to say, kid, that some of those soldiers —maybe most of them—are there against their will, don't know what they're doing, that the Augmenter has 'em over a barrel." I shrugged. "What can I say? I get the picture. But too much is at stake here to play it safe. Those guys'll just have to take their chances along with the rest of us. Those are the breaks."

We rode on in silence for a while.

"Jim," Valerie said.

"Yeah, kid?"

"Don't call me kid, Jim."

"Sure, Valerie."

"I wasn't going to say any of that."

"You weren't, eh?"

"No."

"Well, I'm still glad I said it. You'd have gotten to it sooner or later."

"No."

"No? I don't get it."

"It's dangerous, Jim, for *you.* "

"Me?"

"Perhaps *very* dangerous."

"You're kidding. How? You mean someone'll try and stop me from using the contraption? Let them try! We'll put out a call, get every Moon Base supporter in a hundred miles to come running."

"I don't mean that either, Jim."

"You don't? Well, what *do* you mean?"

"Melissa's Augmenter, Jim, hasn't been tested in two ways. We don't know if it will work, or if it does, to what extent; and we don't know what it will do to its prime conductor."

I sighed. "See," I said to Stokes, "she told me and I still don't understand a word."

"Perhaps you're just stupid?" Stokes said.

"I haven't finished," Valerie said.

"Oh."

"And you're tired, Jim." Valerie said.

"Yeah, I suppose I am," I admitted.

"And it makes your little mind even duller than usual," Valerie said.

"Duller than that," I pointed out, "and I'd be dead."

"Look. Melissa's notes indicate she didn't know how long the Super Ed-Out effect would last. Perhaps weeks, months or even years. But maybe only hours."

"She didn't know?"

"She didn't. And the level of conviction was never measured. A hundred percent? Or something else? And how does a belief induced through the system stand up to challenge?"

"How does it?"

"We don't know."

"Okay. So it's untested. I still don't see what the danger is."

"That comes now. Remember I mentioned the prime conductor?"

"Yeah."

"Well, the Augmenter, as I'm sure you saw, has all sorts of interesting features. But did you notice the small metal skullcap with the wire attachments?"

"Nope. That's the prime conductor?"

"Uh-uh. That's what the prime conductor wears."

"Wears?"

"So his brain waves can be magnified, processed and broadcast in order to achieve the proper convictions."

"His?"

"The prime conductor, Jim, is a person. And a very important one. Because if he thinks the wrong thoughts, say slavery instead of freedom, you might have a bunch of slaves on your hands."

"Oh, brother."

"But that's not the half of it. Melissa didn't know if the prime conductor would survive the experience."

"Survive?"

"She obviously means drop dead," Stokes said. "You might drop dead, old boy."

"What do you mean, *me?*" I demanded.

"Well, you can't expect me or Valerie to use that deadly gadget. And who else can you trust?"

CHAPTER 39

Our moonlight procession hit the city sometime after 3 A.M.

Few lights greeted us. The city seemed to be blacked out. We didn't have long to wait for a reason. The familiar sounds came from up ahead: cannons, machine guns, rifles, handguns. The bloodletting was still in full swing. We used the side streets as far away as we could get from the actual combat. Too much was riding on our mission to chance being done in by a stray shell. Besides, we wanted to go on living. Even in a world that was a wee bit less than perfect.

The Leisure Guild Complex was dark. Troops guarded the two gateways we came to. We rode on by.

"Make out who they were?" I asked Stokes.

"Afraid not."

"Think we can get by those guys with our Bennys?" I asked.

"There are limits to how many times I want to risk my neck, old bean."

"You got a better idea?"

"It's not for nothing I'm president of this establishment. I bet those jokers out there have no idea about the executive garage."

"This is hardly the time to boast of your privileges, Harley."

"Wait till you see where the entrance is. Three blocks north of here. Out in the city. A tunnel takes us right under the wall. What do you say to that?"

"Always knew there was a good reason for being president."

"What are those two guys with machine guns up to by your entrance, Harley?"

"They obviously don't know they shouldn't be there," Harley said. He stepped on the gas. The car gunned toward the garage entrance. My Benny produced a horde of motorcycle troops before us. Behind us, our real-life convoy swung into line. The two guards jumped for their lives. Smart guards.

We swung through the tunnel hitting ninety.

"Won't those men call ahead?" Valerie said.

"Ahead is a lot of places," Harley said.

We swerved out of the tunnel. Darkness was on our side. I was glad something was.

A huge square building loomed up in our headlights. Our car screeched to a halt.

"Quick, now!" Stokes said.

We piled out of the car, began unloading our part of the Augmenter. Behind us, our motor escort came to a noisy standstill. Techs and security instantly began imitating our efforts.

Three security guys trotted over to lend us a hand.

I turned to Stokes. "We'd be better off planning for a pitched battle, Harley; Valerie's right. Those guys we almost ran down are sure to blow the whistle on us. How far can we get before the troops show up?"

"Far enough, old boy. With a little luck."

"That last part blows it."

"This way!" Stokes said, running off.

"This way" was into the square building. Our whole crew came with us, lugging pieces of Augmenter.

No lights lit the marble corridors. Some of the security guys were equipped with flashlights; they lit our way.

"Through that door," Stokes said.

We watched till the last of our crew was through the door, then we followed. Harley carefully closed the door. And grinned. "We're safe now," he said.

"Yeah, eh?"

We were walking down a smooth tunnel.

"That building we were in," Stokes said, "has twenty tunnels which branch off into other tunnels; understand?"

"No."

"Well, partner, there are a hundred and fifty buildings in this complex. And almost each has a tunnel. Get it now?"

"Yeah," I nodded. "We're safe."

"Back again," I sighed, looking around at the interior of Relay Station One. It didn't quite feel like home. But home wouldn't have felt like home either anymore.

"This may take some time; dear me, yes," Wheems said, eyeing the pieces of Augmenter piled at his feet.

"As long as it doesn't take *too* much time," Harley said.

Wheems and his men began busily reassembling the Augmenter.

"Partner," I said, "how come we didn't take one of those tunnels here the last time, when the muties were trying to skin us alive, and almost succeeded. You had us running through the streets, for Christ's sake."

"Well, old man, the president's building is one of the few which *doesn't* have a tunnel. Security reasons, you know. Can't have just anyone wandering in, can we?"

"Na," I said to Stokes, "what kind of world would that be?" To Valerie I said, "You don't really expect me to risk life and limb on that contraption, do you?"

"Then what are we doing here?" Valerie asked.

"Stokes," I said, "what are we doing here?"

"Waiting for you to risk life and limb."

"Valerie, how dangerous is it *really?*"

She shrugged a shoulder. "Maybe Melissa knew."

"She's beyond asking," I pointed out.

"No one knows," Valerie said. "Except Lane, maybe."

"That's the wrong answer!" I yelled.

"Done," Wheems said, wiping his brow.

"Ah," Stokes said.

"It is plugged into the system," Wheems said.

"Plugged in," I said.

"And ready to go," Wheems said.

"So am I," I said. "Anyone seen my hat and coat?"

"He *does* have a case," Valerie said.

"How would *you* like to do it?" Stokes asked.

"I'm a lady," Valerie said.

"Look," I said, "let's be realistic."

"About time," Stokes said.

"We could toss a coin," I said.

"What's realistic about that?" Stokes said.

"But then one of us would have to do it," I said. "And I'm rather fond of all three of us. Especially me."

"Here we go again," Stokes said. "You have someone else in mind?"

"Sure. One of *them.*"

"The security team?" Valerie asked.

"Why not? What's a team for if it won't play ball. Harley can offer the lucky guy a bonus. Right, Harley? Those guys are *used* to taking risks. That's what they get paid for. I've taken enough risks already. I've used up my quota. Let someone else run with the ball."

"But Jim, don't you understand?" Valerie said. "Whoever does this could have *tremendous power* over society."

"Fine. Let's pick someone worthy of it. Which one of your boys can handle this responsibility, Harley?"

"*Tremendous power?* Are you serious, old noodle? None of them."

"Well, let's have Wheems do it."

"Don't be silly," Wheems said. "Wild horses couldn't drag me."

"What about his techs?" I asked Harley.

"Even worse than security. Smarter. More grasping."

"Jim," Valerie said, "we can begin with the voltage way down, and see what happens."

"On *me?* I thought I'd already said no. Aren't you listening? You got to listen if you want to get ahead in life."

The door opened and one of the security guys strode over to Harley, whispered in his ear. Harley nodded and the guy went away again.

"What gives?" I asked.

"The end," Harley said. "We're about to be attacked. Troops are massing all over the place down below."

"See? I said they'd get wise to us."

"That tunnel, old buddy, bought us a good hour. What did you want, a paid vacation?"

"We've got to do *something,*" Valerie said.

"Maybe we could just escape," I said hopefully.

"And leave civilization in the hands of Fulton and company?" Valerie said.

"Civilization," I said, "can take care of itself. It's us I'm worried about."

Somewhere down below a shot was fired.

"Shit," I said.

Three more shots sounded in rapid succession. Something went BOOM! After that, there didn't seem much point in keeping track.

"How much time we got?" I asked.

"A little," Stokes said. "We've blown the chutes."

"That was *our* BOOM?"

"Right. Leaving the staircases. We have them mined. They're relatively narrow, too. We should be able to hold our own for a while."

"Then what?"

"I was hoping *you'd* tell *us.*"

"Listen, Jim," Valerie said. "The Augmenter is the *only* chance we've got. Perhaps I *was premature* in thinking it dangerous. Lane must have used it."

"Yeah," I said, "maybe it turned him into four people. Four of me would be too much. I'm having enough trouble with one."

Something went BOOM! again.

"Back staircase," Harley said.

"Jim," Valerie said.

"Absolutely not," I said.

"But what else can we do?" Valerie said.

BOOM!

"Front staircase," Harley said.

"Leaving what?" I asked.

"Hand-to-hand combat, I suppose. Our men will be able to hold out for just so long. Then the fat's in the fire for sure. The hands doing the combat will be *ours.*"

"I don't think I know how to do that exactly," Valerie said.

"You'll learn," Stokes said, "we'll all learn."

"Oh, dear," Wheems said, "I could never learn that. Why don't you just do what they want, Mr. Morgan, and save the day?"

"Jim," Valerie said, "I'll just *inch* the voltage up—"

"Voltage is what they use in electric chairs," I pointed out.

"If you feel any pain, anything bad at all, I'll stop."

"Never," I said.

"But what's the alternative, Jim?"

A dead silence followed, punctuated by assorted gunfire and screams from somewhere in the building. The damn sounds were getting too near.

Wheems broke into tears. "Oh, *please,* Mr. Morgan. I'm too young to die!"

He wasn't the only one.

"I swear," Valerie said, "I'll kill the power at the slightest hint from you."

I shook my head. "Kill, yet. Sorry. Nothing can make me change my mind."

Just then the screaming started in earnest. It was really close, too; maybe three floors away. Someone had been shot, or blown up or something. But someone wasn't quite dead yet. The screaming went on and on and on.

"Yeah, it seems to be okay," I said.

"You aren't sure?" Valerie said.

"How the hell should I be sure? I've never worn a metal skullcap before."

Stokes came back from the staircase. "I spoke to the men. They're bunched three floors down, armed to the teeth and ready to fight to the last man. Unfortunately, that's not saying much. We're just about scraping the bottom of the barrel. So this better work, partner, or the next stop is the Pearly Gates."

I said, "I'm just the guinea pig. Tell the scientist here."

Valerie shrugged. "I'm doing my best."

Wheems was at the control board. His techs were strategically placed around the room at various lesser panels. Our signal would blanket the city. Anyone watching the entertainies, or tuning into Ed-Out or one of the news alert networks would get us. Even the giant news-flash screens set up outdoors around the city would carry our message, provided, of course, the Augmenter did its stuff and I still had enough brains left—once the juice went on—to think up a message.

"Just yell," Valerie said, "if this hurts."

She flicked on a dial.

Besides the skullcap, I was wrapped up in wires as if I were in a cocoon. I wondered what part of me would start hurting first.

I heard a humming noise.

Stokes leaned over, whispered in my ear, "If the Augmenter lays an egg, partner, we're doomed. Let me take this opportunity to say bye-bye."

"Bye-bye," I said.

"Anything?" Valerie asked.

"Uh-uh."

"I'll turn it up a notch. Now?"

"The humming's grown louder," I said.

"Nothing else?" Valerie asked.

"It tickles," I said.

"Okay," Valerie said, "let's give it some more power."

"Well?" I asked.

"You don't feel anything?"

"Not a darn thing."

"I just upped it."

"Yeah?"

"A whole digit," she said.

"Could be it's a bust."

"Don't say that," Stokes said.

"Think something," Valerie said.

"Like what?"

"End of conflict," she said.

"Sure."

"So?" Stokes said.

"I'm thinking."

Gunfire was still coming from the staircase.

"Maybe you should think harder," Stokes said.

"Let's up it a little more," Valerie said.

"Watch it," I said.

"I am. You *must* feel *something*, Jim."

"If you say so."

"Does it still tickle?" she asked.

"I don't think so."

"He doesn't even know," Stokes said.

"It does look like a bust, doesn't it?" I said.

"Would you mind if I tried just one more notch?" Valerie asked.

"Probably. I'd like to go on feeling no pain."

"It's really still very low."

"Perhaps that's the problem," Stokes said. "Why don't we turn it all the way up?"

"Because it might kill him," Valerie said.

"We definitely don't want to kill him," I said.

Stokes shrugged. "It's either them or us. At least we're his friends."

"No," said Valerie, "just one more notch."

"You heard the lady," I said.

"There," Valerie said. "Well?"

"Don't hold your breath," I told her.

Valerie sighed. "You can't make them stop the shooting, Jim?"

"I can't even make me stop shaking. I could always ask them nicely of course."

"We'd better scrap this," Stokes said, "and find a way out of here."

"Now you're talking," I said.

"I still have faith in Melissa," Valerie said.

"That's the spirit," I said, "never say die. Just get me out of this chair; maybe we can make a run for it."

"Oh, dear," Wheems said. "Can't you see? There *is* no place to run to; none at all."

"Maybe," I said, "we can get the chutes working and take a powder that way."

As if in answer something very loud, unpleasant and very close exploded on the staircase.

"Uh-uh," I said.

I was still wrapped up in a bunch of wires, the metal headpiece firmly in place.

The door burst open.

Our guys came through it.

Some paused to fire a couple of blasts over their shoulders. The rest didn't bother. They were going full tilt as though there were actually someplace to run to.

I couldn't blame them.

The bad guys were right at their heels.

Only bad wasn't the word for it.

Monstrous, maybe.

Two of the muties were of the giant variety which I'd run into earlier. Both were about nine feet tall. A couple of the others were too ugly to describe. The guy with nine hands was no picnic either, especially since each hand held a weapon.

If I hadn't been all tangled up in wires, I'd have gotten up and run too.

Stokes had his laser out, was firing away. Wheems was headed for the back wall as though there were a secret door buried in it. He had lots of company. Valerie was standing stock still, which was probably as smart as anything. And I was seated in my chair, skullcap and all, out in full view, as if on some kind of stupid throne.

The guy with the nine hands had no trouble spotting me. Either did the five things at his side.

I was one of the few stationary objects in the room.

And virtually impossible to miss.

The guy raised all nine guns and pointed them at me.

I did the only thing I could.

I opened my mouth wide and screamed, "STOP!"

And the guy did.

Along with everyone else.

In the eerie silence that followed I heard myself say, "Whaddya know?" And then, "Just the muties stay stopped. Everyone else can move."

And they did.

"Oh, boy," I said.

Stokes turned to Valerie. "Didn't Sussman's notes say anything about vocalizing the command?"

"Not a whisper," Valerie said.

"Well, that's where we went wrong," Stokes said.

"Perhaps she left it out for security reasons," Valerie said.

"Who knows? And who cares?" I said. "The darn thing works! That's the important thing! How much juice did you give me?"

"Not much," Valerie said.

"Well, it's worked like a dream so far. Look at those guys. They haven't moved an inch. And not a sound from the staircases. Why don't we turn the Augmenter up full blast and see what happens?"

"You sure?" Stokes asked.

"Why not?" I asked.

"I really don't think I'd do that, if I were you," Malcolm Lane said.

CHAPTER 40

I looked up toward the ceiling.

A skylight panel opened there; Malcolm Lane peered down through it. He wasn't alone, either; the other three Lanes were on hand to keep him company. Each held a laser weapon.

"How'd you get up there?" Stokes demanded.

"Copter," Lane said.

"See," Stokes said to me. "There *was* a way out."

"Yeah," I said, "all we needed was someone dumb enough to land a copter on the roof during a full-scale war."

"Right." Lane beamed. "And here I am. All of me, in fact. Flown in especially for the occasion."

One of the other Lanes hoisted down a ladder. All four Lanes descended.

"How come they're still pointing their guns at us?" Stokes asked. "I thought they were pals of yours?"

"At least one was. But business acquaintance is more like it."

"Why don't you make them drop their guns, old boy?" Stokes asked.

"Sure," I said. "Why not? FREEZE!"

It almost worked, too. One of the Lanes was so busy laughing he almost let go of his gun. The rest just grinned.

"Is this thing on?" I asked Valerie.

"As on as it was before," she said.

"So how come it doesn't work now?"

"Oh, it works all right," Lane said, "it just doesn't work on *us.*"

"You guys take shots or something?"

"It wouldn't work on *you,* either."

"Why?" I asked.

"Because you've been a prime conductor," Lane said.

"And prime conductors are immune to the Augmenter," Lane Two said.

"Yes," Lane Three, said, "something happens *inside* that changes a man who serves as a prime conductor."

"Indeed," Lane Four said, "and you'll never guess what that makes him *legally.*"

"A scofflaw?" I asked.

"A mutant," Lane One said.

"I grow a third eye or an extra hand?"

"Don't be disgusting," Lane One said.

"You're just immune," Lane Two said, "from the Augmenter."

"Because you're changed inside," Lane Three said. "Your genes will never be the same again. Your offspring will be immune too."

"In short, a mutant," Lane Four said.

"Where'd you guys get this startling news?" I asked.

"From Mama," Lane Three said, "may she rest in peace."

"Your *mother,* eh?" I said.

"*The* expert," Lane Four said.

"Our ma," Lane Two said, "was Melissa Sussman. And if she didn't know, who did?"

"Welcome to the club, fellow mutant," Lane One said.

"I don't think I like this club," I said.

"Well, I for one don't believe it," Valerie said.

"Oh, but it's *absolutely* true," Lane One said. "The four of us would've been the famous Sussman quadruplets. If Mama had had her way."

"But Papa would never hear of it," Lane Three said.

"Papa was already married, you see," Lane Four said.

"We had the best of everything," Lane Two said, "except Papa's name."

"And poor Mama could hardly acknowledge us," Lane One said, "unless she wanted a horrible scandal that could *ruin* her career. And Mama *loved* her career, you know. And she did go on to become president of the Science Fed. So she must have known what she was doing; wouldn't you say?"

"I suppose so," I said. "So who is your dad, anyway?"

"General Manning West," Lane One said.

"Oh, brother," I said.

"We're going to *get* him," Lane Three said bitterly.

"I thought you already did," Stokes said, "at the relay station?"

"To tell the truth," Lane Two said, "he got away."

"But that," Lane One said, "hardly matters. After all, we weren't out to do him in. He *is* our papa."

"Oh, no," Lane Four said, "we just want to destroy his career, that's all. He'd hate that. And change society, too, while we're at it. By making us top dogs."

"Top Lanes," Lane One said, "would be better put."

"Yes," Lane Two said, "Mama used us as guinea pigs. We were all prime conductors, you see. But that was *only* in the early stages."

"There must be a reason," Valerie said, "only I'm afraid to ask."

"Mama feared it might make us cuckoo," Lane Three said.

"And Mama was right," Lane Two said.

Lane One sat down on a workbench, grinned at us. "We used a volunteer for the later stages: Mama's dear, dear friend Captain Charles Ryder. We invited that ass, People's Counsel Barnabus, over for lunch and Charley gave him the works."

"The works," I said.

"Yes, just like you, Morgan, he attached himself to the Super Ed-Out system, put on the skullcap and gave Barnabus the business. Made him pro-mutant, you see."

"But why pro-mutie, of all things?" Stokes asked.

"Why not?" Lane One grinned. "It served to stir things up and that's what we wanted so we could come on as saviors. But poor Ryder went gaga in the process. So I wouldn't really advise you to use the Augmenter at full power. Absolutely not."

"There's one thing I simply do not understand," Valerie said.

"Just one?"

"For starters. If you didn't use Super Ed-Out, how did you get all those soldiers and civilians to follow you?"

"Neo-Ed-Out," Lane Four told her, "proved quite adequate. Slow, tedious work, of course. And far from permanent. But, as you see, adequate."

"How the hell did you guys do it?" Stokes demanded.

"Bribed some technicians," Lane One said. "Used low-power Super Ed-Out on others. And even blackmailed a few. Mama had already given us the locations of the relay stations. Oh yes, we had our ways. And we took all the time we needed."

"So all this is your fault?" I said.

"Hardly all. Fulton had his coup planned *long* before us. And Hess didn't need a coup because he was going to lock up all his opponents and *never* have elections. We just joined the sweepstakes."

"Jeez," I said.

"There, there," Lane One said, "don't you fret. Everything's going to work out just fine. Didn't I save you from Daddy?"

"He means West," Stokes said.

"I know who he means," I said to Stokes. To Lane I said, "Why, for heaven's sake?"

"Why not? So you'd be grateful. You *are* grateful, aren't you?"

"I'm just brimming over with gratitude."

"Oh good! In any case you haven't much choice, do you? Where are you going to go? Fulton? Hess? West? The poor mutants?"

"What are you talking about?"

"It's really quite simple," Lane One said. "We need the blessings of Moon Base to make us legitimate. We need *your* blessings. Neo-Ed-Out has been singing our praises—in selected areas, of course—for ever so long. Even some of the muties don't mind us now. But we couldn't reach everyone. And we don't know how long the conditioning will last. And some people seem to be immune!"

"Is that true?" I asked Valerie.

"True enough. That was one reason Melissa went on to the Super system."

"What's the other reason?" I asked.

"To stop would-be dictators like Fulton," she said.

"What about tinhorn kingpins like the Lanes?" Stokes asked.

"I'm afraid she must have liked them," Valerie said.

"Flesh and blood after all," Lane One said. "It *will* tell. Oh, we were all quite close. Too close, in fact; I told Mama you were coming to Earth. And she mentioned it to Papa. That's how he found out."

"Yes," Lane Three said. "We saved you, Morgan, and let you run free just to demonstrate that your only choice must be the Lane Brothers."

"Sounds like a cough drop," I said, "some choice."

"Oh, we'll make dandy dictators," Lane Two said, "and we're even willing to give *you* a piece of the pie."

"I can hardly wait," I said.

"The alternative," Lane Three said, "is the hoosegow."

"He already had a taste of *that*," Lane One said, "and detested it. I know. I set him free. He owes us."

"Make up your mind," Lane Three said.

"Us or the lockup," Lane Four said, "or maybe we'll just shoot you now and get it over with."

"Why are things getting worse instead of better?" I asked Stokes.

"Because all these Lanes are being unreasonable, old man," he said.

I was still trussed up in my Super Ed-Out chair. The Lanes were immune. But here were twenty-five muties and security guys standing around like statues and going thoroughly to waste. *They* weren't immune.

"Get the Lanes," I hollered.

The Lanes looked around to see who I was talking to.

And twenty-five muties and security guys fell on them.

"Thanks for coming, Mr. Chairman," I said.

"I could hardly decline," Raymond Hess said, seating himself, with some dignity, on a workbench. He was right, too; his own troops had dragged him here. We were still holed up in Relay Station One. Only now it was a matter of convenience, not necessity. A small but important difference.

I nodded at the gray-haired politician. "Don't blame your men for turning on you, Hess; it wasn't their fault."

"Then whom do you suggest I blame?"

I grinned. *"Me.* Stokes here. Valerie. Mr. Wheems and his helpers, even. And, of course, the ghost of Melissa Sussman: her little device turned the trick. If you hadn't gotten greedy, tried to set yourself up as dictator, none of this would've happened."

"You forget the others," he said, "Fulton, West, the generals, the mutants—"

"Yeah, but they had *you,* the top guy, as a rotten example. With all the security outfits around town you could've nipped those plots in the bud. But you didn't. You figured a couple of plots would give you the perfect excuse for a take-over. Too bad things got out of hand, eh? But don't worry, Mr. Chairman, experience counts, and we're going to use yours to put things right again. At least for a while. You still get to run the show. Only now you'll have help from the Lane Brothers, General West, Harley Stokes here, and even me and Valerie Loring from time to time. Lucky you, eh? It sure beats the firing squad, right? I'd even give you Fulton, but I figure the guy who knocked off Melissa Sussman and Senator Tarken ought to be put on trial, no? You'll note there's no more shooting around town. That's because there are no more armies. Stokes and I have Sussman's Augmenter. And at the moment we've augmented a general desire for peace in everyone. At least in all the viewers, and that *means* everyone. This super stuff is only good in short spurts, mainly because I don't want to sit around in a skullcap all day. So we're sticking to the old ways. We're broadcasting a Neo-Ed-Out urge for free elections. In a couple of months even you'll be wanting them yourself. Any objections, Mr. Chairman?"

"And if I have?"

"Save 'em till after election day. And thank your lucky stars I'm going to be too busy to become chairman myself, you miserable creep, you."

"Too busy with *me*," Valerie said.

"Hess won't mind," I said.

We were alone in the relay station. Finally.

"Why, Jim, are you letting those *persons* remain in power?"

"I shouldn't?"

"They're *awful.*"

"Who isn't?"

"*I'm* not."

"True. But you're going to be busy with me, remember? Anyway, it's only temporary. And those guys *do* have experience; at least they won't run the old ship of state into the ground."

"But can you trust *them?*"

"Of course not. But Neo-Ed-Out is going great guns on all channels, broadcasting our message subliminally."

"Which is?"

"Peace, harmony and love!"

"But Jim, what makes you think Hess, West and the Lanes will buy that message?"

"Of course they won't. But like everyone else they'll be affected. And we *do* have the Augmenter as backup. Every once in a while Harley's going to show up and use it, tell everyone to cool it. If that doesn't do the trick, nothing will."

"What happens to the Augmenter *after* free elections, Jim?"

"Who knows? Maybe they'll ban it. Or set up a committee to study the darn thing."

"And the mutants?"

"Another committee, probably."

"But *you're* a mutant too, now."

"Big deal. Who's to know? Think the Lanes'll snitch?"

"And you're *really* immune to the Augmenter?"

"Yep, so it seems."

"What about the Neo system?"

"You mean peace, harmony and love?"

"Especially love."

"Love makes the world go round. And I'm as susceptible as the next guy."

"So what are we waiting for?"

"Beats me, sweetie."

Isidore Haiblum is well known for his science fiction novels, humorous essays, and articles on Yiddish and other Jewish topics. He is the author of eight previous novels: *The Identity Plunderers, Nightmare Express, Outerworld, Interworld; The Wilk Are Among Us, Transfer to Yesterday, The Tsaddik of the Seven Wonders,* and *The Return.* And one book of nonfiction (with Stuart Silver): *Faster Than a Speeding Bullet—An Informal History of Radio's Golden Age.* His novels have been translated into French, German, Hebrew, Italian and Spanish. He lives and works in New York City.